AN INDECENT PROPOSAL

"This isn't the most ideal place to have this conversation, but I can't sleep another night without speaking to you about us."

Nachelle's throat closed up. "Us?"

"Yes, us," Steven answered. "I know you're attracted to me and I'm definitely attracted to you."

Nachelle listened to his confession, but sat numb, unable to move or to speak.

Steven needed no response from her to continue. "I've given it a lot of thought and I've come up with a way we can remove this interfering wall and start making some decisions about our future."

"I'm not sure what you mean . . ." Nachelle's pledge to avoid office romances flashed in her head like a blinking neon sign.

"Nachelle, to determine if this is a passing fad or not, you should spend the night with me, and after we've made love, we can talk about the future." Steven's businesslike tone shifted to smooth and sensual. His dark eyes softened as he ran a single finger down her cheek to her chin and up to her lips. In a honeyed whisper, he stated, "It would settle a lot of things and allow us to move onto more important matters—business *and* personal."

Look for these upcoming Arabesque titles:

July 1996

DECEPTION by Donna Hill
INDISCRETION by Margie Walker
AFFAIR OF THE HEART by Janice Sims

August 1996

WHITE DIAMONDS by Shirley Hailstock
SEDUCTION by Felicia Mason
AT FIRST SIGHT by Cheryl Faye

September 1996

WHISPERED PROMISES by Brenda Jackson
AGAINST ALL ODDS by Gwyn Forster
ALL FOR LOVE by Raynetta Manees

After Hours

Anna Larence

PINNACLE BOOKS
KENSINGTON PUBLISHING CORP.

PINNACLE BOOKS are published by

Kensington Publishing Corp.
850 Third Avenue
New York, NY 10022

First Pinnacle Books Printing: June, 1996
10 9 8 7 6 5 4 3 2

Printed in the United States of America

To Anna Lawrence, my grandmother, and Bonell Fields, my mother. I would be nothing without your strength, your wisdom, your guidance and love. Thank you.

Acknowledgments

Believe me when I say this book would not have happened without the support, kind words and in some cases, swift kick in the pants from the following people and organizations. Thank you all.

Paulara Hawkins
Francis Ray
LaRee Bryant
Angela Washington-Blair
Pam Fields
Javaun Smith
Patrice Robinson
Cheryl Troutman
Rick Rollerson
Rae Graves
Women Writers of Color
North Texas Romance Writers of America

One

Club 2050, Fort Worth's newest night club, was noisy, smoky, and crowded; the New Year's Eve party was in full swing. Nachelle Oliver pushed her way through the elegantly attired women and men standing around the bar, carefully balancing a wine spritzer in one hand, as she made her way to the table she shared with her best friend, Heather Chadwick and Gerald Forrester, Heather's fiancé, who was a professional basketball player.

"Finally," she muttered as she gingerly sat down at their table. "I didn't think I'd ever make it back. Where's Gerald?"

"He saw a friend and went over to say hi." Heather's hazel eyes twinkled with mischief as she eyed her friend's flushed appearance. "I noticed several men eyeing you. I told you red is your color. That dress is simply too devastating for any man to ignore."

"Oh, Heather, give it a rest, will you?" Nachelle's good-humored smile softened the words, but even as she protested, Nachelle had been vaguely aware of the not-so-discreet stares of several men. Secretly, she had to admit that Heather and the saleslady had been right. The red-sequined chemise dress, with its multi-colored bands around its hem, collar, and wrists set off her chocolate coloring and shapely curves to perfection.

"Okay, I'll leave it alone for now, but I've already told you my mission this year is to find you a special man."

Nachelle rolled her usually expressive, doe-brown eyes heavenward and, with an exaggerated sigh, remarked, "Even if you find that special man, I won't have any time to spend with him *this* year." Thoughts of her changing job position and Ralph Hayes's pending retirement pounded in her mind like a jackhammer.

Sensing her friend's thoughts, Heather laid a hand lightly on her arm, "Nachelle, we came out tonight so you could try to forget the news, remember?"

"I know, Heather. But, it's not working." Nachelle took a sip of the soothing drink and continued, "I . . . It's just hard for me to believe that Ralph willingly and secretly sold the Hayes Group to DuCloux Enterprises. I mean, I know it's his company and that technically I'm *only* an employee and he's the boss, but Ralph and I have a history. I can't believe he didn't warn me about this move."

"Nachelle, I'm sure Ralph had good reasons for doing what he did. He's a very shrewd, intelligent man. He has to be or else he wouldn't have been able to build up his company to the point he has."

Nachelle sighed deeply and placed a cheek into the palm of one hand. With resignation, she agreed. "Yeah, I know."

Gerald's booming voice interrupted further conversation between the long-time friends. "Hey, ladies, I'm back from making the rounds."

With a lovesick grin on her face, Heather stepped on tiptoe and planted a soft kiss on his smooth, sable-brown cheek. "I'm glad you're back. Nachelle wants to dance."

Gerald bowed low and with a chuckle in his voice, stated, "It would be my pleasure, madam, but first let me congratulate you on the DuCloux deal. You really orchestrated a big one!" Admiration was evident in his voice.

Simultaneously, two mouths dropped. Gerald saw that he had made a faux pas. His smile quickly disappeared.

Nachelle was the first to regain her senses. "How could you . . . did you find out about the buy-out?" Her normally husky voice threatened to reach a glass-shattering pitch. Sharp, red fingernails gripped Gerald's wrist as thoughts tossed through her mind. She repeated her inquiry, "How do you know about that?"

Gerald looked contrite as he stared at Nachelle's stricken face. "I was in the airport waiting for my return flight and picked up the paper. There it was. A full-page story in the morning edition of the *Atlanta Constitution*."

"You've got to be kidding!" A disbelieving Nachelle sat stock-still. "But how could the newspaper already have the story? The deal was just finalized today."

"I'm sorry, Nachelle. I assumed you knew about the article. You have, after all, been running the Hayes Group for the past couple of years."

Nachelle's initial desire was to call Gerald's bluff; he had a reputation for practical jokes. But judging from the look on his face, she saw that he was just as concerned as she was.

"Yes, well . . . this 'big one,' as you call it, was handled by Ralph and the DuCloux people. None of the Hayes Group executives were involved in the negotiations. Several months ago, Ralph mentioned that he might pursue some sort of deal with DuCloux Enterprises, but he never mentioned it again, so we all assumed that it had been a passing fancy." Nachelle spread her hands in supplication. "Who would have thought Ralph was secretly doing the deal?" Shaking her head slowly in disbelief, she finished, "Anyway, it's finished . . . or will be once they get Harlan's signature on the contracts."

Heather held up a petite hand. "Wait, wait, wait. You didn't tell me that part earlier today. You mean Harlan has to sign some papers to make it official?"

"Oh, Heather, there was just *so* much to tell. But, yeah, since the Hayes Group is one hundred percent family-owned by Ralph and Harlan, both father and son have to agree."

Heather's mind ran a mile a minute thinking about the implications of Harlan's necessary involvement; displeasure reflected on her face. *After all the heartache he put Nachelle through, if I ever see him again, it'll be too soon.* Heather's runaway thoughts concerning Harlan and the past stopped cold when she heard Gerald's next question.

"Has Harlan been notified?"

"I don't know, but I believe someone from DuCloux may have attempted to contact him. I'll know for sure on Monday when I speak with Ralph."

Determined to keep Harlan's name off everyone's minds and lips, Heather asked, "So, when this buy-out or sale or whatever it is happens, it means you could lose your job, right?" Hazel eyes searched Nachelle's face looking for signs of worry, anger, or stress.

"It's rare that new incoming management keeps 'old' employees, especially at the executive level." Nachelle paused to look longingly into her wine glass. Between Gerald's unanticipated news, thoughts of a questionable future, and the steady cadence from the live band along with the shouts and laughter from the party-goers, she could feel the beginnings of a royal headache. "My days are definitely numbered."

"I'm sorry, Nachelle. I know so little about your business . . . I thought this was a good thing." Gerald placed a loving, long arm around Nachelle's shoulders and gave her a gentle squeeze.

"Oh, Gerald, I know. I do appreciate the information. I wouldn't have known about the newspaper article otherwise." A fire lit Nachelle's eyes at the thought of the devious act.

To assure herself that the article could only have been contrived by a DuCloux Enterprises agent, she rewound the mental tape of her lunchtime conversation with Ralph Hayes and decided he wouldn't under any circumstance release this type of information without first notifying every Hayes employee. She had trusted Heather with the news, and knew with infallible faith, that her best friend would never do such a thing as leak the information. Deciding, with complete certainty that it was the work of DuCloux Enterprises, she said, "I definitely have something to discuss with Mr. DuCloux on Monday morning."

A simmering anger boiled within Nachelle at the thought of further implications sure to be caused by the premature news. "I can't believe the DuClouxes are being so insensitive. Why, our employees don't even know yet." Her voice rose several octaves as her anger came to a full boil. "What if one of them gets hold of that paper or hears it on the radio or from a friend or relative? My God, if that damn Steven DuCloux were here, I'd . . . I'd . . ."

"Nachelle, he is here." Gerald spoke softly, looking sheepish. "I ran into him just a few moments ago."

In a voice filled with incredulous wonder, Nachelle asked, "Here? In the club?"

Gerald nodded an affirmative and in one gulp polished off the rest of his ginger ale. Heather groaned in consternation.

Nachelle placed her elbows on the table and supported her throbbing head with interlaced fingers. As she lifted her head to speak, a drawling, Southern, undeniably male voice stated, "Gerald, we meet again. Please tell me one of these lovely ladies is the force behind the Hayes Group."

As if in a slow-moving, freeze frame, Nachelle raised guarded eyes to the face of her new boss. Steven DuCloux was not what she had expected.

Shaking the previous images she had built in her mind, Nachelle stared into the blackest eyes she had ever seen, the darkness of which only seemed to complement the mass of slightly wavy, salt-and-pepper hair that covered Steven's head and his coffee-bean coloring. His nickname in the computer industry popped into her mind: The Silver Shark. Although unequal to Gerald's basketball playing height, Steven DuCloux was tall, his size placing him shoulders above most of the male patrons. He had a subtle predatory air that even now was closing like a cloak around Nachelle. With much effort, she squelched a shiver and turned tortured eyes to Gerald.

Gerald stood and shook Steven's hand. "This is my fiancée,

Heather Chadwick, and this is Nachelle Oliver, Operations Vice President for the Hayes Group."

Steven gave his attention and handshake to the ladies in order of introduction.

"Ms. Oliver, we finally meet. May I say that I'm glad we're on the same team now." In response to her tight smile and slight nod, he added with a quirk of one brow, "I'm not assuming too much, am I?"

Rejecting the emotional upheaval his presence had brought, Nachelle cleared her throat and responded, "I'm aware final negotiations were concluded today, if that's what you're referring to." Carefully extracting her diminutive hand from his oversized one, she removed the last tinges of emotion from her voice, and responded, "Congratulations." She hoped her dry, impassive tone was reflected in her face as well. She had learned, in graduate school and through her experiences with Harlan Hayes, her ex-fiancé, the value of emotional detachment.

Steven smiled, showing a row of sparkling white teeth, and Nachelle noticed a dimple. "Thank you. I'm looking forward to meeting the rest of the staff on Monday."

Innocent, caring people could be hurt between now and Monday, she thought ungraciously.

Nachelle's busy mind stopped long enough for her to ask, "So you plan on being at the office when we announce the news to the employees?" It took all of her training to keep the sneer out of her voice.

His calm, seemingly innocent appearance annoyed her.

"Yes, Ralph and I discussed it today and we decided it would be beneficial. Don't you agree?" Jet black eyes narrowed slightly.

Nachelle's anger raged. She yearned to wipe that slick smile and composed expression from his face. Willing the same control that shepherded her through previous devastating events, she remarked in a staid voice, "The decision's already been made."

After ten years of knowing Nachelle, Heather recognized the telltale signs of percolating fury hiding behind her friend's ice mask. Interjecting quickly, Heather asked, "Gerald—Steven—how do you two know each other?"

"We're both Atlanta natives," Gerald replied. "Although we didn't live on the same side of town, everyone in Atlanta knows of the DuCloux family and DuCloux Enterprises."

That same disarming smile that didn't reflect in his eyes resided on Steven's face when he remarked, "And of course, everyone in Atlanta takes great pride in knowing the NBA's MVP for two years running is Atlanta born and raised."

With love and pride swelling her words, Heather remarked, "Well, Atlanta may claim him as a birthright, but I know Fort Worth has his heart." The innuendo was not lost on Gerald. He stooped and kissed Heather.

The extravagantly attired female singer was softly crooning a Luther Vandross ballad. Gerald remarked, "I believe they're playing our song. Shall we?" Denying Heather an opportunity to think or respond, he whisked her onto the dance floor.

Their sudden departure left Nachelle feeling exposed.

"May I?" Steven didn't wait for Nachelle's response. With an ease she found alarming, he slid his long body into the closest seat to her. A universal hand gesture brought a nearby waitress to the table.

"A refill for the lady and a gin and tonic for me." Happy to do his bidding, the young waitress flashed a dazzling smile and backed away from the table.

Steven took no notice of the flattery, but turned slightly in his seat toward his new vice president. His mind flitted to the information contained in Nachelle's dossier. He had taken extra time with her bio and personnel file. After all, although it wasn't common knowledge, it was by her hand that the Hayes Group had managed to sidestep the previous two buy-out attempts initiated by DuCloux Enterprises. For that alone, he applauded her, but no one had bothered to mention to him that she was as delectable looking as a ripe mango. Even in the darkened atmosphere, he could discern full generous lips, large almond-shaped eyes, and a healthy mane of coal black hair that begged for a man's gentle teasing and caress. The caveman in him longed for a satisfying look at her body and legs; unfortunately, the table hid her from his appraising eyes.

"Ralph speaks very highly of you." His bass voice rippled in the air.

"I'm very lucky to have had Ralph as my mentor. He's an exceptional businessman." Nachelle quelled a beneath-the-surface jeer. Pictures of the newspaper article still pierced her thoughts as she struggled to maintain a sense of professional decorum.

The primary-colored strobe lights suspended over the dance floor began rotating crazily, and the pace of the music picked up as the band transitioned to a fast dance number. Nachelle caught a glimpse of Gerald's tall frame and Heather's considerably shorter one. Her silent wish that they return to the table floated unanswered in the air. Their bodies simply moved apart as their steps quickened to keep time with the music.

"What do you think the employees' reaction will be when they hear the news?" Steven's eyes roamed from her attractive face to the collar of her jewel neckline to the small hands that occasionally surrounded the wine glass. A visual picture of those hands caressing his body flashed through his mind.

"I wouldn't presume to speak for every Hayes employee on staff." Nachelle couldn't control the tightness in her voice.

A silky thread entered his voice. "Right now I'm interested in the feelings of one employee. How do you feel about the change, Nachelle?" Steven interlaced long fingers and sought an answer from the most influential Hayes employee, the unofficial, official leader of the Hayes Group. His penetrating eyes never left her face.

The headache that had earlier plagued Nachelle renewed its presence by thudding harder against her left temple. She was in no mood to converse with the man who with one quick signature had changed her life. "Change can sometimes be good."

Steven leaned closer to Nachelle and stated boldly, "That's not really answering my question. What type of support can I expect from you?"

At his direct, forceful tone, Nachelle's composure shattered. Finding out about the buy-out, the newspaper article, meeting Steven, her headache, thoughts of an impending job search were all too much for her crowded mind. Her nerves, previously on edge, shattered. She reacted with blind fury and pent-up frustration.

"I understand your question! What I don't understand is why you're even bothering to ask it when it's obvious you don't care how I or the other employees will feel!"

Nachelle knew she should put a brake on her emotional outburst, but it was already too late. She had yelled at her new, short-term boss. With her initial anger exorcised, she suddenly felt better. She thought with dismay, *I'm going to lose my job anyway, so I might as well let him know what type of opponent I can be.*

She continued, "Did you or your people stop to think of the damage that could be done by printing that news article before the official announcement?"

Steven leaned back slightly at her onslaught. Women in both his professional realm and in his personal life used honeyed words, overt glances, and nature's feminine gifts to try and win his attention. Here this woman sat, inches from him, appearing to be unaffected by his reputation or position, using a tone of voice he wasn't accustomed to hearing directed at him.

A fleeting look of annoyance crossed his face. "So you know about that error." Steven stroked his chin before continuing. "You have every right to be angry. That article wasn't due to be released until Monday. Someone jumped the gun."

"And you don't know or care who that someone is?" Nachelle asked with barely concealed scorn. "A situation of this importance would never have been handled so poorly at the Hayes Group." A dramatic crescendo in the music punctuated her bold statement.

Steven was surprised to discover his anger rising to match hers. No one, absolutely no one, talked to him in such a challenging way. This attractive little woman had obviously been running things for too long. Mastering his anger, he stated coolly, "What difference does it make? The harm, if any, has been done. The only thing we can hope for is a smooth recovery." After a slight pause, he continued, "Now, back to my original question, if the employees know or don't know, how will they feel? How do *you* feel?"

Nachelle rubbed a hand across her forehead, wishing she could smooth away the problems facing them both as easily. Knowing they wouldn't be so lucky, she placed her emotions on simmer and turned what she hoped was a blank face to Steven.

"Having worked with a good many of them for years, I feel comfortable in saying they'll be worried and sad. To many of them, Ralph isn't just 'the boss,' he *is* the Hayes Group."

Before Steven could respond, an older, harried waitress dumped a bucket of ice surrounding a bottle of champagne, four glasses, and their earlier order on the table.

"Do you think it'll ease their fears to know that no changes will be made until a comprehensive study on how best to merge the two companies is completed and that the merger itself will take six to eight months, possibly longer?"

Nachelle thought again of Steven's reputation as the Silver Shark. His words were as skilled as his looks were handsome. Could she afford to give in to the hope that his words offered? She thought of the tenured, dedicated employees who hadn't had to look for work in years. She thought of Ralph and Adele Hayes, who were trusted pillars in the Fort Worth community. She thought of the small beginnings of the Hayes Group in the Hayes's garage so long ago and its current standing as the premier provider of specialized computer hardware and software. Her thoughts darted to Harlan Hayes, her ex-fiancé, who could have led the company to even greater heights if. . . . Her eyes misted over as she realized that even the bad years hadn't been as devastating as the buy-out news. The emotional roller coaster ride she'd been on all day continued its dangerous course: dipping, diving, tilting, snaking its way through memories of the past then heading toward future problems. Finding she could no longer hold onto even the handrail for safety, she shuddered in resignation and blinked furiously at the surface tears which threatened to spill over her eyes. Her train of thought cocooned her in the past, making her momentarily forget that Steven DuCloux, President and CEO of Du-Cloux Enterprises, sat a baby's breath away, completely in the present, watching the struggle raging within her with curious, dark eyes.

Steven reached into the inside pocket of his black, hand-tailored suit and withdrew a silk handkerchief. A thumb and forefinger of one large hand gently coaxed her face fully toward him. With surprising care, Steven dabbed at the tears, his touch firm yet pleasing.

A lost-spirited Nachelle sat zombielike, allowing Steven to care for her. His ministrations brought her face closer to his own. Brown eyes, glittering with emotions and still-unshed tears, met black eyes, which appeared to be devoid of any life. Staring into the bottomless depths, Nachelle felt like she was being sucked into a black abyss.

A fluttering awakening in the pit of her stomach made her breathing constrict and grow shallow. She could feel the heat from his body radiating, drawing her into his silver and black web. She willed the energy to draw away from him; however, the invisible string drawing them together grew tighter. Steven moved slowly towards her, his eyes maintaining black-magic contact with hers. Inexplicably, her lips parted to accept the unavoidable.

They were a breath apart when a big bang reverberated throughout the club. Startled, Nachelle jumped back and away from Steven. Shocked at what she had almost allowed to happen, she focused on the brightly colored confetti falling from broken piñatas. Her ears picked up the beginning strains of "Auld Lang Syne" and the popping of champagne bottles.

"Happy New Year, Nachelle!" Heather's laughter followed Nachelle's descent to reality. She managed to muster a smile when Heather's comforting arms surrounded her in a minute bear hug.

"Happy New Year to you!" Nachelle ended the hug, stood, and turned to Gerald. A quick exchange of words and greetings followed, mirroring the actions of the other club patrons.

"I would have thought y'all would've had that bottle of champagne open by now. We've got some catching up to do," Gerald remarked, rubbing his hands in anticipation.

With a devilish wink, Steven explained, "We got wrapped up in other things." He popped the cork on the bottle and filled four glasses. One would never have guessed he and Nachelle had just been involved in a serious moment.

Nachelle flushed, thankful for the dark atmosphere. Still, she could feel Heather's quizzical gaze on her composed face. She refused to meet her eyes.

Heather held her glass high and proposed a toast, "To old friendships . . . and new."

After a clink of glasses, Gerald stated playfully, "Okay, time to hear those New Year's resolutions. I'll start first. I resolve to set a date for our wedding."

Heather looked sheepish and remarked, a little deflatedly, "We'll see." In a cheerier voice, she stated, "I've already told Nachelle my resolution and it's not repeatable in mixed company, but it has something to do with a special man."

The men weren't having that and initiated a chorus of "No fair," and "Come on, tell," comments. A mixture of lighthearted laughter followed their refrain.

Heather saucily countered with, "You can beg, plead, and

bribe, but I'll never tell, so, Steven, you might as well tell us your resolution."

"Gladly. I resolve to make the most of my recent acquisition and wrap up my work on acquisition number two, a wife."

Nachelle was stunned by Steven's words. She couldn't believe that he was prepared to kiss her knowing he was engaged to get married.

Unaware of Nachelle's distress, Gerald piped up, "Well then, we can hopefully count on two weddings this year." He held his hand up to show crossed fingers. His eyes never left Heather's.

Heather smiled, but turned to Nachelle and asked, "Nachelle, what's your New Year's resolution?"

"I . . . I don't plan to make any resolutions." Hurriedly, Nachelle added, "My track record with them stinks." *And so does my new boss,* she added silently. By her count, he was living up to his reputation. The rumors she'd heard at trade shows must have been true. The Silver Shark specialized in devouring young businesses and young women, then spitting them out in a mangled mess. She was not going to be one of the conquered and she pledged to do everything in her power to ensure a significant portion of the Hayes Group stayed intact!

"That's our Nachelle. Never intent on making the same mistake twice." Gerald placed long arms effortlessly around each woman, although he spoke to Nachelle, "We wouldn't have it any other way."

Picking up the last bars of the traditional year-end-and-beginning song, Heather and Gerald joined in.

After the last note dissipated, Steven replied, "I hate to leave such good company, but I've got a hectic day tomorrow." Turning to Nachelle with an unreadable look, he stated, "We'll finish on Monday."

Nachelle's heart somersaulted and her pulse sped up. *If he thinks for one minute I'm willing to finish what almost happened, he's in for a rude awakening.*

When good-byes were complete, Nachelle breathed a sigh of relief. She knew, without the benefit of a crystal ball, Monday would be a day she would never forget.

Two

Monday, January 3rd—the first working day of the new year—heralded overcast skies and bitterly cold temperatures. Nachelle pulled the lapels of her wool winter coat together as she covered the short distance from the parking garage to the Hayes Group building, a four-story, red brick office building situated on the outskirts of downtown Fort Worth.

Despite the additional layer of clothing, she found herself shivering. *Admit it, Nachelle,* she gently scolded herself, *you're not reacting to the cold, but rather, anticipating the reactions of the employees after they hear the news and . . . how Steven DuCloux will handle Friday night's incident.*

The soft swoosh of the heavy glass entrance doors closing behind her was the only sound that greeted her as she stepped into the lobby. As if walking into the Hayes Group building for the first time, she stopped and looked at every detail. Everything from the pink marbled floors to the large potted ficus trees to the brass directories positioned by the elevators took on a new facet. Her throat constricted as she realized the logo she had taken for granted for the past seven years would soon be replaced by the bold design depicting DuCloux Enterprises.

"Ah, Nachelle. Here you are."

Nachelle whirled around to see Ralph Hayes and Steven DuCloux approaching her.

Ralph continued with a warm, friendly smile on his ageless face. "I was just telling Steven you would be arriving soon." Even with present company, Ralph greeted her in his usual cordial way—a quick peck on the cheek and a brief hug.

Nachelle forced a lukewarm smile. "Good morning,

Ralph." With concentrated effort, she pulled her eyes from Ralph's comforting ones to meet Steven's. "Good morning, Mr. DuCloux." Memories of Friday night rushed forward, crowding away thoughts of the unprecedented meeting soon to come and . . . escalating her body temperature.

With no regard to pleasantries, Steven remarked, "Steven. Call me Steven. We don't hold with certain formalities at Du-Cloux Enterprises."

Nachelle nodded her agreement and offered a tight smile.

Steven continued, "Why don't you go unload your things and then meet me and Ralph in the cafeteria? We have just enough time to review the agenda and some minor details before the meeting."

"Sure." Nachelle walked stiffly into the elevator the two men had just vacated and punched the fourth floor button.

The Silver Shark is living up to his reputation, she thought glumly. *He didn't show a flicker of recognition or emotion. Nothing at all to indicate we almost . . . oh, God, I can't believe I almost kissed him.* Nachelle cut off her thoughts. She didn't want to consider the actions and principles she had almost compromised two days ago.

The distant whir caused by the upward ascent of the elevator didn't intrude on her thoughts as she tried to focus on the big meeting scheduled to take place in less than an hour. But these thoughts led her right back to Steven. This morning of all mornings, he should have shown signs of nervousness and strain. Instead, he looked assured, undaunted; self-confidence oozing from every pore. The charcoal-gray suit, crisp white shirt, and abstract tie containing colorful splashes of red, olive green, and gray only added to his appeal, highlighting his ebony skin and silver and black hair. Nachelle reluctantly admitted he was incredibly good-looking, and as sexy as hell.

"Enough of this, Nachelle!" she muttered, as she entered her office. "You've got enough to worry about without reminding yourself of how utterly attractive the man is."

Nachelle quickly deposited her coat and briefcase. A thor-

ough, but hasty look in the mirror confirmed all was intact—
from the tightly coiled French roll which bound her baby-fine
hair, to the navy, double-breasted suit. She silently congratulated herself on achieving the professional, formal look she
had hoped to present. With restored confidence, and a renewed commitment to use past experiences as a learning tool,
she grabbed her portfolio and rode the elevator down.

Ralph and Steven sat at a table near the entrance. Nachelle
descended two shallow steps and briefly looked around to
confirm that they were the only people in the cafeteria. Looking around the comfortable room brought to mind the time
when Ralph had had the space converted to a cafeteria. He'd
insisted on having it feel like walking into one's personal dining room at home. Square, pine wood tables covered with
cotton green and white tablecloths accented the leafy green
plants scattered throughout the room. Candid photos of employees at work and sometimes at play lined the creamy walls.
Microwaves, a stocked pantry, and a varied hot and cold menu
completed the environment.

With a sigh, Nachelle turned her attention to the men at the
table. She couldn't help but note their differences. Whereas
Steven was tall and appeared to have not an ounce of fat on
him, Ralph was short with a belly like Santa Claus. Steven's
thick head of hair contrasted vividly with Ralph's balding pate.
The one thing they shared, besides a keen business mind, was
that deep brown skin coloring that made women do a double-
take. Clearing her throat to signify her return, she walked
toward the table in the same mood as a convict walking to the
electric chair.

Steven was on his feet, pulling out a chair for her before
she could think about affixing a smile to her face.

"Ah, Nachelle, perfect timing. Steven and I were just talking about you."

Nachelle's grip on her portfolio tightened, but that was the
only sign of anxiety she allowed. Not trusting herself to speak,

she tilted her head and lifted one brow as a sign to proceed. Ralph did so.

"Steven told me you two already met. Quite by accident, no less." Ralph looked pleased to hear that information. "Isn't that remarkable."

"Yes, it is." Even though she could feel Steven's piercing eyes boring into her, she refused to make eye contact with him.

Giving Nachelle a fatherly pat on the arm, Ralph continued, "It'll help make the transition easier for the employees, you know, if you two can achieve the same kind of comfort level that you and I share."

Nachelle was thankful for her dark skin coloring, so as not to give away her sudden embarrassment. *If he only knew just how comfortable we almost were,* she thought wildly.

"I agree with Ralph, Nachelle. As leaders of two dynamic organizations, I daresay that before the merger is complete, we'll be very close."

Nachelle wasn't sure she actually heard the velvety undertone in Steven's deep voice, or imagined it, considering where her thoughts continued to dwell. To confirm or deny her imaginings, she looked questioningly into his fathomless eyes. They offered neither a clue nor an answer. Chalking her imaginings and increased heartbeats to a restless weekend, she turned her attention to Ralph.

"Now . . ." Ralph continued, "I want to inform you of my weekend decision. As I told both of you on Friday, I'm retiring. What I haven't told either of you is that my retirement is effective today. As soon as this meeting is over, I'm gone."

Nachelle gasped and both hands flew to her face. Of course, she knew Ralph had planned to retire, but she had at least counted on his presence through the merger. Things were going from bad to worse. "Ralph, I . . . we need you here."

"Yes, and I wanted to stay, but after discussing the situation with Adele, we decided it would be best for all if I just made a clean break of it. Besides, you'll still be here and the employees respect and admire you." Ralph chuckled, a jolly sound that echoed through the nearly deserted room. "Heck, most of them consider you the boss anyway." Seeing the stricken look on Nachelle's face, Ralph took her hands in his and stared her straight in the eye. "Nachelle, you know that since my last stroke when Harlan left, I haven't been the leader of this organization. You have. You stepped in, took the reins, and have done a spectacular job leading the company. I know I can count on you to continue in that vein, right?"

Nachelle fought a tremendous war. Yes, she had been, almost single-handedly, directing the company for several years now, but Ralph had always been there in the background, a source of strength and wisdom. With her safety net gone and with a previous competitor now in the driver's seat, could she continue to lead the charge? She stared into Ralph's supportive eyes for the answer.

Checking his watch, Steven prompted, "Nachelle, we're running out of time. The meeting will start soon. I'm okay with Ralph's decision. Are you?"

Steven's voice acted like a cold-water dousing. The Silver Shark had witnessed her in another moment of weakness. Anger at Steven for buying the Hayes Group, thus upsetting her nice, safe world blazed through her—hot and intense. Using her anger constructively, her doubts disappeared like a bubble as she turned determined eyes to Steven. In a clear, bold voice, she stated, "Of course I'm fine with the decision. What's the format for the meeting?"

With only a slight pause, Steven launched into a discussion of the meeting. He commanded the floor, with Ralph interjecting a few words intermittently. No sooner had they finished briefing her when small groups of employees started arriving.

"Showtime," Ralph said, with a hint of regret. He stood and left Nachelle and Steven to gather their notes. Ralph's usual welcome—a warm handshake, a friendly smile and a kind word—greeted every unsuspecting employee as he or she stepped into the cafeteria.

Nachelle watched as the employees returned Ralph's infectious greeting. The scene made her think again of how difficult this transition would be for the employees. They all, including herself, were fond of Ralph. He had the endearing and sincere ability to make people feel like they were part of a close-knit family. She recalled the first time she had met Ralph and Adele Hayes. Acting on Harlan's impulsive behavior, she and Harlan had decided to take a long weekend break from their graduate studies at the University of Texas at Austin. They had ditched their Friday classes and had driven to Fort Worth to visit his family. Although she and Harlan had been dating for only a few months, Ralph and Adele had opened their arms to her, and at the end of the three-day weekend, they had even entrusted her with a key to their lavish home. It was that same caring, trusting quality that had made Ralph Hayes and the Hayes Group a success. And now Ralph was retiring, Du-Cloux Enterprises was taking over, and the Hayes Group would be no more.

Nachelle sniffed and made a move to dab at her eyes, but was stopped when a gray silk handkerchief appeared magically. That was when she remembered Steven DuCloux, President and CEO of DuCloux Enterprises, was within whispering distance. *Damn it to hell! That's the third time I've let my emotions run amok around him. He must think I'm a loose canon.* Seconds later, she scolded herself. *What do I care what he thinks of me? In a couple of weeks, he won't even remember my name.* Such was the direction her thoughts had been taking since New Year's Eve—stable and sound one second and erratic and illogical the next.

Taking the handkerchief, she avoided his eyes and murmured in the vicinity of his tie, "Thank you."

"You're welcome." Steven's low-pitched, masculine voice caressed her ear. "Have you recovered from Friday night?"

With great appreciation, his magnetic eyes fastened on her full lips and he wondered if they tasted as good as they looked.

Disappointed in herself for allowing Steven to see her revert to an emotional level yet again, Nachelle snapped to attention. Despite her short-term length of employment with DuCloux Enterprises, she still had a professional position to maintain, and now more than ever, due to Ralph's announcement.

With more casualness than she felt, she shrugged and replied, "There wasn't anything to recover from." Nachelle wasn't about to admit that for the past two days she had turned their near-kiss scene over and over again in her head. She had reviewed it so often that, at times, she felt she could smell his unique blend of aftershave and natural male scent.

Steven pursued the conversation, as if intent on discovering what effects their brief social contact had had on her. "Oh? It seemed like you were responding quite well to the . . . stimulants." Steven crossed powerful arms across an equally impressive chest. His expressionless face revealed nothing.

Nachelle was lost, confused. She didn't know if Steven was attempting to trap her in a word game or if he was sincere in his inquiry. She regretted their encounter Friday night and wished she could rewind the clock and erase the time. But, all the wishing in the world wouldn't eliminate that five minutes from her life, if indeed that was what he was referring to. He was impossible to read!

Feeling out of control, Nachelle fell into a mode that had on more than one occasion saved her—aloof and professional. "I'd rather not continue this conversation. It's not important, and anyway, we have a meeting to start." She refused to meet his eyes for fear he would trespass through her cocoa-colored smokescreen. Yes, she had responded to him and if she didn't put distance between them now, she felt she would fall into the black magic spell his eyes and lips promised to weave.

I am NOT going to have a repeat performance of Friday night, she commanded herself with strong conviction, *no more emotions, and definitely no more tears around Steven DuCloux.*

Nachelle half turned from him and stated, "I see some of the other vice presidents. In case you don't know, Ralph met with each of them this weekend. They know what the meeting is about, but I think it would be best if you meet them now."

Nachelle waved a perfectly manicured hand to catch the attention of Mike Adams and Percy Mitchell. They acknowledged her presence and soon joined her and Steven. Nachelle made quick work of the introductions and then discreetly stood aside to observe Mike and Percy as they faced their new boss.

Steven took control after the introductions and in a low, subdued voice imparted the same information he had shared with Nachelle earlier. Using the repetitiveness as a means of escape, Nachelle excused herself to mingle. But she would rather have her tongue yanked out than admit she needed distance from the Silver Shark.

A few minutes later, Ralph started the history-making meeting and for the next two hours, her mind managed to stay focused on business matters.

Nachelle and two of the four vice presidents for the now defunct Hayes Group stood in the gallery on the fourth floor. All of their offices were housed on this, the executive floor, and occasionally on Mondays they met in the gallery to exchange weekend stories before starting a grueling work week. This morning, their talk centered, not on frivolous matters, but on the buy-out announcement.

"He seems like an okay guy. I got the feeling he was honest when he answered the questions. That's a plus since it'll make our jobs a little easier." Mike Adams, Sales Vice President, spoke in his usual lightning quick manner. His slick tongue and ability to accurately "peg" people led to an impressive sales record and a successful bottom line for the Hayes Group.

"I trust your judgment," Percy declared. As the Logics and Designs Vice President, he had little desire to deal with people, preferring to spend his time with bytes and pathways. However, he had just the right amount of people skills to deal with the analytical, technical staff he controlled. "If you think the almighty DuCloux is worth staying with until the end, whenever that might be, I can go along with that."

None of the vice presidents lived under false pretenses. They knew that eventually they would be handed their walking papers. Their willingness to stay until that point in time spoke to their loyalty to Ralph, the Hayes Group, and their employees.

Nachelle spoke hesitantly, "Mike, did you really get the feeling DuCloux was being honest? He doesn't have a very good reputation in that category. And, I already told you about the newspaper article. We're lucky only a handful of the employees read about the change of ownership in the weekend edition. Thank goodness it was a busy New Year's weekend for the majority of our employees."

"Yeah, I can't figure it. I expected to pick up bad vibes." Mike scratched his bald dome and snorted, his version of a laugh. "Heck, on the contrary, he seems to be 'Mister Personality.' Did you see the charmed looks on the faces of some of the women? I still don't think they know DuCloux Enterprises bought the Hayes Group."

A chorus of nervous laughter broke out.

Nachelle had to admit that she too noticed the admiring stares directed toward Steven . . . most noticeably from the single women. She ignored the wild dip her stomach took and stated, "I hate to leave such pleasant company, but I have a nagging suspicion that DuCloux will want financial reports pretty quickly. Meet you guys for lunch, okay?"

Affirmative remarks followed Nachelle's retreating back.

Hurried strides carried her down the carpeted hallway to her corner office, and the same momentum solidified her mental stance regarding Steven. *I've got to remember to stay cool around that man. I can't let my emotions rule me.* With a negative shake of her head, she continued in a slightly different vein with a look of pure confusion reflecting on her face. *How could Mike not pick up bad vibes?* she mused. She had no doubt Steven DuCloux was trouble.

She recalled one particular story about DuCloux Enterprises and their business practices. It had happened years ago, when Harlan was Executive Vice President of the Hayes Group and Nachelle was then the Finance Director. A major manufacturing company had selected both the Hayes Group and DuCloux Enterprises as final contenders for a customized software contract worth millions of dollars. The Hayes Group had performed their demonstration, and although their product had a few bugs, the manufacturing company's officials had been very impressed. A few days later, DuCloux Enterprises demonstrated their product which turned out to be an exact replica of the Hayes Group's, only without the flaws. The contract was awarded to DuCloux Enterprises. Upon hearing the decision, Ralph, Harlan, and the design team had been greatly disappointed. Winning that contract would have catapulted them all from a national to an international company. Even though the Hayes Group went on to win other major contracts, sometimes beating out DuCloux Enterprises, no one ever forgot that first major battle between the two companies. And certainly no one forgot when, several months after the contract had been awarded, rumors started circulating within the computer industry that DuCloux Enterprises had planted a spy at the Hayes Group's demonstration. When those rumors finally reached the executive offices of the Hayes Group, it had taken both Nachelle and Ralph to stop Harlan from flying to Atlanta to demand answers from Steven Du-Cloux. Instead, Harlan had called Steven. The telephone call had ended with the Hayes Group no closer to the truth. Ralph had then insisted that since there was no proof to leave it alone. Harlan had followed his father's lead, but he, like Nachelle, never forgot.

As Nachelle entered her office, she shook off memories of the past, but also noted that it was right after the awarding of that manufacturing contract that Steven was dubbed the Silver Shark by industry people.

Sighing deeply, Nachelle ran a hand down the side of her face and shook her head slowly. *Who would have ever thought that one day we would all be working for the Silver Shark.* She was halfway to her desk when, just to her right, she saw a movement. She turned to see the man who occupied her thoughts. *Speak of the devil,* she mused.

"Hi. I've been waiting for you." Steven looked purely at ease, lounging on her couch. "Join me for coffee." He had unbuttoned his jacket and one ankle was crossed casually over a knee. On the low coffee table in front of him was a silver tray loaded with coffee, pastries, and even a single fresh carnation.

Taking a deep breath and then expelling it slowly, Nachelle reluctantly did as commanded. *Don't forget who you're dealing with, Nachelle,* she warned herself. *Despite the outside packaging, the man is a two-legged shark, fully equipped to tear and shred in a heartbeat.*

"I was just getting ready to review the December financial report. I assume your finance department will want it." Nachelle eased into an opal-colored, wingback chair. She crossed her legs and arms, not caring that she was giving "closed communication" body language.

Steven ignored her business reference and picked up a yellowing picture of a young couple in a lead crystal frame. "Your parents, I assume?"

"Yes."

"I see where you get your good looks. They're a handsome couple."

Silence met his statement.

He returned the photo to its usual resting place and continued. "I understand they sold their insurance business in Austin many years ago and retired."

Large brown eyes got even larger as she reacted in surprise to his statement. "How do you know that?"

Steven uncrossed his leg and leaned forward. "I make it a business practice to have every executive in my employ investigated." Steven poured another coffee for himself and then a cup for her. Handing her the cup and saucer, he continued. "The more you know about a person, the better you can gauge their work performance."

Nachelle didn't respond. She couldn't! A smoldering anger was closely edging all sensibilities out of the way. She struggled to remain professional, despite her planned intentions.

In a hard tone, she stated, "If you want to know anything about me, you should ask *me*. I don't appreciate your prying."

Totally unnettled, Steven replied, "You're right, I should have asked. But, regardless, I still would have commissioned the report." Steven sat back, immediately dwarfing the small settee. "DuCloux Enterprises takes nothing for granted. No matter how attracted I am to you, it won't make me forget the hardships my family went through to build this company."

Nachelle stared into her coffee. Her hand tightly gripped the rounded surface of the delicate china cup as if she were holding onto a life preserver. Her mind traveled back in time, thinking of all the events and people who had touched her life. What else had his investigators discovered? Did they unearth the reason for her promotion to vice president at such a young age? Did he know of her engagement to Harlan Hayes? . . . And why, for that matter, Harlan was no longer with the company? And, did Steven just say he was *attracted* to her? No, she was sure she must have misunderstood. Like vultures waiting to land, a million questions whirled in her mind.

Steven picked up an intricately carved pewter frame and said, "Since your parents had two children, this must be your brother, Vincent." Steven pinned her with an unnerving direct look. "He's every bit as handsome as you are beautiful." When she remained mute, he continued, "I understand he's a career military man stationed at the Pentagon."

In an icy voice, she declared, "Your informants are very good."

"And you seem to be as committed to your career as your brother is to his."

Nachelle met his stare; the challenge in his eyes was unmistakable. Suppressed anger and indignation made her own eyes glitter like diamonds. Her voice vibrated dangerously as, in short, clipped words, she answered, "I can agree with your need to have loyal, dependable executives, but, I don't agree with your methods, and furthermore, I don't have to discuss this with you."

Not releasing the bottled emotions caused her voice and body to tense; her neck and shoulder muscles grew taut. She stood on shaky, yet determined legs.

"I'm committed to staying here until the dust settles because Ralph asked me to for the sake of the employees, but if it weren't for that, I'd walk out right now. I've already paid my dues, and I won't start over again. You'll just have to take me at face value."

Turning abruptly, she covered the short distance to her desk. It wasn't until she sat down that she realized Steven had shadowed her.

"Your words are contradictory." Large, brown hands landed on either side of her appointment calendar. "With just a few words from me you're ready to walk away from a high ranking position with a prestigious company because it doesn't have the mom-and-pop feeling that the Hayes Group had. Yet, it only takes a glance at the want ads to know that vice president jobs aren't readily available. If you leave now, you'd be doing exactly what you don't want—starting over again."

In a tightly controlled voice, Nachelle replied, "The Hayes Group is *not* a mom-and-pop organization." She stood to obtain a better vantage point. "May I remind you that we managed to stave off your company's advances for years, and the only reason you won this time is because Ralph initiated the deal. May I also remind you that he's still recovering from his last stroke."

"You're wrong, Nachelle. The only reason DuCloux Enterprises 'won' this time is because Ralph had the good sense to realize the world—our industry—is changing, and he isn't prepared to lead his company to and through the 21st century. He's tired, and rightly so; he's a pioneer for which DuCloux Enterprises is eternally grateful." Steven spread his large hands in an expressive gesture. "Ralph opened the door for a lot of African-American companies, including mine, but there's a time for everything, and Ralph realizes that." His point-blank words would have made a person with common sense cower, but Nachelle was too angry to heed the carefully blank expression on his face. "And, even with all your skills, accomplishments, and abilities, you're not ready to lead that charge either. You've cocooned yourself in the lap of comfort . . . here . . . in these safe walls. Yes, it was good for the Hayes Group, but bad for Nachelle."

Steven straightened to his full six feet, two inches, and in a calm, emotionless voice added, "For Ralph, it was either give in to DuCloux Enterprises, a company whose basic philosophy is the same as the Hayes Group, or sell to another company and risk losing everything down to the very principles on which this company was founded."

Steven walked to her door. He rarely lost his temper and when he did, it never showed. His voice and mannerisms gave no indication that she had treaded where few dared go. His voice was soft and calm when he said, "It's a new day and a new age. And with it, a new way of doing business. I suggest you get used to it." Steven was almost out of the door when he spoke again. "I'm going to Atlanta to clear up some business matters. I'll be back at the end of the week." With that, he was gone.

Nachelle had watched his progress to the door with a mixture of relief, anger, and dread. Frustrated, she collapsed into her chair and folded her arms across her desk. With a heavy sigh, she laid her head in the folded crook of her arms and rolled it slowly back and forth. A melange of emotions crowded her senses; her thoughts were a discombobulated mess. Had he really let loose a private investigator on her and the other executives? Did he really think his "rescue" of the Hayes Group was a good thing? How dare he refer to the Hayes Group as a diamond in the rough. *Why, we've outperformed DuCloux Enterprises in a number of key areas. And, he's out of his mind to even suggest I shorted myself by staying on here for seven years.* Her thoughts jumped from one subject to the other, with no rhyme or reason, leaving mass confusion.

Nachelle stood and walked to the ceiling-to-floor window. *He said he was attracted to me.* That thought rose from the midst of all of her other thoughts to shine as brightly as the Eastern star. *That would explain his behavior Friday night,* she thought. *But, so what!* her mind protested. *He's made it clear that business will be first, personal feelings second.* This should have comforted and relaxed her. It didn't.

Nachelle pressed her forehead against the cold glass. She looked out and down at the scene below her. Delivery boys and truck drivers were the lone souls on the streets and sidewalks at this time of the morning in this industrial district. *They perform their jobs in cold angry winds. Can I do any less?* Although the DuCloux climate was harsh, she'd suffered worse situations in the office environment and survived. She would survive this drastic change as well by staying focused and committed to her personal and professional objectives. Fortified for the time being, she made up her mind to confer with Steven as soon as he returned. She had a few things to tell him, one of which being her stand on office romances.

Nachelle could feel some of the anger and frustration confined within her small frame melt away. Although she was still shaking slightly, she made herself visualize a rainbow in the future of the Hayes Group employees, herself included.

She was so intent on her mental exercise that she didn't notice Millie, her grandmother-like secretary, slip into her office to drop off the morning mail and collect the serving tray.

Three

Nachelle knew she should place the heavily loaded grocery bag on the floor and then unlock the door, but that was too easy. Leaning into the door, she inserted the key and heard the imperceptible click of the lock being released.

Great going, Nachelle! She congratulated herself on managing to maintain her hold on the assemblage of groceries, briefcase, and purse, without losing a piece of mail or her balance. With a steady foot, she kicked the door shut and headed for the kitchen.

"Oh, thank goodness, food! You have nothing in the fridge."

Heather's tinkerbell voice rose from behind, startling her, and causing everything in Nachelle's arms to hit the floor.

Swinging around quickly, she shouted, "Heather!" Looking down at the mess crowded around her feet, Nachelle reproachfully stated, "I've told you before, don't walk up behind me! You're not going to be satisfied until you give me a heart attack."

A sorrowful expression showed on Heather's face for a split second before it resumed its usual cheery glow. "You know I'm sorry, Nachelle. Here, let me help you." Heather stooped and stuffed groceries back into the bag. "Ummm! Cream cheese. Did you get bagels, too?"

Nachelle looked at the upturned face of her best friend. The thought of taking her spare key back from Heather passed flittingly through Nachelle's mind, but the benefits of a trusted friend having an extra key to her condominium outweighed the problems. Besides, no matter what the situation was, she had never been able to be mad at Heather for long. This time was no exception.

"Yes, I did." Nachelle bent and began gathering the spilled items. "What are you doing here? I thought you and Gerald were dining with your parents tonight."

Dryly, Heather responded, "I don't have parents. I have a mother who marries for money every two years."

"Oh Heather, quit being so melodramatic."

"I'm serious, but to answer your question, Roger's presence was required in Washington, D.C., and you know Mother, any trip for Roger is a shopping trip for her. They left this afternoon." Heather spoke without malice about her stepfather's and mother's sudden trip and subsequent dinner cancellation. "I'm so relieved. I'm not up to hearing Mother rattle on for hours about life as a Senator's wife and my nonexistent wedding plans. She just can't get it through her head that I'm not in a hurry to tie the knot."

Nachelle followed Heather to the kitchen where they stocked the pantry and refrigerator with the salvaged groceries. "I thought you were going to talk to her . . . try to make her understand your point of view."

"I tried. We had lunch, oh, I guess about three weeks ago, right before Christmas, and it was like talking to a Barbie doll."

"And what about Gerald," Nachelle gave Heather a pointed look. "You heard his New Year's resolution. He's ready to get married. You can't keep stringing him along."

"Oh, I'll talk to Gerald." Heather replied evasively. With a mouthful of bagel and cream cheese, she continued. "Anyway, I didn't come here to talk to you about my family." Heather's hazel eyes sparkled with mischief. "I've got some great news, and I couldn't wait to tell you."

Nachelle groaned. She had seen that look on Heather's face many times before. "Please, Heather, don't tell me you've met my 'Mr. Right' again!" The gentle smile on Heather's face and the animated head nod only confirmed Nachelle's statement. "Thanks, but no thanks. I don't have the time or energy to waste on dating."

Heather ignored her friend's words and followed Nachelle to her bedroom. She playfully retorted, "Nothing you can say or do will knock me off course."

"I'm not interested, Heather," Nachelle replied in a sing-song voice.

"At least let me tell you about him."

Nachelle shrugged out of her suit jacket and threw it on the bed. She placed her hands on her slim waist and gave Heather a hard stare. "I'm going to have my hands full with this buy-out. I won't have a personal life for several months. So forget it."

Heather adopted a sad, puppy dog look and tilting her head to the side, said, "I promise I'll stop sneaking up on you if you just listen to me—just for a second."

Nachelle knew by the gleam in Heather's eyes and the stubborn set of her chin that her appeal was falling on deaf ears. She sighed and threw her hands in the air. "Okay, okay. I'll give you fifteen minutes. Then, I'm throwing you out. I have a lot of work to do."

In her best rendition of a Southern belle, Heather replied, "Oh, honey, fifteen minutes is all I need. But, I think you'll find you'll want more at the end of my time." Heather flashed a big Cheshire-cat grin and assumed a lounging position on Nachelle's four-poster bed.

"We'll see." Nachelle opened dresser drawers and pulled out casual clothes. In seconds, she transformed herself from corporate employee to college coed. In dated, baggy sweat pants and a sweatshirt which depicted the insignia of her sorority, her hair in a ponytail clip, and a minimum of make-up, she looked like she belonged on a college campus.

"Alright. Who's this fabulous guy who's hit the front page of the Heather Chadwick newspaper?" Nachelle threw herself across the bed and pinched off a piece of Heather's bagel.

"I learned today that your new boss is single."

A frown wrinkled Nachelle's forehead. "I thought we were talking about one of Gerald's handsome, single, successful friends? What does Steven DuCloux have to do with this?"

Heather rolled her eyes heavenward, then focused them on Nachelle. "Nachelle, you're absolutely the best in the world at business stuff, but sometimes you can be a little dense regarding men. Didn't you notice Steven's reaction to you on Friday night? You totally captivated him."

Nachelle opened her mouth, but it took a couple of starts before words formed. "Heather, you can't be suggesting that I consider Steven DuCloux as a . . . a . . ." An incredulous look reflected on Nachelle's face. "That's ludicrous!"

"What's so crazy about it?" Heather retorted. "The man is unattached, sexy as hell, and accomplished. Mixing his business knowledge with yours would create an indestructible company, and you wouldn't have to worry about finding another job or employee layoffs."

As slow as the morning sunrise, it dawned on Nachelle that her friend was dead serious. "Oh Heather, I wasn't trying to be callous, but this isn't and will never be the typical boy meets girl story. There are so many other things to consider."

Heather defended her matrimonial choice for Nachelle. "Such as?"

"Well, such as, he may be officially single, but he told us Friday night about his engagement."

"Ah ha!" Heather jumped up, excitement moving her around the room. "Mother found out today that he has been seeing some socialite in Atlanta, but he hasn't popped the question. Her sources said it isn't likely that he will. And besides, he didn't actually say he was engaged."

"Sources?" A puzzled frown was replaced with sudden understanding. "Heather, don't tell me your mother called long distance to question her friends about Steven DuCloux?"

"Of course she did. You know Mother has never denied me *anything*." Heather winked and recovered her spot on the bed.

Nachelle dropped her head into her hands. "Heather, how could you? You must know that I would never consider Steven as anything other than a temporary boss." It was Nachelle's turn to pace the room. "The man is unyielding and untrustworthy. Do you know he had the audacity to have my background investigated?"

"Noooo! Really?" Heather's eyes grew large with interest.

"Yes! He knows all about my family, and he probably knows what type of cereal I used to eat as a child." Nachelle plopped down in her windowpane chair and stated in a derision-riddled voice, "According to the great Steven DuCloux, it's a common business practice at DuCloux Enterprises."

"Isn't that something?" Heather allowed a few moments of silence to slip by while Nachelle's comments sank in. After a time, she surprised Nachelle by laughing.

"It isn't funny, Heather." Nachelle threw a pillow at her friend. "You don't know how angry I was, still am."

Heather shook her head, laughing harder. "No. No, Nachelle. I'm not laughing at you. I'm laughing because while he was investigating you, Mother was discovering all *his* little secrets. She probably knows what type of cereal he ate as a child." Heather chuckled in her high-pitched voice. "You know how nosy Mother is."

Nachelle sat on the edge of her chair, watching her friend. A mental picture of Mrs. Wolfe, Heather's mother, "spying" on Steven flashed vividly through Nachelle's mind. Nachelle couldn't stop the smile from spreading across her face.

Heather continued, talking between spurts of laughter, "And knowing my mother, she probably got more information on him than he got on you."

The knowledge that Heather's last comment was probably true made Nachelle shake her head in surrendering grace. Between Heather and her mother they could bring the KGB to their knees. With teasing politeness, Nachelle asked,

"Maybe I should tell Steven to hire your mother for future PI jobs?"

A new round of laughter followed Nachelle's last remark.

Eventually, their laughing fit subsided and Heather continued, "I know my fifteen minutes is up, so I'll quickly tell you what else Mother found out." Heather polished off the last bite of bagel and in a matter-of-fact voice rattled off the DuCloux family information. "Adolphus and Nadine DuCloux had four sons. The three older boys are married with children. And, of course, they all work in the family business. Then there's Steven, the baby."

"Some baby!" Nachelle interrupted.

Heather chuckled. "Yeah, well, the baby was always targeted to run the business after Adolphus's retirement."

"Really? Even with three older brothers?" Nachelle asked, unconsciously biting the inside of her cheek while storing the information in her mind.

"Mother says there's a family practice that guides the family in their selection. It's a pretty serious decision, and whatever the choosing method looks like, it's been pretty accurate so far because there's always been a strong, male DuCloux at the helm, and the business has prospered with each succeeding generation. They're a very tight-knit group and a non-family member can only go just so far up the ladder in DuCloux Enterprises."

To take some of the doom out of her words, Heather beamed a glorious smile, and added, "That is, until they met you. You showed the DuCloux that they couldn't just ask and receive. You made them fight for the Hayes Group."

Nachelle shrugged her shoulders and crossed the room to her vanity table. She sat down and fiddled with the toiletries laid out in an orderly fashion. Her mind was like a sponge, soaking in all of Heather's information.

Heather continued, "Anyway, back to Steven. After he graduated from Morehouse and Harvard, he apprenticed with his dad. Mother says the company experienced unprecedented growth under the dynamic duo's guidance. But, everything is cyclical and oddly enough, at the same time Ralph was recovering from his first stroke here in Fort Worth, Adolphus had a heart attack. At that point, Steven took complete control of the business."

Heather leaned forward and assumed a dramatic facial expression. Wiggling her eyebrows in a Dudley-Do-Right fashion, she commented in an abysmally secretive voice, "I'm afraid I didn't learn any deep, dark company secrets or strategies that you could use against the mighty DuCloux." Cheerful, bright Heather fell back against the plump pillows and spread her hands wide. She adopted another cartoon voice and said, "That's all, folks."

Nachelle chuckled as she always did when Heather displayed her acting ability. The two women had known each other since they were freshmen at the University of Texas at Austin. Although Heather had most of her classes in the drama building and Nachelle's classes were in the business school, they shared the same dorm and fell easily into a complementary friendship which blossomed into a relationship stronger than most family relationships.

It had been no surprise to Nachelle that after graduation, Heather used her acting talents—and her Mother's never-ending supply of funds—to start her own children's puppet theater. It was the perfect venue for Heather's talents: her love for children and her bubbly, positive personality.

"Thank you for sharing that information." Nachelle stood and stretched. "I don't know what I'm going to do with it . . . yet, but it's comforting to know he doesn't have *all* the cards." Nachelle gathered their dirty dishes and walked to the kitchen.

Heather followed Nachelle and watched as she rinsed and stacked the dishes in the dishwasher. "Nachelle, the main thing is to keep an open mind. I know you think my matching you up with Steven is crazy and that I imagined his reaction to you on Friday night, but the bottom line is, he's a man and

you're a woman. Everything else is unimportant, *especially*
the past."

"That's easy for you to say. You were always the one break-
ing hearts. You can't possibly know what it feels like to have
your heart and dreams ripped to shreds. To be embarrassed
and humiliated in front of my colleagues. To have most of the
Hayes Group employees whispering and gossiping behind my
back. I'd be a fool to open myself up to that again."

"You don't know that it would happen like that. Steven isn't
Harlan."

"No, he isn't, but there are enough similarities to turn me
off." Nachelle turned from the sink and gave her friend a tortured look. "Even if Steven is interested in a romantic relationship, which I highly doubt, I learned enough from Harlan
to know office romances, especially with the boss, are guaranteed to fail."

Heather knew from experience when Nachelle used that bold
tone of voice that there was no reasoning with her. Even so, her
persistent nature wouldn't let go. "Look, Nachelle, I certainly
don't want you to go through another office affair gone bad. I
love you too much to see you hurt again, but don't confuse the
issue. It's not the location . . ." Heather raised her hands in a
quote sign to emphasize her words. *". . . but the people* and quite
honestly, Harlan was not the man for you. At the risk of sounding
negative, I have to say that the romance would have failed even
if you and Harlan hadn't worked together."

"Heather, I don't think you're being realistic." Nachelle
stated. "The job, the office politics, the boss/subordinate role,
all of those intangible pressures added to our downfall."

"Okay, then don't broadcast a new relationship like you
and Harlan broadcasted your old one. Keep it discreet."
Heather smiled mischievously and wriggled her brows.
"That'll make it all the more spicy anyway."

Nachelle leaned back against the kitchen counter and
crossed her arms and legs. "Why are we still talking about
this? It's not going to happen."

"But, you yourself said you'll lose your job eventually anyhow, so it's not like he's going to be your boss permanently. And, if for some reason it doesn't work out, *which I highly doubt,* you won't have to deal with those petty, backbiting folks at the job. You won't be there!"

Silence and a stony set face met Heather's declaration.

Heather knew she was running out of debate points. In a weaker voice, she cajoled, "Well, say at least you'll mull it over?"

"No, absolutely not." Nachelle thought about the decision she'd made at the office earlier today. After hearing Heather speculate about Steven's "reaction" to her Friday, the fact that Steven said he found himself attracted to her, and his newly learned "unattached" state, she was even more determined to speak with him when he returned. She would deflate this balloon before it started expanding. And, as soon as she met her commitment to Ralph to stay and iron out the future for the Hayes Group employees, she was out of there. Softly, Nachelle stated, "Heather, look, I really appreciate you for caring, but sometimes I think you focus too much on the fairy-tale happy endings that signify the conclusion of your performances. Please understand this is serious stuff."

The women had been friends for too long for either of them to be offended by the other's position. Truth and a genuine concern for each other had made their relationship strong.

"I know this is your heart and mind that we're talking about, Nachelle, and you're right that I want everything to be colored bright yellow, but I'm afraid for you. It's been months since you've had a date and you're never going to get over your fear of falling in love again if you isolate yourself within the walls of the office." Heather held up a hand when Nachelle opened her mouth to speak. "I've resigned myself to your decision, for the time being . . ." she winked boldly. "But, I have to ask, what about Harlan?"

Nachelle's look changed from one of steely determination to confusion. "What about Harlan?" she repeated.

Heather opened the refrigerator and took out fixings for

chicken salad and soup. "Remember you told me the only thing left to make this transaction complete is Harlan's signature on the dotted line."

"Yes, and . . ."

"What are you going to do when he returns to sign the papers?"

"First of all, he doesn't have to physically be in Fort Worth to finalize the deal. He can stay in Phoenix and just sign and notarize the papers, then mail them back certified. Second, even if he comes to Fort Worth to finish the deal, which he won't, we both know there is nothing left between us."

"Are you sure there's no chance you two could get back together?"

Nachelle looked suspiciously at her friend. "What are you getting at, Heather? I can tell you're up to something."

Looking as innocent as a nun, Heather spread her hands and stated, "Nothing. I'm just asking."

"Yeah, right," Nachelle remarked skeptically. "Just make sure you don't make something happen. Mind your own business."

Heather snapped to attention, saluted, and playfully shouted, "Yes, sir!"

Nachelle shook her head and smiled. Heather was as good a friend as any person could ever ask for, but sometimes she was as nutty as peanut butter.

The two friends sat down for a simple meal and talked of inconsequential things. An hour later, after eating and cleaning up the kitchen, Heather stretched and reminded Nachelle of the work waiting for her.

"I've taken enough of your time. Call me tomorrow for lunch." Heather tugged on her gloves and coat. Before she closed the door she asked, "Please call Gerald for me. Tell him I'm on the way. And thanks for dinner."

"Sure thing." Nachelle locked the door behind Heather, then walked to the window in the living room to watch her journey to her car.

With Heather safely enclosed in her fire engine red Porsche, Nachelle walked to the entry table in her foyer and retrieved her briefcase. With papers, reports, and ledgers spread before her, Nachelle found it impossible to concentrate. She realized after a time that she had read the same paragraph twice and still didn't know what it said.

Her thoughts were focused on the conversation she had shared with Heather. She trusted and loved Heather, but Nachelle knew she would not be able to commit to the open mind Heather wanted her to use in approaching Steven, or, for that matter, love. Heather was a dreamer, and in her dreamlike state, she sometimes missed reality. The reality was, Nachelle and Steven were not just a woman and a man. They were subordinate and boss; democrat and autocrat; commoner and aristocrat. There could be no middle ground for them—only a battle ground. Nachelle had no doubt that Steven would fight for the new, fortified DuCloux Enterprises. For as long as she could, she would work to save as much of the Hayes Group as she possibly could, and, despite Heather's urgings she would remain committed to her personal pledge—avoid office romances at all costs. It hadn't worked with Harlan and he, too, like Steven, had been the head of the empire. His addiction to drugs had forced Harlan to a rehabilitation center in Phoenix, which had sheltered him from the snide remarks, the backbiting, the gossip, and the rumors when the engagement had ended. She had been the one to pay emotionally, physically, and mentally for the love affair. Only a fool would relearn a painful lesson, and she was no fool. She hoped Heather didn't have any contrary plans in mind. But, she also knew Heather could be as stubborn as a spoiled child. Still, she had ways to deal with Heather. Just the mere mention of Heather's fear of commitment would throw Heather offtrack.

Her thoughts were interrupted by the ringing of the telephone. Realizing she had forgotten to call Gerald with Heather's message, she jumped up and ran to answer it. Expecting it to be Heather, she answered casually, "I'm sorry. I forgot."

A silent pause followed her opening. "Nachelle, you were obviously expecting someone else." Steven's deep Southern drawl floated through the ear piece.

"Ummm, yes." Nachelle spoke slowly until she realized who was on the other line. "But, what can I help you with?"

"If nothing else, you certainly recover quickly." After a pause, Steven continued, "I'm calling to find out how the rest of the day went. Are things settling down?" Even at nine o'clock at night, and after what must have been a very long, tiring day, his voice sounded clear and powerful.

Remembering he was as crafty as a traveling salesman, she cautiously answered, "We've had more productive days. This is obviously a major change."

"Yes, that goes for the employees at both companies." Steven continued, "I'm here at the DuCloux offices right now. My vice presidents here tell me even this office was a buzz of gossip."

Nachelle stated, "I've never been through this type of upheaval before, but I imagine it will take several weeks before things quiet down and full productivity resumes."

"You're right, of course." After a brief pause, Steven changed tracks. "I wanted to apologize for my harsh words this afternoon. Please don't think that I'm not considering you for continued employment. You have some skills that are beneficial to DuCloux Enterprises."

"Thank you," Nachelle murmured. She felt safer keeping her responses to a minimum.

"What I should have asked you this afternoon is if you regret having spent all of your professional life at one company?"

"No. As I stated before, Ralph is a great mentor. He's very patient, kind, and intelligent. I consider myself blessed." Nachelle thought to herself that even with the bad times, she would walk the same path if she had the chance to re-do her life.

"I see." Steven spoke slowly, as if cataloguing the information. With an abrupt change of subject, he asked, "Do you think the employees fully understand the situation they are in?"

Nachelle silently admitted that she herself didn't fully understand all the nuances. Aloud, she commented, "Judging by the questions that I and some of the other executives received today, a great deal of confusion still exists among the employees. And, of course, they're all concerned about their futures. This whole change of ownership happened so quickly and without any warning, leaving them all feeling disoriented."

"That's to be expected." Steven expelled a deep sigh. "If the shoe were on the other foot, I'd have expected the same from DuCloux employees."

Nachelle was surprised at his acknowledgment. She hadn't expected the company-eating predator to display empathy.

Steven's direct business manner prevented her from having to think of a gracious remark. "It looks like my business matters here in Atlanta will be wrapped up by Thursday."

Nachelle's heart dropped when she realized that that meant he would be returning sooner than expected. She ignored the wild dip, the rapid beats of her heart, and sat as patiently as possible waiting for him to deliver the rest of the bombshell.

"I've made arrangements to return to Fort Worth on Thursday night, but I won't be in the office Friday. Instead, my secretary, Dorrie Hall, will be flying back with me and she'll be in the office on Friday to arrange, with your help, a business meeting for that night at my hotel suite."

Nachelle gulped and ground out, "Friday night. You want to conduct a business meeting on a Friday night?"

"Friday's as good a night as any. Dorrie will call you tomorrow with additional details."

"Excuse me, but what's wrong with Friday during the day? You just said you're flying back on Thursday."

"Nothing's wrong with Friday during the day except I already have plans." Steven continued, "I'd—"

Being the efficient person that she was, Nachelle saw the need to point out the obvious. She persisted, "In case you don't realize it, some people may still have guests in town for the holidays, or already have plans for Friday night."

A lengthy pause greeted her remark. "Is it the others you're concerned with Nachelle, or do you have a date you don't want to cancel?"

Her retort spewed forth before she could temper her response. "Didn't your investigators tell you the answer to that? Since they were able to obtain my unlisted number and tell you my professional career history, I assumed they also briefed you on my social calendar."

Steven's voice rumbled deep in his chest, and when he spoke, it was in a slow, controlled manner. "Look, Nachelle, let's cut through the bull. I'm having a business meeting for the executives of both companies. It will start at eight o'clock on Friday night in my hotel suite at the Worthington. I'll consider any absence insubordination and that person will be replaced in the blink of an eye. Do you understand?"

Commitment forced the words from Nachelle's convulsively working throat. "Only too well, Mr. DuCloux." Nachelle silently counted to ten to control her temper and thought for the umpteenth time that day, *if it wasn't for the uncertain future of the employees, he could count me among the insubordinate.* She looked down and saw the half-moon marks her nails had left in the soft flesh of her palms. Nachelle took a deep breath and in a strained voice asked, "Is there anything else?"

"As a matter of fact, there is."

Nachelle could hear him shifting papers and her tension grew. She wanted nothing more than to end this conversation. But, it appeared Steven had other plans.

"I've asked Dorrie to also speak with you about—"

As Steven spoke, Nachelle hung her head. All the emotions

and feelings from the past three days crowded her senses, making her feel as if she were caught in a whirling vortex. She realized in just one brief day an exorbitant amount of freedom had been siphoned away. With Ralph's quickly scribbled signature on the bottom line of a binding contract, her days of job freedom and growth were gone.

How uncomplicated it would be to walk out and never look back, she thought, with a sigh. But, if she did so, would she be able to sleep? Would she ever forgive herself for not fighting? She already knew the answers to those questions. And it was those very answers that forced her to stay and bend to Steven's domineering ways.

"Nachelle? Did you hear me?"

Nachelle tuned in to realize Steven was trying to get her attention. "I'm sorry. I didn't quite catch that."

"I said, I've asked Dorrie to work with you in planning Ralph's retirement party. I figured you'd be the most likely candidate since you know him and his family so well."

Nachelle wasn't sure she actually heard him. She mumbled a response. "Uh, yes." Surely he hadn't said what she thought he said? A retirement party for Ralph?

"You may want to have some ideas ready to share with Dorrie when she calls. Naturally, DuCloux Enterprises will pay all associated expenses."

Was the Silver Shark actually doing something nice? Nachelle couldn't believe her ears. Steven was authorizing an event that wouldn't add to, but rather detract from the bottom line. She pinched herself to make sure she was still awake.

"Okay," was all Nachelle could manage. Inwardly, she thought, *how could the man be so mean and harsh one minute and then kind and generous the next?* Her mind tried to work out the puzzle.

"It's late here and I've kept you long enough. I'm a night owl, but I have a feeling you lead a very regimented life, early to bed and all that. See you on Friday." Steven briskly ended the call.

"Bye." Nachelle hung up the receiver, but continued to stare at its slick surface.

The man is an enigma, she thought, *a Jekyll and Hyde.* Nachelle looked at the brief notes she had taken during the conversation. Noting the name of his secretary, she felt pity for the woman. *How does she keep up with him?* she wondered.

Deciding she'd had enough of this eventful day, Nachelle stood and walked to her bedroom to begin her nightly bedtime ritual.

Shucking the faded college clothes, she donned a pink terry cloth robe and matching slippers. While she washed her face and brushed her teeth, her mind wandered back through the events of the day and the most recent phone conversation. *Is it possible I'm reading the man wrong?* she thought. *Am I really being fair and giving him a chance? Or am I so brainwashed with previous assessments of Steven and DuCloux Enterprises that I'm the one being too judgmental?* She recalled Mike Adams's earlier statement that Steven didn't appear to be harmful. She valued the Sales Vice President's opinions and those of Ralph and Heather. All opinions seemed to concur that she should keep an open mind about Steven.

On the other hand, when he invades my privacy and threatens my job because I question his decision, how am I supposed to see him as anything other than a cold-blooded, domineering machine?

Nachelle shook her head in dismay. She opened the ponytail clip and bundled her hair into a shower cap. "Oh, well," she said to her reflection in the mirror, "I don't have any other choice but to hang in there. I'll just have to step carefully."

It's going to be tough, she thought. *I've had all the power for so long. I've got to get used to him and his style quickly, not only for my own sanity, but also to ensure the merger is advantageous for the Hayes Group employees. I'll play it safe, concentrate on business first and always keep my emotions out of it.*

The mere thought of emotions brought her to Heather's conversation. She had recoiled at Heather's suggestion that she look upon Steven as an available man, but looking in the mirror, she blinked, and for a minute instead of seeing her own reflection, she saw that of Steven's. In the privacy of her own bathroom, she admitted he was a very handsome man, and under different circumstances, she might actually enjoy his company. But, as her boss, she could never see him in another light. She knew from experience that a personal relationship with the boss didn't bring happiness.

Even with the personal pledge sealed in her heart, Nachelle couldn't stop her mind from wondering what kissing him on New Year's Eve would have felt like, or what it would have felt like to run her hands through his wavy thick hair, and feel the long length of his thighs pressed against her own.

To stop the treacherous thoughts, Nachelle turned the water to scalding temperature and concentrated on cleansing her body . . . and mind.

Four

To Nachelle's amazement, the meeting date was upon her before she knew it. Since the announcement of the change in ownership to the staff, she had been extremely busy getting the employees somewhat settled and fielding calls from what seemed like every radio station and newspaper office in the Southwest region. The news of the buy-out was apparently front page reading.

As she parked her red Cadillac Allante in the hotel's parking garage, she realized she was very tired from the hectic pace and extra long hours she had maintained over the past days. She turned off the engine and rested her head on the steering wheel. *Pull yourself together, Nachelle. The meeting will only last a few hours. As a treat, you can vegetate all day tomorrow if you want.* With that uplifting thought in mind, she eased her size eight frame out of the car.

As she walked to the express elevator that would take her to the penthouse, she noticed several cars belonging to Hayes Group executives. She expelled a sigh of thanksgiving; the last thing she wanted was to make small talk with Steven DuCloux while waiting for the management staff of both companies to arrive. She had already spoken to him more times this week than she preferred.

A tall, stately man took her wool coat at the penthouse door and ushered her into the grand room. Automatically, her eyes sought and found Steven. Even with his back to her, she recognized his tall form. He, like the other employees, was casually dressed, sporting blue jeans and a chambray shirt. As she started forward, she watched Steven bend down and pick up a napkin which had fallen to the floor. The action accentuated the muscles in his legs, fully outlining his buttocks. Nachelle's heart caught in her throat. She thought she had never seen a better physique. *Get a grip, Nachelle,* she admonished, *he's your boss. You have more than one reason to avoid thoughts of this nature.* Plastering a smile on her face, she approached Steven and the small group of people clustered around him.

"Hi. How is everyone this evening?" Nachelle directed her comments to all, affording Steven very little eye contact. She surveyed the group, noting that the strangers were probably DuCloux Enterprises executives.

Others in the tight group murmured their greetings or nodded. But, Steven responded in a cheerful voice, "Hello. It's good to see you."

Nachelle was taken aback at his enthusiastic greeting. His accompanying dazzling smile looked genuine, too.

His gaze swept her from head to toe, then upward again, resting longer than necessary on her glossed red lips.

Nachelle felt a flush spread throughout her body. Even if she didn't feel like it after his appraising look, she knew she was completely clothed. Her outfit of black and white herringbone pants, a white turtleneck, and a black and white patterned sweater didn't feel as much like armor as it had when she'd dressed. Of course, she had dressed to battle the cold winds, not Steven's prying eyes.

Shifting her eyes from his dark, secretive ones, she stated, "Judging by the crowd, it looks like everyone's here. I'm sorry if I'm late."

Steven said, "You're not late at all. Here, let me introduce you to my staff from Atlanta."

Steven placed a firm, yet gentle hand under her elbow. Introducing her first to the people nearest them, he then propelled her around the large, elegantly furnished room to meet the remaining executives.

When the final rounds of introductions were completed, Steven steered her to a side buffet piled with stacks of papers of varying heights.

He leaned casually against the buffet, crossed his muscular arms and asked her, "So what do you think?"

The open-ended question left her momentarily bereft. Nachelle decided to go with the first thing on her mind. "I think I'd like to know why DuCloux Enterprises doesn't have a female in upper management? With the exception of Dorrie, I'm the only female here."

Steven's eyes narrowed and grew more intense, "Does that bother you? Surely you should be used to such circumstances?"

"Just because I'm used to a certain situation doesn't mean I condone it. I happen to have attended a university which produces women with outstanding leadership skills, yet I see very few of them whenever I attend business functions."

"I see." Steven rubbed a hand down the side of his chin. He pinned her with a steady gaze, leaned forward so that only inches separated their faces, and lowered his voice to a spine-tingling octave. "Well then, Nachelle, I would have to say I was waiting for someone like you."

Steven's eyes offered Nachelle no clue to his level of seriousness, and even if they had, she was suddenly busy trying to regulate her breathing and prevent her body from burning up.

Before she could break the spell Steven was casting, Nathaniel Johnson, DuCloux Enterprises' Vice President of Operations, interrupted them.

Nathaniel said, "Steven, we have some people who are ready to roll on their assignments. Maybe we should begin." Nathaniel pushed his glasses up on his nose and waited for Steven's response. His Napoleon style height and build forced him to look up at Steven.

In the blink of an eye, Steven took charge. He walked away from Nachelle as if he hadn't just shared a private word. Nachelle was left standing by the buffet, feeling like fuzz occupied the space where her brain should have been. *I just don't know what to make of him,* she thought, as she walked with Nathaniel to the arrangement of chairs around the board-room-style table. *I know his business dealings aren't always above board and that he drives his company with a single-minded purpose—to win at any cost—but tonight he seems to be showing a human side. He definitely deserves special handling.*

Four hours later, a depleted Nachelle closed her portfolio and leaned back into the cushions of the chair. *I'm definitely going to treat myself to that full day of rest,* she thought wryly.

"That wraps it up for tonight. Are there any questions?" No one spoke in response to Steven's question. Most were too exhausted. Steven was the only one who still looked fresh and ready to go an additional ten rounds.

"Then, with the exception of Nathaniel and Nachelle, the meeting is adjourned." Slow moving men and Dorrie gathered papers, briefcases, and coats. Moving more like zombies in a horror flick than company executives, they filed out of the penthouse and packed into the waiting elevator.

Steven wasted no time dishing out the final details.

"Nachelle, I've decided to appoint you as the vice president in charge of the merger. You'll be working closely with me to ensure the integration of both companies happens smoothly. Nathaniel, I'll need you to step in and act as in-charge President for the Atlanta office since most of my time will be spent here in Fort Worth."

Both Nachelle and Nathaniel were visibly shocked at Steven's words. Nachelle had naturally assumed either Steven himself or Nathaniel would lead the charge; she hadn't even considered that he would appoint her since she was from the "opposite" side.

Nathaniel sputtered his disappointment, "Ste . . . Steven. I . . . I'm not questioning your authority or judgment, but is that the best decision for the company?"

"Nathaniel, we've been working together long enough for you to know my decisions are always based on what's good for the company." Turning his attention to a stunned Nachelle, Steven continued, "Now, Nachelle, the first step is to complete the merger study in a short time so we can be fully integrated within a year. DuCloux Enterprises invested a lot of money in this deal and we've got to make that investment start paying as soon as possible."

Nathaniel nodded his head affirmatively and inserted, "I agree, Steven, and that's why I wonder if you might reconsider your appointment. Nothing against Nachelle, but she may not have the experience to lead such an aggressive project. Merging two giant companies can be a challenge even for someone who's been around the block a few times."

As tired as she was, Nachelle sat up straight. She experienced a frightening déjà-vu. Three years ago, when she was named the Operations Vice President for the Hayes Group at the age of twenty-six, she had encountered similar resentments and anger from the men who had ended up reporting to her. Back then the men had quoted her engagement to Harlan Hayes as the basis for her promotion. They had totally discounted her graduate school training, her many hours of private tutoring with Ralph as her mentor, and the extensive hours she spent during the summer and after school helping to run her parents' insurance business in Austin. It had taken months of stellar performance from her for them to finally acknowledge what Ralph Hayes had already known— Nachelle was a qualified, highly competent, intelligent woman capable of running any company. Now it was Nathaniel indicating that because of her lack of experience, she shouldn't receive this position. Was she going to have to prove her worth all over again? Didn't her track record mean anything? She shook with fury and angry words formed in both retaliation and defense.

Steven spoke before Nachelle could protest. "Nathaniel, I know you are disappointed that I named Nachelle to this position. It's an opportunity that doesn't come along often, but the fact is the Hayes Group outperformed us in a number of key areas over the last year. As you know, she was instrumental in leading the employees to achieve those high results. It's because of that that I need her as my right hand person and as the catalyst for the merger." Steven paused and fixed Nathaniel with a look that would have stopped a runaway freight train. "May I remind you that you'll have a free hand in directing the Atlanta office. In essence, you won't be reporting to anyone. That's how much faith I have in your abilities."

Both men sat as still as statues. Nachelle noticed that the air grew taut and some of her own anger dissipated upon hearing Steven's comments.

Nathaniel started to speak, but Steven completed his thoughts. "I assure you that when we've completed the merger, you'll maintain a comparable position. In the meantime, I know Nachelle will appreciate all the assistance you can give her."

Nathaniel looked directly at Steven, "Steven, I've worked for DuCloux Enterprises for more years than she's been a vice president, and I've supported the company in ways too numerable to mention. I expected that to be considered when assigning responsibilities."

"That was noted and taken into account. Again, this was a business decision, Nathaniel. One which had nothing to do with personalities, but with the continued growth of the company." It was only because of Nathaniel's long-standing friendship with Adolphus DuCloux that Steven had even allowed Nathaniel to continue his arguments this far without being fired. However, Steven had reached the end of his patience. He threw the final dice on the table and impaled the older man with a deadly look. "Now, Nathaniel, I need to know if you're going to continue to provide the support and loyalty you've given to DuCloux in the past. Will you assist Nachelle in the work to form a bigger and better DuCloux Enterprises?"

Recognizing that he was treading on thin ice, Nathaniel dropped his eyes and backed off. He gathered his papers and stuffed them into his briefcase. "Of course I'll continue to support the company. I love DuCloux Enterprises as much as you do, Steven." Nathaniel stilled his movements and turned a twisted, angry face towards his boss. In an acid-filled voice, he stated, "I wonder if your father would agree with your decision."

From her viewpoint, Nachelle could see a muscle jump viciously in Steven's jaw. His hands clenched in big fists at his side. If it were possible, his face grew even harder. His attractive features twisted in unmasked fury. She tried to make herself one with the chair and forgot to breathe while waiting for the storm to erupt.

Long, determined strides carried Steven to Nathaniel. When he was inches from his father's trusted friend, Steven said, "My father's health is of the utmost importance right now. The less stress he has, the better his chances of a full recovery from his last surgery." A dangerous undertone entered Steven's voice and he spoke slowly, clearly enunciating every word. "I'm sure neither you nor I would do anything to upset him or threaten the future of my family's business."

Nathaniel recoiled from the veiled threat and Steven's arctic words. He scooped up his briefcase and turned to Nachelle.

Nachelle noticed that his light complexion had turned red, and she could almost see the animosity radiating from him like a heat wave. In a tight voice, he stated, "I look forward to working with you." Without another word, he turned and exited.

Nachelle exhaled a long breath. She couldn't quite believe what she had just witnessed. *I'm going to have problems with Nathaniel,* she thought wearily. However, the more pressing thought was that she had just witnessed Steven's transformation to the Silver Shark. Watching his deadly approach, seeing his eyes and face harden, and hearing firsthand how a few words felled an unsuspecting man made her realize how blessed she'd been, considering how she'd lost her temper with him on more than one occasion. Still, in all the harshness of the scene, she hadn't been able to quell a tremor of excitement while watching Steven. Crazily, her senses had come alive and her body had tensed with charged energy.

Her thoughts returned to the present when Steven rejoined her at the table. Warily, from the corner of her eyes, she watched him extend his long legs out in front of him and, with his eyes closed, press his back into the comfort of the tapestry-covered chair. His hands rested on his knees and she saw that they weren't as tightly balled as they had been seconds before. She stayed attuned to any residual anger that might still dwell in him.

"I'm sorry you had to witness that." Steven spoke softly and released a long sigh. His eyes were still closed as he brushed one hand across his brow and asked, "Would you like something to drink?"

The swift change of conversation stumped Nachelle for only a second. "No, thank you," she answered primly. Now that she was completely alone with Steven, and more than a little leery of his current state and her own reaction to him, she was anxious to escape. To cover her nervousness, she asked, "Was there anything else you wanted to discuss this evening?"

Steven took so long in responding to her question that for a moment she thought he might have fallen asleep. When she turned to fully face him, she noted his breathing was shallow. Tentatively, she queried, "Steven?"

"I heard you and yes, a couple of things." Steven pulled his legs in and reached for the folder containing his notes. Nachelle couldn't stop her eyes from focusing on his movements, the way his arm muscles rippled seductively under the soft fabric of his denim shirt.

The ringing of the telephone abruptly pulled her back from the imagery her mind was conjuring. Steven stood to answer it.

"Excuse me. It must be my mother. She's the only one who would be calling so late." Steven walked towards an open doorway to the right of the living room. Before he vanished into the room, he stated, "I'll only be a minute."

Left alone with her thoughts and inactivity, she reviewed the past few hours. Steven seemed eager to make the merger as smooth as possible for both sets of employees. *He's not making any guarantees, but at least he seems to be openly communicating,* she thought. And of course the one bright spot from the evening was being named Operations Vice President to oversee the merger. *I'm not going to let Nathaniel's negativity put a damper on this victory for me and the Hayes Group employees. This appointment will allow me more leverage and more influence to save as many Hayes jobs as possible. On the flip side, I'll be working closely with Steven and that's nothing to celebrate.* Nachelle let her head roll back. She closed her eyes and recalled the energy-charged scene she had just witnessed. *Steven's a double-edged sword. I thought he was going to tear Nathaniel's head off, but then, in a New York second, he switched gears and was polite and all business again.* Nachelle shook her head slowly back and forth, unknowingly disturbing the curls that laid protectively around her neck. She sighed, consciously giving up her attempt to piece together Steven's complex personality, at least for the moment.

"One thing I know for sure, I'm going to have to better control my physical reactions to the man and temper my emotions," she scolded herself quietly. "Otherwise, he'll eat me alive." Even as she reprimanded herself, a visual image of Steven filled her head. *Like Heather said, he is sexy and very attractive. How I would love to feel his beard rub gently over my* . . . Nachelle sat bolt upright. She couldn't believe the thoughts entering her head. She looked around the room as if someone else was guilty of the unprofessional thought. Noting she had no one to blame but herself, she leaned back into the cushions and allowed a slight smile to curve her mouth. *It's only because I've been celibate for years that I'm thinking such ridiculous thoughts,* she chided herself. *Still, I might be interested in a romantic relationship with him if only it had been another time, another place.* Nachelle sighed wistfully.

She checked her watch and the slim gold hands told her it was almost one in the morning. She yawned and settled deeper in the chair. Tiredness washed over her in giant waves, reminding her of the long, grueling work days and little sleep she'd had this week. With eyes closed, she thought, *if nothing else, the next few months will be exciting.* Before she could form another coherent thought, the Sandman claimed her as a victim.

Five

As much as Steven loved the daily updates he received from his mother regarding the antics his nieces and nephews continually pulled on any human being who had the misfortune of making their acquaintance, his attention was fixed on the living room where the intelligent, beautiful, and shapely vice president awaited him.

"Steven . . . Steven. Are you listening to me?" his mother asked, concern lining her voice.

"Yes mama, I'm listening." Steven told a white lie. He was only half listening to his mother. His thoughts were centered on Nachelle, the rare jewel he'd found hidden in the shell of the Hayes Group.

Even before the buy-out, he'd learned a lot about the dark beauty. After all, it had been her recommendations and maneuverings that had kept the Hayes Group out of "enemy territory." And because of that, the fire of curiosity about the woman herself had been ignited. When DuCloux Enterprises had finally, successfully acquired the Hayes Group, his first order of business, after celebrating, had been to read her personnel file from front to back. It hadn't provided enough information to satisfy his appetite, hence the private investigator. The PI had done a much better job of filling in some of the gaps of Nachelle's life than Steven had hoped for. Armed with that additional knowledge, the initial seeds of interest in Nachelle on a personal level were planted. And, of course, once he met the real thing at the New Year's Eve party, his interest bloomed to full maturity.

As a single, red-blooded man in his mid-thirties, Steven knew the time had come to think seriously about settling down. His mother stayed on his case constantly, and with what she felt to be good reason.

The DuCloux family, whose roots were deeply grounded in Georgia, subscribed to long-lasting traditions which were as natural and commonplace to the DuCloux family as serving black eyed peas on New Year's Day. It was assumed that all the male DuCloux would be educated at Morehouse, work in the family business, marry, and produce heirs to work at DuCloux Enterprises. Above all else, each succeeding generation was expected to ensure business growth, prosperity, and most importantly, that the business remain in the hands of family.

Their time-honored family edicts passed from generation to generation and it would be hell to pay for the person who broke with tradition.

Preserving the family name and history relied heavily on selecting a woman with certain inherent and learned qualities. Those standards had been categorized and developed into a criterion list which all of the men in the DuCloux family used to select a wife. The criterion list had been in their family for as long as there was a DuCloux, and it had served the men well. Steven, as did his brothers, abided by the long-standing tradition, especially considering the demands of the DuCloux legacy and the success so far gleaned from the checklist. His three older brothers had wives and children who were excellent fruits of the custom.

At age thirty-four and as the CEO of DuCloux Enterprises, Steven needed a wife. It wasn't for lack of trying that he was not married. His dating experience was extensive and varied, but had failed to produce a woman who had passed all checkpoints.

Cradling the phone between his ear and shoulder, he rifled through some papers on his desk until he found the folder containing the criteria sheet for selecting a wife. While his mother rattled on, he scanned the checklist containing five checkpoints. *I wonder . . .* he thought. An idea was forming, one that was taking on great appeal. *Nachelle just might be a candidate for this list. The initial beginnings are there. She's smart, physically I'm attracted to her and she has already passed checkpoint number one—professional background check.*

Steven was pleased with his idea and with Nachelle's potential. She had four more items—personal background, social skills, sexual compatibility, and family suitability—to pass before he could propose a personal merger. And what better way to compare her character to those checkpoints than to work day and night with her for months? He smiled slyly in anticipation. Yes, all of the reasons he had shared with Nathaniel on why he had selected Nachelle to lead the merger were true, but now there was an extra bonus in it for him if things worked out. Could she possibly be the elusive wife he'd been searching for?

Steven reverted to the present when he heard his mother state she was tired. He grabbed the bait and ended the call with assurances of a return call the next day.

He stood, stretched, and checked the time on his Rolex. Fifteen minutes since he'd left Nachelle. It seemed like an eternity. Just the thought of being near her broadened his smile, and he spoke in a deep tone as he entered the living area.

"If we don't wrap up in a couple of hours, we'll have to order breakfast."

Nachelle was always a light sleeper, especially in alien environments. Her eyes fluttered open at the sound of his voice. She bounced up from the chair like a guilty child caught in the act of stealing cookies from the cookie jar.

"It is late." Nachelle spoke softly, resisting the urge to rub her neck where a crick had settled. An embarrassing flush suffused her body at the knowledge that she had allowed herself to fall asleep. To gain more adjustment time, she studied her watch as if she had never seen it before. *I can't believe I was that lax,* she admonished herself. *What if he had found me asleep? What a terrible impression that would have made.* An even more disturbing, feminine thought closed fast on the heels of her logical thoughts, *I must look a mess.* She reached a tentative hand to her hair and casually ran her fingers through the sleep-flattened curls.

Nachelle stated as she turned to face Steven, "Steven. If you don't . . ." A soft tearing sound stopped her commentary and her forward steps. She looked down with a wide eyed stare. A half inch tear near her knee on the backside of her pants gaped at her. "Oh, no," she moaned, as she bent at the waist to further inspect the damage.

Reacting with the quickness of a track star, Steven joined

her and knelt on one knee beside her chair, pushing her hands aside.

"Let me." The command in his voice was not to be denied. Nachelle relinquished the inspection to his prying hands. "There's an exposed nail here . . ."

What an appropriate ending to a crazy, event-filled week, she thought, a week filled with more gloom than a haunted house. Nachelle didn't often admit defeat, but she'd had enough of this trying week.

Her downcast eyes slowly gravitated to Steven's bent head. His kneeling position afforded her a generous view of his salt-and-pepper hair, the classical shape of his head and shoulders which rivaled a defensive lineman's. *What a perfect male creation,* she thought absently. Steven looked up suddenly and met her stare. It took the remaining reserves of Nachelle's strength not to shift her eyes away with the guilt created from openly admiring her boss.

"It looks like the braiding has separated from the upholstery; somehow your pants snagged on the exposed nail." Steven stood and framed his narrow waist with his hands. His cold black eyes bored into her gentle brown ones.

His measuring, bold look made Nachelle almost forget her name. She felt like those captivating eyes knew she had been scoping him and sensed the direction her thoughts were headed. *But, that's ridiculous. He can't read minds, and besides I don't even know what my next thought would have been,* Nachelle reasoned internally. *Yeah, but you have an idea where things were going. He is a very sexy man.* The counter argument silently framed and shaped her reality.

"I know the damage has been done, but I'll call the hotel staff in the morning and get them to take the chair out for repairs. I'm sorry your pants are ruined."

Nachelle blinked, but it did nothing to erase the onyx orbs that stared through her. She wanted relief from the black cage of Steven's eyes, within the depths of which she thought she saw a flicker of something—caring, desire, humanity, she wasn't sure what.

She wet her lips and shifted her eyes, with great effort, to the ragged material that was once her favorite pair of pants.

"That's okay. They were old pants." Nachelle attempted a small smile which failed miserably.

"Still, I'd hate to think, either by design or carelessness, that any part of your lovely body was marred. You could have been cut." Steven's comment forced her eyes to meet his.

The resulting impact left her feeling like an elephant was sitting on her chest. *How could he say that?* she thought in shock. *What a forward statement to make to someone you work with!* Never mind that her own thoughts about him had been of a similar theme. She hadn't voiced them aloud. Struggling for normalcy, she admitted defeat when she felt her heart running like a race horse.

Steven's hormones were sending a powerful message to kiss her senseless. He tried to stamp down his desires and concentrate on discovering the depths of the real Nachelle. *I have to know if she passes checkpoint two and three before I lay claim to those inviting lips. Still, there's no need to be totally chaste,* he thought compromisingly. Leaning forward slightly, he stated in a low, confident voice, "I'm looking forward to working together. I've never had the pleasure of teaming up with such a beautiful woman."

Convulsively, Nachelle's throat worked, but produced no sound. When he closed strong, brown hands around the upper flesh of her arms, her throat remained paralyzed. The thick sweater material covering her flesh wasn't enough protection to stop the sensations that caused quivers in her stomach.

"I'm looking forward to learning more about you. It should be an exciting time for us both." Steven's eyes devoured her lips. He moved closer still to position his head just inches from her own. He wanted to kiss her, the desire was stronger than the need to breathe, yet his thoughts stopped him. *Was now the time to move their relationship to a different level?*

What if she turned out to be just like the other women in his past—beautiful, but inadequate? Could he risk the damage to his company, his image, his future, if she turned out to be a disappointment and he had to end her employment? An image of the press smearing his family's name and company loomed into view and stopped his advances.

Nachelle broke his imprisoning gaze and looked at his dark hands holding her captive. Harlan had held her in a similar, domineering fashion the night he had accused her of stealing his position in his parents' hearts and in the company. That same night he had humiliated her and she had broken off their engagement. That awful heart-ripping image served as an alarm clock, causing her to quickly regroup her emotions. She shrugged out of Steven's grip and maneuvered around him, gathering her things from the table and stuffing them in her briefcase.

"It's late. I think I'd better be going." Nachelle almost ran to the coat closet. Without a backward glance, she slipped on her coat and headed for the elevator. She had pressed the button and was waiting impatiently when she felt Steven's presence.

"You may need this." Steven handed her her purse.

Nachelle blushed with embarrassment. "Thank you," she murmured with a very succinct look in his direction.

"If you're too tired to drive home, I can arrange transportation for tonight and have your car delivered tomorrow."

"I'll be fine on my own." Nachelle spoke more harshly than she had intended. She needed to hear those words as much as she needed for Steven to hear them.

"Nachelle, I know you're capable of taking care of yourself, but you've already had one close encounter with a wicked object tonight."

Make that two, Nachelle thought.

"This just isn't a safe hour for any woman driving alone." The bell announcing the elevator's arrival resounded throughout the small foyer. Nachelle stepped in as soon as the doors opened. She'd decided that the conversation was over.

Steven took one look at Nachelle's face and knew there would be no compromise. He followed her into the elevator and pressed the appropriate button.

"You're as stubborn as my mother," Steven muttered with a defeated sigh. He turned to Nachelle, letting his gaze roam over her face, imprinting it in his mind. He opened his mouth to speak, visibly changed his mind, and turned front and center.

Nachelle gave Steven a sly, sideward glance, and thought, . . . *his mother? Why would he compare me to his mother?* Nachelle let the thought slide into nothingness. Tiredness crept back into the present. She slouched under the heavy wool coat and was thankful that the ride in the elevator and the brief walk to her car was anticlimactic. She longed for solitude and time away from Steven's imposing figure.

Steven slipped naturally into his role as a Southern gentleman: carrying her briefcase, unlocking the door, and checking the interior of the car—all without a single spoken word. To an outsider, it looked like a normal business relationship between colleagues, minus speech.

As he shut the car door, Steven said in a soft tone, "Call me when you get home."

"Fine." Nachelle didn't look in his direction. She started the motor and backed out of the numbered space. As she headed for the side street exit, she could see Steven in her rearview window, standing like an ancient African warrior: tall, dark, and commanding. She released the breath she had been holding and slumped in her seat.

My God, she mused, *what the hell is going on? That's the second time I've almost succumbed to that man! I've got to pull myself together and quit acting like a sex-starved teenager. Steven is just like Harlan. If I let him, he'll use me, dump me, and leave me with a damaged reputation and a broken heart. I'm not stupid enough to fall for that again.* Nachelle screeched out of the parking garage and soon entered the fast-paced freeway. She drove like the devil himself chased her.

Six

A new work week had arrived. The second week as a Du-Cloux Enterprises employee felt no more comfortable than the first, but at least the initial anxieties had lessened. For Nachelle, some of her acquired calmness stemmed from Steven's decision to give her direct control over the merger. On the flip side, she would have to interact closely with him and that was an unnerving prospect. For a reason she had yet to explore and name, all of her sensibilities and self-control seemed to scatter when he was around.

On her drive home early Saturday morning, she'd convinced herself it was exhaustion making her act like a nervous filly around Steven. To cement her reasoning, she had called Steven as promised. In addition to assuring him she'd arrived home safely, she had requested to meet with him first thing Monday morning. She intended to make it clear to him that she wanted only a strictly business relationship—and to prove to herself that she was more than capable of maintaining things that way.

Nachelle was glad this was one of those mornings when she beat Millie into the office. Though an excellent secretary, Millie was sometimes a bit of a mother hen. Nachelle didn't require nor want any extra attention this morning. She wanted peace and a few minutes to focus on her upcoming meeting with Steven. She leaned back in her soft leather chair and closed her eyes. The stillness of the morning and the mellow tunes floating from the radio acted as a sedative. Unfortunately, her tranquillity was short-lived.

"Oh, Nachelle, I didn't know you were already here," Millie said as she bounced in, surprise evident in her actions and words. "What are you doing here so early? It's barely 7:30." Millie made a clucking sound and started fussing around her desk. "You did go home this weekend, didn't you?"

Nachelle was determined to put a stop to any non-essential conversation and movements in a polite but effective way. "Millie, I have a very important meeting with Steven this morning. Please hold all calls, messages, and visitors. I need this time to prepare, okay?"

No one had to hit Millie over the head to convey a message. "No problem. I'll bring you some fresh coffee and then I'll leave you to your plans."

True to her word, Millie reentered several minutes later with a steaming cup of the hot brew. "Nachelle, I forgot to bring this in with the other mail. It's for you."

Nachelle sprang to attention. Millie laid a brown papered package, the size of a shirt box, on her uncluttered desk. A puzzled frown furrowed her forehead as she mentally searched for the reason why a package would be delivered to her on this particular day. It wasn't her birthday and Christmas was over.

Maybe it's that present Heather mail-ordered that didn't show up for Christmas, she mused.

"Did this arrive this morning?"

"I'm not sure when it arrived. I assume it came with the late mail on Friday afternoon." Millie spoke as she backed out of the plush office. "I'll leave you to it now." She paused at the door. "If you need any files for the meeting let me know."

After nodding her head in acknowledgment, Nachelle ripped into the wrappings. She acknowledged a small prickle of excitement as she lifted the lid of the white box and hunted through the layers of pastel pink tissue paper. Her breath caught in her throat as her eyes fastened on the gift. With slightly shaking hands, she picked up the gift card and read:

Nachelle—
    Please accept these with my apologies.
    No strings attached!

                                                    SDD

Nachelle let the card flutter down to her desk and picked up the pair of perfectly sized black and white herringbone pants, exactly like the pair she had ruined at Steven's hotel suite.

"Steven D. DuCloux," she murmured aloud. "Well Nachelle, what do you do now?"

She put the pants back into the box and then rose to pace the length of her office while riotous thoughts crowded her mind. Pausing at the window, she opened the vertical blinds to absently view the scene below. People and cars moved frantically as they scurried to reach their downtown offices.

I wonder if any of those people have a boss who's as complex and dangerous as Steven D. DuCloux? She turned her head toward the surprise package on her desk. *No strings attached! Yeah, right,* she scoffed. Her troubled gaze snagged on the brief meeting outline she had started before Millie had interrupted her.

Quick as a finger snap, she refocused on her goal. She now had one other item to place on her agenda. Mr. *DuCloux won't know what's hit him when I'm through,* she gloated. *He won't have a choice but to see me as the confident, well-qualified vice president I am and consequently leave the personal remarks unspoken!* With fire in her bones, she returned to the desk and began writing furiously.

Almost an hour later when she was satisfied that she had clearly captured all her points and issues, she placed her notes in her portfolio and set it aside to busy her mind with the morning's mail and the financial reports. At 8:25 sharp, Nachelle picked up her portfolio and headed for Steven's office. She was determined to be on time for her 8:30 appointment with the boss.

As she rounded the corner to Steven's office, she could see Dorrie, Steven's secretary for the past twelve years, juggling the phones, the mail, and her work on the computer. The older woman with a short, graying afro barely spared Nachelle a glance. While holding the telephone against her ear with her shoulder, she motioned with her head and eyes for Nachelle to enter the president's office. Squaring her shoulders almost imperceptibly, she knocked once, then opened the door to the office that had till very recently belonged to Ralph Hayes. She couldn't count the number of times she had passed through that door. The office had once represented a haven of love and support. Now, due to circumstances dictated by timing and chance, the office represented the lion's den and she was Daniel.

Steven beckoned her forward. He put a hand over the mouthpiece of the phone and whispered, "I'll be through in a second."

Nachelle sat down in a generous, paisley-patterned chair which squarely faced Steven's mahogany desk. She took the grace period he offered and reviewed the notes she had drafted in her office earlier this morning. Satisfied that she had missed nothing, she crossed her legs and tried to concentrate on anything other than Steven. She gave it a valiant effort, but after noting the small changes he had made in the office, mostly pictures of his family in place of the pictures Ralph had had, her attention returned to Steven. He looked devastatingly handsome in a black Brooks Brothers' suit. He had already shucked his jacket and had rolled up his sleeves to show brown muscular arms. He was casually marking on a report while the person on the other end of the line rattled on.

How small his silver pen appears in his hand, she thought faintly. That thought brought her back to Friday night at his hotel suite when he had used that same hand to examine the tear in her pants.

He had been so concerned, and what a surprise to receive a replacement pair. *Harlan would never have done that,* she couldn't help thinking. The unintentional reference to Harlan whipped her into shape and brought to mind the commitment she held dear. *So what if he shows a little humanity at times. It's all part and parcel of being the Silver Shark. I'm still not interested in him, and he'll know that today. Now, concentrate Nachelle. This is going to be difficult enough without these traitorous thoughts.*

"How was the rest of your weekend?" Steven asked as he hung up the phone and put the report aside to give her his full attention.

"Good, thank you," Nachelle quickly answered, caught up short. She'd been so engrossed with her thoughts, she hadn't realized that Steven had ended his conversation. Now that she was back in the present, she saw how his midnight eyes roamed freely over her figure as if trying to judge for himself the validity of her response. When his eyes lingered on her full breasts and narrow waist, she wished that she had chosen a different suit in which to confront him today. She had forgotten that the black-trimmed red crepe power suit accentuated her figure. "And yours?" Nachelle asked, hoping to eliminate the personal edge that had crept into the room.

"I was tied to the phone with the Atlanta office most of the weekend. The rest of the time I spent thinking out a strategy to a very interesting problem."

Nachelle was glad he finally met her eyes. She relaxed—a little. "Anything I can help with?"

Steven laid his pen down and leaned back in his chair. His eyes narrowed to slits. "Probably, but it's a little too early to know yet." After a brief pause and an intense look in her direction, he sat up quickly and asked, "You want to finish what we started Friday night?"

Nachelle stopped breathing for a second. Her eyes widened as a vivid image of them standing face to face, only inches separating them, his hands warming her flesh even through layers of fabric, flitted through her mind. "I . . . As I stated . . ."

In a cool tone, Steven cut her off. "I'm referring to the business plans we didn't discuss because of the late hour . . . and you'd also mentioned a few items you needed to talk about." Steven studied her with hooded, secretive eyes. "What did you *think* I meant?"

Nachelle felt like an idiot. Her mutinous thoughts had taken her down the wrong road yet again. She had wrongly assumed his reference pertained to their very personal encounter at his suite. Her confidence fizzled and started a downward spiral. The monologue she had practiced in her office seemed ill-fitting now that she might be barking up the wrong tree.

Perhaps I imagined his personal interest in me on Friday night. I was tired, it was late, maybe I was just punchy. After all, the gift card—"no strings attached"—written in his own handwriting, proclaims his intentions. Nachelle looked deep into his eyes and, seeing nothing readable in their depths, decided to take him at face value.

She looked down at the notes she had recorded about personal relationships at the office. Flipping them over, she looked up and answered, "Exactly what you said. The unfinished agenda items . . . and that's it. The things I wanted to speak with you about have been resolved." Turning to a fresh sheet of paper, she blotted out of her mind the notes she had written just this morning. She and Steven were on a new playing field.

"Good. Let's get started then."

Steven barged into the business details like a freight train. Nachelle eased into her second-in-command role, her earlier embarrassment at assessing the situation incorrectly fading like smoke. She listened intently while he communicated his ideas, his requests, and his dreams for the company. She sought clarification when needed and offered recommendations and suggestions when appropriate. This was a role she was comfortable with and one in which she could excellently perform.

Two hours later, Steven ended the meeting. "Let me know

if your people have trouble getting the reports from Atlanta. The people here aren't the only ones scared of what the future's going to bring. Since it came out that I'll be spending most of my time here, rumors that the Atlanta office will be closing are flying rampant."

"Sure." Nachelle back-tracked to a time when she too had been a victim of the ugly rumor-mill. She could understand and appreciate Steven's concern for controlling the hurtful barbs.

"There is one other thing before you leave." Steven leaned forward in his chair and pinned her with a direct stare. "I was informed by my legal staff that they have not yet received the signed papers from Harlan. They have tried to reach him, but have so far been unsuccessful."

Nachelle frowned and gripped her pen tighter. Presenting a calm face to Steven, she asked, "Have you told Ralph?"

"Yes, actually, I spoke with Ralph several times this weekend about the matter. It's Ralph's suggestion that we continue forward. He feels pretty confident that Harlan will sign with no problem."

"I see." Nachelle bit the inside of her lip. Her face was a composite of concentration.

"What's your opinion? You know him very well, perhaps you even know a side of him his family doesn't."

You can say that again, Nachelle thought sarcastically. Immediately after that thought the light clicked on. She was reminded of Steven's use of PIs. *Oh, so they did discover Harlan and I were engaged. I wonder how much Steven knows.* Nachelle squirmed in her seat as she recalled the unpleasantness she'd been subjected to at Harlan's hands.

"Nachelle, I'd really like to hear what you're thinking."

"It's probably an oversight." Nachelle shrugged her shoulders. No way was she going to tell him Harlan was an irresponsible, self-centered man who couldn't give a flip about licking a stamp let alone about signing some important papers that had hundreds of lives attached to it. Where Ralph was optimistic, Nachelle was not. Steven was right. She did know some things about Harlan that Ralph and Adele in a million years would not even begin to guess.

"I hope that's all there is to it. If he doesn't come through, this could be a real disaster." Although his words expressed concern, Steven's countenance gave nothing away. His handsome face was a mask of granite. "I'll give it more time, but I've already warned Ralph that his and your assistance would be required if it takes much longer."

Nachelle nodded. She didn't trust herself to speak. She knew this was a major coup for Steven and he would not let a missing signature stand in the way of his grandiose plans. She had no doubt he would put action to his words and if that turned out to be the case, she would be forced to interact with Harlan. They hadn't spoken in over eight months and their last conversation had been anything but polite. Nachelle looked at the business notes she had written and fervently prayed that Harlan would sign and return the papers soon.

Steven stood and walked around the massive desk. He half-sat, half-leaned on the desk, crossing his arms. "So, how did the pants fit?"

His question jolted Nachelle to a subject she had decided not to broach. *Well, there's no beating around the bush on this one. I might as well tell him and get it over with.* But, how did she tell her boss that she had returned his token gift because she had thought that he was using it to make a play for her? How did she tell her boss she was wrong and showed poor judgment after he had entrusted her with the responsibility of merging two dynamic companies?

"The pants were . . . are just fine. I appreciate your taking the time and effort to replace them." Nachelle paused before continuing. She would just have to admit the truth. "I had Millie return them to the boutique. As I told you previously, the pants were old and due to be replaced this season anyway."

Steven didn't reply immediately. He stared at her, looking

like she'd just spoken in some foreign language that he didn't understand.

"Why did you do that?" he asked softly.

"I just told you." Nachelle fidgeted in her seat. The Cross pen her father had given her glinted in the light as she twirled it round and round. "The pants were a wash. After one more wear I would have given them to charity." Nachelle held onto her accurate if somewhat stretched story like a lifeline.

"Why don't you save us both some time and tell me the real reason why you returned them?" Steven's voice was a fraction lower. A close relative would have known this was a sign that his iron-fisted control was slipping and that he was fighting to regain it. He didn't like the idea that his well-intentioned gift had been returned.

She wasn't surprised at his ability to see through the thin veil of truth she was hiding behind. "What makes you think I'm not telling the truth?" Nachelle asked.

Nachelle would have elected to have bamboo shoots placed under her nails rather than to tell Steven that Harlan used to give her presents and then use them against her. Harlan had been her boss, her lover, and then later, her nemesis.

Determined to protect every bit of her visible and invisible self, Nachelle forged ahead. "It was a kind thought, but an unnecessary one. Thank you just the same."

"Unnecessary?" Steven said, fighting to keep his cool. No woman had ever spoken to him in such an unconcerned tone . . . and it was obvious she was hiding something. "It's nothing more than I would do for any employee."

Nachelle recalled the words he had scrawled on the card, "No strings attached!" A bitter bile rose in her throat as past ugly memories demanded her attention. "There are always strings attached." Nachelle let the words slip before she could package them.

"Is that the voice of experience speaking?" Interest in her answer caused him to lean forward. "Has something happened in your past that would cause you to confuse the meaning of three simple words?" A demanding tone had snaked into his voice.

Immediately on the defensive, Nachelle sat back in her seat and crossed her arms. A threatening sense of discovery spurred her to hide behind the cool professional veneer she usually found so comfortable. She wished she had donned it prior to now. "My past experiences have nothing to do with you. You need only concern yourself with the attributes I currently bring to your organization." Her face glowed with defiance.

"I already know about your present attributes. I'm more interested in the past right now. So, please, explain your statement." The challenge in Steven's voice would have made most heavyweight champions back down. Nachelle was too agitated to bow to his request.

"I've given you my position. There's nothing else to discuss or explain." Nachelle spoke as if the Arctic was contained in her small body.

With deliberate purpose, Steven stood straight and towered above her. "This doesn't have anything to do with Harlan Hayes or your broken engagement to him, does it?" His voice was low; his stance self-possessed.

His unexpected reference to her ex-fiancé made her ice mask slip slightly. She recovered sufficiently enough to respond. "I'm committed to keeping my business matters separate from my personal affairs. Any information you would like regarding the business relationship Harlan and I had is contained in my personnel file." Nachelle couldn't resist a back-handed comment. "As to my engagement to him, surely your PIs informed you of any pertinent information, especially since you hinted earlier I know him better than his family."

Steven leaned over and grasped the arms of the chair Nachelle sat in, effectively capturing her in a jail of strong dark arms. The decidedly musky scent of his expensive cologne assaulted her senses as he leaned in close.

"Actually, no. The PIs didn't get the full scoop on you and Harlan's business or personal relationship."

Kneeling in front of her with one knee on the floor, Steven brought their eyes to the same level. His movement caused his stomach to brush against her stockinged legs. She felt his washboard muscles through his starched white shirt and fought hard to keep her vivid imagination from entering dangerous territory. As it was, she was having a great deal of difficulty matching his eye contact.

To avoid the disturbing physical contact, Nachelle uncrossed her legs and sat up straighter as Steven continued in a controlled but persuasive tone.

"It's obviously a story that a number of people want buried," he said. "But, I have faith in my PIs. Or, you can make it easy on both of us and tell me about your affiliation with Harlan. He still plays a very important part in the present."

"There's nothing to share that would impact the present or future." Nachelle clamped her jaws together and wished she had the guts to walk out of this newly transferred company. But, running from a worthwhile battle had never been in her nature, even if it meant personal sacrifices.

Steven ran his capable hands up the sides of the chair and although her arms were pressed tightly against her, she could imagine the feel of them against her yielding flesh. She did have Friday night's memory to refer to.

In a voice that left no doubt to the sincerity of his words, Steven stated, "I'll let this conversation stand for now, but if anything in your past stands to impact the future of this company, you'd best tell me now while I'm in a good mood."

Nachelle spoke with more bravado than she felt. "You have nothing to worry about."

Steven let several seconds tick off before he spoke. "I hope not, or you'll have hell to pay." Steven gave her her personal space back, but didn't rise from the floor.

Nachelle dared a deep look in his eyes and saw the truth

within their midnight color. She knew at that moment that he was capable of hurting anyone or anything that threatened DuCloux Enterprises. Despite her tough resolve to remain unaffected, she shivered but was rooted to the spot.

Dorrie was the one to break Steven's black spell. "Sorry for interrupting, Steven, Nachelle," she said, poking her head in the doorway. "Nathaniel's on the line. He says it's important."

"Thank you, Dorrie." The look he gave Dorrie was a generation different from the dark gaze with which he'd pinned Nachelle.

After Dorrie shut the door, Steven resumed eye contact with Nachelle. "The Fort Worth Metropolitan Black Chamber of Commerce banquet is in a few days." Steven stood and returned to his side of the desk. "I'll pick you up."

Nachelle opened her mouth to refuse the off-hand invitation, then realized it would be silly to do so. Several representatives of the Hayes Group always attended the function since they belonged to the Chamber. And, with Ralph's retirement in effect, she had no choice but to accompany Steven. She hoped and prayed Mike Adams and his wife would be there as they usually were.

Nachelle nodded her consent and exited the office without granting Steven a good-bye glance.

Steven picked up the phone, but didn't take the call off hold. Instead, he watched Nachelle leave his office. He could not for the life of him remember a time when a woman could move him to anger and then desire in only a millisecond of time. It had taken all of his self-control to keep his hands off her. The chair had been a poor substitute for the flesh he was sure would have been soft and warm. His blood still thundered through his body in unfulfilled protest.

His last thought, before picking up Nathaniel's call, was that he couldn't wait to receive and read the final PI report. They promised to have the full scoop on her love affair with Harlan Hayes. With that report, he would be able to fully assess her personal background and compare it to his family's checklist. As long as there were no surprises and she passed the criteria, he could check off that item as complete.

Seven

With only one shoe on, Nachelle hobbled to the vanity. "Where is the other blasted shoe," she moaned. Ignoring her dilemma for the moment, she grabbed her silver evening bag and began throwing cosmetics, cash, and identification into it. The thought of Steven waiting in the living room with Heather spurred her to equal the speed of light.

Heather's dangerous enough by herself, she thought. *Adding Steven to the mixture would be pure suicide.*

Nachelle searched one final time for the missing silver pump that complemented her black and silver dress. The dress itself left everything to the imagination. It had long sleeves with rhinestone buttons, a high collar, and layers of sheer black organza which flared enticingly around her knees. Only a rhinestone belt accentuated her tiny waist and completed the picture. She recalled the previous time she had been appropriately dressed only to discover that one appraising look from Steven had left her feeling naked and vulnerable. *I don't need that tonight,* she thought with dread.

After leaving Steven's office on Monday morning, she had been certain Steven wasn't interested in pursuing a personal relationship. Now, days later, she wasn't one hundred percent sure. It wasn't anything she could concretely pinpoint, but rather, the rumors she kept hearing regarding his professional battle cry. It was said that, when faced with an imposing challenge, Steven would stoop to any level to win. Nachelle had heard that again today when having lunch with Angela Myers, the Human Resources Manager of the Hayes Group. Supposedly, Angela had had a lengthy conversation with her peer in Atlanta who indicated Steven played for keeps and that he was not opposed to giving directives that meant his subordinates sometimes performed duties that crossed the legal line on employment, compensation, and other personnel matters. It appeared that he cared more for DuCloux Enterprises than for the people who were the wheels that made his big company move forward. Based on that lunchtime conversation, the past run-in that the Hayes Group had had with DuCloux Enterprises over contracts and bidding and the fact that Steven himself told her DuCloux Enterprises was his reason for breathing, Nachelle had reached the conclusion that maybe she'd been too hasty in trusting his verbal and written words.

With his reputation as a deadly business opponent, he'd probably say or do anything to throw me off.

She flushed with renewed embarrassment. After the lies and degenerate antics Harlan had pulled, she should have been more in tune with Steven's unscrupulous ways. *Well, no more,* she thought vehemently. *I won't fall for another innocent act.*

As to her physical reactions to him, Nachelle saw Steven for what he was—an incredibly sexy, handsome, and confident man. She felt sure her body was betraying her because of his dark attractive looks and the celibate state she had been living in since the break-up of her engagement to Harlan, two years ago. She made a secret oath to do a better job of ignoring the man and sticking to her own agenda—positioning the merger favorably for the Hayes Group employees and avoiding office romances.

One thing I know for sure, and that is he's left no doubt as to where his heart lies. With his forceful statements, Nachelle knew he would rather die than jeopardize the future of his company.

Nachelle took off the one shoe in her possession and went to her bedroom doorway. "Heather! I need you for a second."

Down-to-earth Heather returned the call. "I'm entertaining Steven. What do you need?"

"I need you in here, please." Nachelle stood in the doorway and shuddered. What in the world could they be talking about?

For the past week and a half Heather had been on a Steven DuCloux fan club kick. Every time she and Heather had gotten together or spoken over the telephone, Heather had made it a point to inquire about Steven or make a comment pertaining to Nachelle developing a personal relationship with her boss. No matter what Nachelle said, Heather was unshakable. She was like a dog with a bone. And now she was in the living room with Steven, talking about God only knew what.

Nachelle heard the shuffle of Heather's tennis shoes coming down the hallway. Almost instantly Heather appeared, munching on raisins and sporting a tri-color jogging suit. She looked not like the thirty-one-year-old woman she was so much as a teenager. "What's up? Do you need help with the zipper?"

She rattled on, barely stopping to take a breath. "He is an absolute ten! Wait till you see him in that tux. It's going to knock your pantyhose off." Heather's hazel eyes twinkled innocently when she added, "By the way, your other shoe is in the living room."

Nachelle froze in her tracks. "The living room? What is my shoe doing in the living room?" Confusion showed, like an uncompleted five-hundred-piece puzzle, on her dark face.

Heather sighed. "When I went to let Steven in, I had the shoe in my hand." She popped a raisin in her mouth and perched precariously on the bed.

Nachelle placed her hands on her hips and sent a thunderous look in Heather's direction. "And?"

"Well, Steven liked the shoe."

Nachelle crossed her arms and patted her foot. "Am I going to have to prompt you through this whole story?"

"Just hold on, Ms. Impatient. I'm getting there." Another raisin disappeared into Heather's mouth.

"Where? Where exactly are you going with this sketchy exposé?"

Heather replied as if her response was the most natural and only possible answer. "I'm trying to tell you that Steven has your shoe. Since I was playing the perfect hostess, in your absence I might add . . ." She sent Nachelle a tsk, tsk look. ". . . I poured us drinks and he held your shoe. He still has it."

"Heather!" She stumbled through a series of half-formed words and expressions. After trying for several seconds and still unable to frame any type of intelligible remark, she gave up.

"Are you ready?" Heather grasped Nachelle's arm and tapped the face of her watch. "Time's a ticking and didn't you say potential clients are meeting you at the banquet?" Heather moved behind Nachelle and gently steered her towards the door. "You look like two million dollars. Now, go and meet your Prince Charming."

Nachelle gave Heather a scowl that could have caused snow to fall in the Caribbean. Coaching herself to expect the worst, Nachelle squared her shoulders and entered the living room.

Steven sat in an overstuffed easy chair balancing Nachelle's shoe between his two index fingers. Absently, he moved it back and forth, watching as the light threw colored beams off the silver pump. He looked up when he heard the women enter the room and almost dropped the object when he saw Nachelle. The conservative, yet body-conscious dress framed her full, high breasts, thin waist, flared hips, and knock-out legs. Although it hid her flesh, Steven's imagination of what lay underneath the fine fabric skyrocketed. He stopped himself from ogling, but wasn't as successful at stopping the delicious fingers of desire from touching every potent part of his body.

Nachelle stated truthfully. "I'm sorry I kept you waiting. I was looking for that. I didn't know it had beat me to the living room." She gave Heather a pointed look.

"No problem." Steven stood and took a baby step away from the easy chair. He pointed at it with the high-heeled pump. "Sit down and I'll put it on for you."

"That's okay. I can do it." Nachelle grew faint-hearted.

Having him touch her feet, she thought excitedly, *was much too intimate of an act!*

"I know you can do it." Steven, again, used her shoe as a pointer, while his deep sensual bass voice reached across the room and wrapped itself around her like raw silk.

"Go on, Nachelle. You're already running late." Heather egged her on, then moved out of striking distance.

Torn between compliance and refusal, Nachelle decided it wasn't worth making into a federal case. She edged forward and took the appointed seat, but not before sending Heather an *I'll kill you later* look. Steeling herself for the brief encounter, she took a deep breath and recited her earlier vow to discipline her thoughts and actions.

I can handle this, she thought logically. *He's just putting my shoe on.*

As Steven took the other shoe out of her hand, a wicked half smile played on his face and caused her heart to skip a few beats. "Feeling like Cinderella?"

Nachelle thought he might have been joking, but she couldn't be sure because he immediately bowed his head, effectively hiding his face. Nachelle stared at his bent head and begrudgingly admitted Heather was right. He looked very attractive in his black tuxedo. Instead of the traditional black cummerbund and bow tie, he had elected a print pattern with gorgeous fall colors—gold, bronze, yellow, turquoise, and burgundy—and had replaced the cummerbund with a vest. His bow tie was of the same print. The well-fitted suit emphasized the breadth of his shoulders and the muscular build of his body.

Buried beneath his slick and tough exterior, he should have a heart in there somewhere, she thought. Yes, he had agreed to sponsor a retirement party for Ralph and he had agreed to take the merger slow so as not to send all of the employees into shock, but those acts didn't begin to make up for the cold-blooded business acts that were his trademarks—unscrupulously landing contracts, underhanded recruiting, buying smaller companies that threatened his market share. No doubt about it, Steven DuCloux was a complex character, one who caused her to tread lightly but also one who had a strange pull on her.

So intent was she on her internal thoughts that she was unprepared for the caress of Steven's hand on the underside of her calf. Inwardly, Nachelle's heart surpassed the Indy racing speed, but outwardly she appeared unmoved . . . until she accidentally met Steven's eyes.

For the first time since meeting her new boss, she saw a definite readable emotion reflected in his dark orbs. What she read made her throat constrict. Desire . . . pure, undisguised desire. And, as if his visual message wasn't enough, his hands completed the message by moving sensually over her lower legs and feet.

An intense, racking bolt of sexually-heated electricity shot through Nachelle's body. She grabbed the cushion and squeezed it between her hands. The action did little to lighten her reaction to his touch.

"You have nice legs." Steven spoke slowly and pinned her to the chair with his desire-laden gaze.

"Thank you." She squeaked the words and even to her truthful ears, her voice sounded unnatural. Thank God Heather had gone to the kitchen for more raisins.

Some sane part of her conjured up the reason for his being in her living room on this particular night, causing her to mutter in a thick voice, "I . . . uh . . . We have guests tonight. Mike invited several potential and existing customers to the banquet. Perhaps we should get a move on." When Steven didn't make a move to create space for her to get up from the chair, she carefully brushed past him. "I'll just get my wrap and we can leave."

Nachelle fled from the private sanctuary he had created and on rubbery legs arrived at the coat closet breathless. Once there, she made a big production of choosing the most appropriate evening wrap and . . . steadying her breath and heart-beats.

Now Nachelle, she scolded herself, *you just told yourself to exercise discipline around the man. You call that discipline?* She looked at her hands and saw they were still trembling. Even her stomach was aquiver.

Closing her eyes for a second to gather inner strength, she opened them and grabbed her black satin swing coat. *The last thing I need is for Steven to help me into my coat.* She already knew the havoc his masterful hands could wreak.

Tacking on a forced smile, Nachelle walked to the living room entryway. "I'm ready."

Heather returned from the kitchen in time to escort the couple to the door. She spoke in a sugar-induced voice. "You guys have a great time." She boldly winked.

"I'm sure we will." Steven spoke with a great deal of authority in his voice.

Nachelle refused to meet either pair of eyes.

On the way to the hotel, in between small talk and the almost requisite business discussions, she tried to remember that Steven was her enemy. Everything negative she had ever heard about him she recalled and played like an album with a scratched groove. But, in between the justifications, memories of his touch and smoldering looks vied for equal attention. Feeling the beginnings of a headache, she gave up on the internal debate and decided to just concentrate on making it through the night.

Luckily for Nachelle, upon their arrival at the hotel throngs of people flocked to Steven like he was some kind of a demi-God. Nachelle took the opportunity to escape his guiding hand.

After a pass in the crowded women's restroom, she returned to the mayhem and found their corporate table. Although Steven was seated, he still had a small group of local politicians and businessmen situated around him. She quickly scanned their table and discovered that two empty seats remained—one, three seats to his left and the other right next to him. Before she could slip into the farthest seat, Steven stood and pulled out the chair next to his.

She silently cursed his gentlemanly habits and sat down with great reluctance. While Steven politely shooed his entourage away, she introduced herself to the potential customers they were wooing. She was glad to see that Mike, their Vice President of Sales, and his wife were comfortably ensconced across the table.

"Please everyone, excuse my manners. I'm afraid I'm not being a very good host." Steven smiled as he recovered his seat. "Now that my hostess has arrived, I can depend on her to keep me honest." Steven turned his head toward Nachelle and gave her a conspiratorial wink.

Nachelle's reaction to his bold action was swift and no less powerful than his heated look. Her stomach took a wild dip and the butterflies that had developed inside it went crazy.

"And a very beautiful hostess you have," one of their guests responded, saving Nachelle the trouble of having to come up with a fitting response.

"Yes. Indeed." Steven agreed, looking appreciatively at his VP.

The seductive picture she created in the mysterious black and silver dress almost made him forget his mission for the evening—rating her performance in the social hostess category, a skill much needed for a DuCloux wife. Steven was honest enough to admit he was becoming down right attached to Nachelle. In their short time together, he had already witnessed and approved of her logical decision-making, her accuracy with financial numbers, and her nurturing spirit that appealed to the numerous employees she was responsible for. However, too much was at stake for him to rely on his caveman instincts. He was looking for a woman worthy of being a DuCloux wife. The future of his family's company rested on his decision.

Nachelle tried hard to ignore the magnetism of the man

sitting so close. But, he was every bit as charming as Heather's mother's investigation and office rumors had indicated. The ladies at their table were all practically in love with him by the end of the evening, and she could tell the men equally respected him. Even her ally, Mike, seemed to have forgotten that Steven DuCloux was the man who had turned their lives upside-down.

The evening ended with a mild uproar of good-byes, and other parting pleasantries. With the guests safely on their way, Mike and Steven congratulated each other on successfully sewing up two new contracts. Nachelle was pleased that she had a few moments to restock her emotional banks before she was forced to be alone with Steven—again. Soon, however, she was whisked away by Steven's domineering hand and shepherded into his midnight-colored Lotus.

"I'm glad that chore is over." Steven remarked as he pulled his expensive sports car away from the portico and into the merging traffic. He flipped on the wipers to erase the light drizzle of rain falling around them.

"I imagine with the influence your company has in Atlanta, you're always attending these sorts of functions," she stated flatly, while looking out of the window. She absently noted that they were getting more rain than usual for this time of year.

"You're right. But regardless of what city or organization, I still don't like them. I always feel like a kid playing dress up." Steven shifted gears and soon they were accelerating beyond the posted speed. He sighed heavily, "But, of course they're necessary for business. Tonight is a good example of that."

Steven allowed an extended pause to exist before continuing.

"So, I put my own personal feelings aside and try to play the perfect host. And, by the way . . ." Steven glanced quickly at her side profile, ". . . you were great tonight. You've obviously done a lot of business entertaining. That's good and very important."

Steven made a mental note to check off that category on his checklist. He had gotten the final report from the PI firm earlier than he had anticipated, but it had generated more questions than answers. *I don't know if she broke off the engagement, and if so, was it a mutual decision? And why did Harlan leave his dad's business, give up his rightful heir position, and move to Phoenix? Most importantly, does Nachelle still love Harlan?* Steven didn't know the details of her relationship with Harlan and it was driving him crazy. Disappointed but undaunted, he decided he was going to have to get the real answers from Nachelle. He wasn't sure how he was going to get her to fill in the gray areas but he was going to fill them! In the meantime, he couldn't check off personal background on the list. Even so, he reflected, based on his initial review, she was sizing up nicely to the DuCloux list. She had definitely passed the social hostess category, which left only three more categories to rate—personal background, family suitability, and sexual compatibility. *Who knows, she just may be the one.* Steven smiled in the dark. Soon, he might be able to get his parents—especially his mother—off his back about marriage and the family decree. In a flash, he decided to enact his strategy, tonight, for determining sexual compatibility.

Steven stared straight ahead through the windshield, thinking how best to position his proposition. He didn't want to offend her, but, on the other hand, he had to make sure she was potential DuCloux material, for once a DuCloux man married, he lived by his vows—to have and to hold from this day forth till death do us part.

Taking the plunge, Steven spoke, "This isn't the most ideal place to have this conversation, but I can't sleep another night without speaking to you about us."

Nachelle's throat closed up. She had been silently ticking off the miles to her house and enjoying the absence of conversation. He'd spoiled the companionable atmosphere by mentioning the very subject which made her most uncomfortable. "Us?" Even though he was concentrating on the tricky road conditions, she didn't dare look at him.

"Yes, us. I know you're attracted to me and I'm definitely attracted to you."

Nachelle listened to his confession, but sat numb, unable to move or speak. A myriad of complex thoughts bombarded her mind, but she refused to dwell on any one for more than a split second.

Steven needed no response from her to continue. His encouragement came from the sexual pull he felt between them and his desire to run her through the list successfully. "I've given it a lot of thought, and I've come up with a way that we can remove this interfering wall and start making some serious decisions about our future."

"I'm not sure I know what you mean. I . . ." Nachelle started the denial process automatically. Her pledge to avoid office romances flashed in her head like a blinking neon sign.

"Nachelle, I hope you're not going to tell me I'm imagining this sexual magnetism we have for each other. Give me more credit than that." Steven steered sharply to the left to avoid an obstacle in the road, causing Nachelle to bump lightly against his shoulder. "Sorry," he murmured.

A web of indecision closed around her. If she told the truth, she would be opening up old wounds and setting herself up for more hurt. If she told a lie, Steven would see through it like rice paper. And then what would that do to the tenuous future of the employees who were depending on her? More importantly, what would it do to her?

Steven continued, "You probably haven't given our situation as much thought as I have, so you'll need time to think about it." Steven pulled up to her condominium building. He shifted to park, engaged the emergency brake, and turned in his seat, throwing his right arm over the back of her seat. "While you're letting that sink in, think about this as well. To determine if this is a passing fad or not, you should spend the night with me and after we've made love, we can talk about the future."

Simultaneously, Nachelle gasped and her head swiveled in his direction. One small-boned hand covered her mouth and her already large eyes grew even larger.

"I know it's unorthodox and a bit presumptuous on my part, but it's the only thing I could come up with." Steven paused, searching her doe brown eyes. She had no way of knowing that he was on a mission. "If you have a better suggestion, I'll consider it."

In a small, disembodied voice, Nachelle answered, "I can't. I don't."

Steven's businesslike tone shifted to smooth and sensual. His dark eyes, similar in color to his car, softened as he ran a single finger down her cheek to her chin and up to her lips where he traced their delectable outline. In a honeyed whisper, he stated, "It makes sense, Nachelle. It would settle a lot of things and would allow us to move onto more important matters—business and personal."

Nachelle didn't care that a horrified look showed on her face. Pushing his hand aside, she shook her head and whispered, "You're crazy."

As if a pack of hungry wild dogs chased her, she flew out of his car and up the stairs to the lobby door. Her very existence depended on her getting away from Steven and his farfetched, insulting idea.

Eight

It took a considerable amount of time for Nachelle to complete the simple task of unlocking her front door. It seemed her hands had digressed to the motor skills level of a two-year-old child. It didn't help that her blood thundered savagely in her small body as Steven's forward proposition echoed repeatedly in her head.

Finally, the dead bolt gave, causing the door to swing open to reveal her private, secure sanctuary. She slipped inside and leaned heavily against the door, inhaling massive gulps of air. She raised her hands to smooth her brow and felt a fine sheen of moisture housed there.

"Good God," she breathed. "I can't believe him."

Nachelle forced herself to move away from the door. She felt like she was caught in a dizzying array of kaleidoscopic patterns as her emotions alternated between shock, frustration, and anger. "How dare he make such a proposition! I'm his VP! An employee, for goodness sakes!" As she talked aloud she trekked a path to her bedroom, leaving in her wake a trail of discarded, forgotten articles—purse, banquet program, coat, shoes.

As if emerging from the twilight zone, she found herself in her bedroom, staring at her reflection in the vanity mirror. The shock of Steven's words finally wore off, leaving Nachelle disgusted with both herself and him.

"What kind of a woman does he think I am?" she asked herself angrily. "Just because I had a romantic relationship with one boss doesn't mean I'm available for any man who signs my paycheck." Nachelle wiped fiercely at a few angry tears. "I'm going to call him and tell him just what I think about him and his stupid proposal." As she dialed his hotel suite, she muttered frostily, "I've hinted to him that I'm not interested in a personal relationship, yet he continues to bring up the subject as if he's testing me. His head is thicker than Harlan's."

Nachelle stopped the tide of words as she considered her last remarks. A bright light went on. *A test. Yes that's it. He's testing me. Maybe he's testing my character, just to see if he'll keep me on after the merger.* She latched onto a rational, logical thought, but after tossing it about for several seconds, all the while listening to his phone ring, she discarded it.

After letting his phone ring for an unmeasurable amount of time, Nachelle finally slammed the receiver into its base.

"Damn him! He's got nerve." Staring at the phone, she stated, still visibly upset, "You're not getting off so easily, Steven DuCloux. You owe me an explanation and an apology."

Frustrated, Nachelle sunk down onto her vanity bench. *I'll bet he wouldn't persist in making me uncomfortable if I retaliated by using the press.* No sooner had the words pushed forward to Nachelle's consciousness than she regretted them. Without a shadow of a doubt, she knew she wouldn't do or say anything to hurt Steven. The thought made her eyes widen and throat constrict. She dropped the cold cream jar she had been toying with. Thick, white globs splattered over the counter and mirror as honesty colored her black and white thoughts.

"I can't hurt him." Aloud, she echoed her thoughts. *And, even in his car, I so much as admitted, at least to myself that Steven was right. I am attracted to him. That's why I was so dumbfounded, and later, angry.* Nachelle squeezed her hands into fists and admitted the hurtful truth. She *was* drawn to Steven. She could no more control or stamp out the feelings she now acknowledged than she could retract the buy-out. It was as clear as day that she wanted to know Steven as thoroughly and intimately as she had hoped to know Harlan. The really scary thing was, she didn't even know why she was attracted to him. Based on what she knew about him, she should be leaning in the opposite direction.

Nachelle slumped on the bench, cradling her face between her hands. Staring deep into her own eyes, she reflected that her relationship with Harlan had started as unsuspectingly.

As first semester MBA students, she and Harlan had had some of the same courses. He had noticed her right off and quickly talked her into teaming up for group projects. They had worked well together and before the semester had ended, Harlan had snared her heart. Before they had completed their graduate studies, they were engaged, and as everyone had assumed, after graduation they both started promising careers at the Hayes Group.

Harlan naturally started at a Vice President level, working as his father's right-hand assistant. Nachelle, as the Director of Financial Operations, felt blessed to be part of a loving family, which was much like her own small family in Austin. The major difference in their families being that her parents had used more discipline in the raising of Nachelle and Vincent. They had required them to take on more responsibilities at an early age, due to the long hours the Olivers had worked in their privately owned insurance agency. Nachelle counted it as a blessing to have a bright future with a strong, competitive company. To top it off, she had the commitment of marriage and motherhood. For four years she had lived a fairytale life.

In the fifth year, as Nachelle made wedding plans, Harlan had grown exceedingly anxious and restless. Ralph was seeking Nachelle's opinions more and more, and he had even promoted Nachelle to her current position without consulting Harlan beforehand. Instead of celebrating Nachelle's success, Harlan had let his own insecurities develop into feelings of resentment and competition. Then, to help him cope when the scales started tipping in Nachelle's favor, he had turned to drugs and other women.

The chasm between the young couple was complete, and when it was evident Harlan preferred his drugs to his family, Nachelle, or his job, Ralph—considering the future of the company he had created in his garage so many years ago—gave Nachelle Harlan's job responsibilities and forced Harlan to take a leave of absence. Ralph had continued to try and reason with his son, but Nachelle knew she and Harlan could never go back to their original plans. By that time, he had lied to her, degraded her, and crushed her heart. Harlan was out of control.

After many sleepless months, Nachelle made the painful decision to call a halt to the wedding plans. The night Harlan came to her condo so she could give him his ring back, he was flying high. The peaceful, reasonable exchange Nachelle had envisioned was quickly shattered. Harlan was belligerent and violent. He accused her of conspiring to take his place in his family and at the company. After throwing the ring at her, he slapped her across the cheek, then stormed out of her house. It had taken Nachelle many hours to pull herself together and regain some semblance of control.

Later that same night, after she had tossed, turned, cried, and finally given up on sleep altogether, she received a call from a hysterical Adele. Nachelle had rushed to the Hayes's residence in the exclusive Woodhaven neighborhood of Fort Worth, and upon entering the house had overheard the horrendous argument Harlan was having with Ralph. A tearful Adele pleaded with Nachelle to stop Harlan's tirade. Given her own humiliating encounter with Harlan earlier during that day, she was fearful, but went to Ralph's aid. What she got for her effort was a string of vindictive, foul words thrown in her face by the man who had once proclaimed to love her. And then all of the shouting, crying, and screaming had ceased for a few horrible moments as Ralph had clutched at his heart and fallen down. That argument, along with the other stresses which Ralph entertained, led him to have a massive stroke. Nachelle had called 911 and within minutes paramedics had strapped Ralph to a multitude of machines and had loaded him into the ambulance with a disoriented, wailing Adele by his side. After locking up the house, Nachelle had jumped in her car and anxiously blown her horn for Harlan to join her. Trancelike, Harlan had refused her invite, got into his own car, and roared off down the road behind the ambulance. Nachelle joined the procession, but moments later was thrown off when Harlan took an exit before the ambulance. Deciding Adele needed her more, she continued on to the hospital and comforted Adele through the night and well into the following morning until the doctor emerged with a cautious report of Ralph's condition. Later that morning, when her parents had arrived from Austin to support Adele at the hospital, she took off in search of Harlan. She visited all of his friends, his town house, his unsavory hangouts, every place she could think of. Harlan had disappeared. Several days later, when he still didn't show up, she filed a missing person's report.

With Ralph in the hospital fighting for his life and Harlan missing, it fell on Nachelle to run the business and keep the press at bay. The office grapevine had grown long tangles of lies and half-truths. What employees didn't know, they made up and the rumors were not kind to Nachelle's receiving ears. They sounded too much like the accusations Harlan had tossed at her. For many a night she had closed the door to her office and then shed a river of tears. Had it not been for her parents' comforting, open arms, Mike's supportive, non-judgmental nature, Millie's nurturing manner and wisdom, Heather's friendship, and her brother Vincent's humor and courage, Nachelle was sure she would have given everything up. Work became her salve, and it was at that low point that Nachelle vowed she would never get involved in another office romance.

A few weeks after filing her report with the police, they called to inform her that Harlan was in Phoenix, Arizona at a drug rehabilitation center. Apparently, when Harlan made what seemed like a wrong turn on the way to the hospital, he had kept driving and driving, stopping only for gas, breaks, and sleep. Fortunately, his car broke down at a service station in Phoenix. The owner, noticing his disheveled appearance and vacant expression referred Harlan to a nearby mission who managed to admit him to the rehab center. With the uncertainty regarding Harlan's whereabouts resolved, Ralph's recovery became more progressive and Adele's shoulders seemed to lift a little higher.

Four months from the date of his stroke, Ralph was back at work part-time, and together Ralph and Nachelle rebuked DuCloux Enterprises' second buy-out attempt. Six months from the date of Ralph's stroke, Harlan was released from the rehab center. He had called his parents and informed them of his decision to live and work in Phoenix. The couple was disappointed but supportive. His second call was to Nachelle. He apologized for his treatment of her and asked that they remain friends. She had breathed a sigh of relief and accepted his olive branch. It had been a tough year for her and she was glad Harlan hadn't suggested that they try and pick up where they left off. Her scars were still too fresh, her senses too raw, the lesson he had taught her weighed heavily on her soul. Later, she was glad she had only agreed to a friendship status since as fate would dictate, Harlan began using drugs yet again, starting an abusive pattern of admitting and releasing himself from the rehab center. He could not seem to get it together and during his down periods he would call his parents or Nachelle for money for drugs. They would refuse and he would retaliate by cutting off contact, sending them all into a state of worry. Such was the emotional roller coaster they had been on for the past three years. They never knew if Harlan was good or if he was horrid. It had not been easy, but Nachelle eventually learned to turn a deaf ear to Harlan's pleadings when he called, and although she could not turn her heart to stone, she had it sealed pretty tightly in a steel vault where Harlan could not play with it. Adele and Ralph had a harder time refusing their son his wishes, especially since they had been catering to his demands his entire life. It had been eight months since she had last spoken with Harlan, and their last conversation had not been pleasant.

The chiming of her grandfather clock brought Nachelle back to the present. She shook her head. *I can't believe after all I've gone through with Harlan that I would allow myself to be attracted to Steven.*

Deep in thought, Nachelle padded into the kitchen and poured herself a Kahlua and milk. She had tried so hard to deny her attraction to Steven only to realize she had been transparent even to a man she hadn't known very long. Had she in some way led him on to his proposition? Had she unknowingly given him a sign that she was willing to have more

than a professional association with him? Thinking back over
the last few weeks, she reviewed every scene when the two
of them had been alone. *Perhaps he mistook that almost-kiss
at the party and my letting him hold me at his hotel suite as
encouragement to pursue a personal relationship.* Nachelle
turned to the living room and curled up on the sofa using a
pillow as a lap tray. Following a deep sigh, she admitted, *Okay,
so the truth is out. I'm attracted to Steven and don't want to
be, so what do I do now? Regardless of my part, if any, in this
mess, I still have to hold true to my commitments to help the
employees make it through this merger and just as important:
to avoid another office romance!* Sipping slowly, she felt the
chocolate liquid spread throughout her body, but didn't expect
the mild drink to erase the haunting thoughts she would en-
tertain tonight.

"There's no sense in pretending," she whispered. She had
wanted to accept his offer even as boldly as he had presented
it. *That's what scares the hell out of me,* she thought. She
wasn't sure how or when Steven had claimed her thoughts,
mind, and body, but he surely had them.

She now knew her earlier shock and anger was not an aver-
sion to the man or his proposition, but rather, to the manner
in which he had proposed. *It was so clinical, so businesslike,*
she mused. *Almost as if he were reading from a script. How
could he treat such a special, wonderful act between two people in a businesslike way? Is DuCloux Enterprises so integrated into his soul that he can't separate himself from the
company?*

Nachelle returned to the bedroom and slowly undressed.
The lateness of the hour, the mellow drink, and an invisible
Steven played with her mind. She imagined, not her hands on
her supple dark skin, but rather the larger, stronger hands of
Steven DuCloux. Mental images of them played like a movie
in her head and she could almost feel his hot breath on her
lips, breasts, legs. From head to toe, her body throbbed in
unanswered passion.

Stop it, Nachelle. she scolded herself. *I will not succumb to the power of the man. I will not let him make me forget the painful lesson I learned from the past.*

Nachelle walked purposefully to the shower and turned on the cold water. Before she could change her mind, she stepped under the tingling spray and gritted her teeth. After five minutes in the water, she relented, and eased on the hot stream. Later, she slipped a satin gown over her head and slid between the flannel sheets.

Try as she may, she could not stop her thoughts from returning to Steven and the follow-up conversation that was destined to happen.

I won't do it, she thought with a sigh. *I've just got to be strong and tell him I'm not interested. I'll stay with the company through the merger and as soon as it's firmly in place, I'll leave the company, even if he offers me a permanent position. I have to do what's right for Nachelle.*

She turned off the bedside light with her renewed commitment cemented in place. Still, the shock of knowing that she wanted to share a night of love with Steven left her trembling, so that when she finally drifted off, she dreamed a patchwork of sweet yet languished dreams of the two of them coupled in lovemaking. Steven affected her even in her dreams.

Nachelle slowly turned her head and cracked open one eye to look at the clock—8:00 A.M. She was late for work!

Springing out of bed, she raced for the shower. *I'll bet the Shark is already up and making a breakfast of some company or employee,* she thought ungraciously.

Loading her toothbrush with paste, she studied her reflection in the bathroom mirror and noticed with disdain the slight puffiness under her eyes and the pinched lines around her mouth. *Not good,* she thought, *considering Steven will probably sport his same unruffled good looks.*

For the first time in her career, Nachelle toyed with the idea of playing hooky from work, but squashed the notion.

I've faced worse days and survived. Besides, I'm ready for the Shark. I've got my decision and my prepared response. After his morning meeting with Nathaniel, I'll just march in there and tell him no.

Nachelle arrived at the office at 9:30—two and one half hours later than her usual start time. The carefully applied makeup hid some of the stress she'd encountered through the evening and night, but a closer inspection would tell the truth. She planned not to let anyone get that close.

"Good morning, Nachelle. Your mail is on your desk and Steven wants to see you as soon as you get in." Millie greeted her with her customary smile.

Nachelle stopped dead, halfway to her office door. "I thought he was with Nathaniel all morning?"

"Dorrie said he wanted to meet with you first."

"Oh." Nachelle entered her office and closed the door. Yet again, the Shark had caught her off guard. She had been counting on having the morning to rehearse her words. Apparently, Steven wanted to tackle this issue immediately. She should have known.

She walked on rubbery legs to her desk and absently hung up her coat, emptied her briefcase, and sorted through the mail. When she could delay no longer she glanced at her image in the compact mirror, picked up her portfolio, and walked on reluctant feet to her boss's office. The determination and bravado she felt earlier this morning diminished with each step.

Nachelle rounded the corner and saw Steven bent over Dorrie's left shoulder at the secretary's desk. He was scribbling on a thick document, giving Dorrie his additional commands. Nachelle would never know what it was that caused him to look up at the precise moment she appeared, but he did.

Steven straightened to his full six-feet-plus height and scrutinized her from top to bottom as she took her final steps to his secretary's work area.

"You're looking a little tired this morning. Are you okay?" Steven commented in his unmistakable Southern drawl.

Nachelle bristled a bit at his perception, but didn't allow her composure to slip. "Fine, thank you. Good morning, Dorrie."

Dorrie nodded in return.

"Go on in. I'll be with you in a minute." Steven didn't give her a chance to refuse; he turned back to Dorrie and the document.

He can be so inhuman, she thought. *One would never know he made a pass at me.* Nachelle entered his domain and allowed herself a few luxurious moments of worry.

"Have a seat, Nachelle." Steven closed the door and his long muscular legs made quick work of the distance from the door to his desk.

Nachelle was not surprised to see he looked totally at ease and unaffected by last night's incident. His attire, consisting of a black and white glen plaid suit with his usual heavily starched white shirt and abstract tie, added to his calm appearance. Nachelle felt a glancing stab of regret about her decision. But, her mind was made up and her heart was sealed up.

Nachelle complied, sitting and clenching her hands together. "I wanted to speak with Dorrie this morning so that we could finalize some of the retirement party details."

"Yeah, I know you and Dorrie had a meeting planned. This is more important." Steven leaned back and slightly to the side in his leather chair. He looked her square in the face and stated, "I apologize for my behavior last night. I was *way* out of line. It won't happen again."

It took Nachelle several moments to digest his remarks. She had been geared for the worst, not something this straightforward or simple.

"That's it?" she croaked, spreading her hands in disbelief.

"Yes. Unless you have something to say." Steven never broke visual contact. His eyes were hard and automated in their tracking of her slightest movement.

"No. I just . . ." She stopped herself from asking why.

Steven arched a thick black brow and said, "If you were expecting something more dramatic, I'm sorry to disappoint you."

Disappointment was indeed what she was feeling and it tied back to the unwise attraction she had for him. *But, that's silly. I should be glad he's apologizing and willing to put this unfortunate incident behind us.* Feeling very edgy and transparent, Nachelle responded diplomatically. "Apology accepted." She surprised herself by managing a slight smile.

Steven folded one large hand around his coffee cup. He regarded her with half-closed eyes. Nachelle thought it must be his favorite sizing-up-the-prey position. She had already seen him focus on employees using that same expression on more occasions than she could count. "The truth of the matter is, I'm more interested in keeping you on staff. You're too valuable an employee to lose because of such nonsense."

Nachelle was speechless. She felt split in two. One self—her professional, already heart-broken half—clapped in glee at his decision; the other—a passionate woman who wanted to be recognized as such—was disappointed that he saw her greater importance as an employee and not a desirous woman. She knew she was thinking like a crazy woman. She'd come to work today prepared to give him a piece of her mind and reinforce her position—*no office affairs.* Her heart and reputation couldn't survive another blow. Now, here she sat, in the face of Steven's rescinded proposal, stunned and disappointed by his words.

She regrouped her splintered thoughts and concentrated on the positive. *With his decision, at least I'll be able to totally concentrate on the merger without having to watch my every word or action. And, I can keep both my commitments.*

"Nachelle?" Steven queried softly.

"Yes?" Blushing, Nachelle realized he'd been studying her as she assimilated her thoughts. "I'm sorry." She hadn't heard what he was talking about.

"I said . . . I'm sorry to have to ask you to reschedule your meeting with Dorrie, but we need you at this morning's meeting. Be sure and bring the fourth quarter financials and first quarter projected reports. Nathaniel will join us in the executive conference room in half an hour."

"Okay. Anything else?" Nachelle stood, anxious to gain a little freedom if only for a few minutes.

"Just one other thing. We still haven't received the papers from Harlan. Call him and do whatever it takes to get those papers here this week."

Nachelle's heart dipped and began a frantic double time beat, matching the double blow she'd received in less than thirty minutes. Even though she had Harlan's telephone number and address in Phoenix, she hadn't had occasion to use them in months. With Ralph and Adele off vacationing, she couldn't be cowardly and defer to Ralph. She had no choice but to make the call.

Nachelle bravely nodded and turned to walk out. She was almost out the door when Steven's voice arrested her progress. "Nachelle?"

She turned and saw that he stood, his face an unreadable mask. Her heart began an erratic pace that threatened to send her into cardiac arrest.

"Are you sure you don't have anything else to say?"

She lifted her shoulder in a dismissive gesture. "I'm positive."

Steven nodded slightly and Nachelle closed the solid walnut door behind her.

She scarcely breathed until she reached the safety of her office.

In the president's office, Steven cursed his luck. *Damn! Of all the women I could have fallen for, I had to pick one who's as mysterious as they come.* Steven slammed a folder shut.

He didn't know if he loved her, but one thing he was sure about: she moved him like no other woman he had ever known.

He chose to believe she felt the chemistry between them, but for some reason decided to hide behind a carefully erected shield. He wondered how much her past with Harlan Hayes had to do with that. Although anyone in his legal department could call Harlan and ask for the papers, he had specifically asked Nachelle just to see what her reaction would be. She'd maintained a perfect poker face, reflecting not a clue to her past with him.

One thing for sure, he thought, *if I don't find a wife soon, my mother will start a nationwide search on my behalf. That kind of pressure and distraction I don't need.*

At thirty-four and quickly approaching his next birthday, Steven thought daily about his family's edicts. He was far behind his brothers in both the marrying and having children game. There had never been a specific age with which to fill the family's commandments, but still, as the leader of the family company, he was held in stricter compliance. He was doing a great job at keeping the company profitable and family-owned and controlled; however, his personal side was failing miserably.

An instinct as primitive as a caveman's pointed to Nachelle as the woman he had been searching for to help him achieve his family's goals. She was smart, loyal, and generous, not to mention beautiful, and sexy.

The big hurdle was finishing the checklist when Nachelle was so private in her own personal dealings. She had erected a professional barrier that was difficult to penetrate and which offered no avenue to her personal nature. He couldn't read her thoughts, her behaviors were well-guarded, and on only a few rare moments had he witnessed her emotions take control.

He'd been bluffing last night when he told her he knew she was sexually attracted to him. But, her response to his advance had proved only that he'd succeeded in shocking her. Bringing him no closer to knowing if he was on or off the mark concerning their physical aptitude. His bluff had also pointed out the very obvious fact that he had used the wrong approach to determine sexual compatibility. Although he still had every intention of pursuing action in that category, he had the good sense to know damage control was now necessary. His rescinded offer had been his damage recovery act and it appeared Nachelle had bought it. In the meantime, Dorrie was working on a more subtle strategy to determine their sexual compatibility.

Steven punched Dorrie's extension, "Have you reached Heather Chadwick yet?"

Nine

Nachelle made it to her desk, reached inside her purse, and pulled out her old leather address book. She easily found Harlan's number and hesitantly picked up the receiver. Taking a deep breath, she rehearsed her words and then dialed.

The phone rang four times before an answering machine picked up. Nachelle wasn't prepared for it; she had only rehearsed lines for a human conversation.

At the beep, she improvised. "Hello, Harlan. This is Nachelle. I . . . Can you give me a call when you get this message? My telephone numbers are the same. Thanks."

Nachelle laid her head on folded arms and expelled a deep breath. Her stomach, however, was still in knots, thinking about Harlan and his reaction once he received her message. Well, no time to worry about it now. It's off to fight with Steven and Nathaniel. Nachelle grabbed files, reports, and other necessary materials and headed for the executive conference room.

Hundreds of miles away, Harlan watched the light flicker off and on on his answering machine. Wrapped in only a towel, he'd raced from the bedroom only to hear the tail end of Nachelle's message. *She sounds great,* he thought wistfully. Desires he thought had long since died stirred in the pit of his belly; her voice still had that husky undertone that brought to mind pleasurable times. He toyed with the idea of calling Nachelle back immediately, even had his hand on the phone, but an idea struck him.

Within the hour he'd arranged for time away from his job, a flight to Fort Worth, had packed, and was on his way out his apartment door. The smile on his caramel-colored face rivaled the sun's rays as he stepped lightly over the threshold into what he hoped would be the beginning of a brighter future.

It was seven o'clock in the evening and Nachelle was wiped out. The meeting with Steven and Nathaniel had ended up taking all of her morning and part of the afternoon, leaving Millie to juggle and reschedule her other appointments. Although the meeting had been a battlefield, she felt good about their decisions and about Steven's apparent willingness to be open-minded and give her free rein over the merger. For the most part, Steven had been fairly quiet during the meeting, only interjecting a point or comment on non-negotiable matters. As she had expected, Nathaniel had been the bear. He'd tried to run her over in speech, continually bucked her ideas, and had generally acted like a world-class sore loser. Being in a similar position years ago, she'd had no difficulty in controlling the flow of the meeting or Nathaniel. It was clear to her that Nathaniel was still interested in upending her temporary position of heading the merger even though Steven had made his position clear.

After returning to her office, she went about the task of "catching-up" and it wasn't until her stomach reminded her she hadn't eaten since the sandwich lunch Dorrie had arranged for them that she looked up and noticed the time.

"Seven o'clock." She looked at the stack of papers needing

her attention and shook her head. "They'll just have to wait until tomorrow." She yawned, a clue to the long, exhausting day she'd had and the equally long, restless night she knew was waiting for her. "I'll just check and see if Harlan called, then I'm out of here." She flipped through the pile of messages and, not seeing one from him, laid all of them neatly by her other piles of work. She folded her arms under her breasts and bit the insides of her lower lip. "What in the world could he possibly be thinking of? Surely he knows he's jeopardizing his father's future."

Nachelle tried to think about the situation from Harlan's side of the fence, but she was too tired, mentally and physically, to complete the exercise. Her coat beckoned from its resting place, and delaying not a moment longer, she gathered it up with her purse, stuffed some priority papers in her briefcase, and headed for the elevators. The quietness surrounding her at this late hour was a great contrast from the beehive activity during normal office hours. And, although she didn't see another person as she made her way to the first floor lobby, she knew some of the programmers and design engineers were probably still at work creating and designing future award-winning software programs. The elevator doors parted and she walked to the front door, her heels clicking loudly in the tomblike silence.

"Good evening, Ms. Oliver." The night security guard making his rounds startled her. "If you give me five minutes to finish my rounds, I'll walk you to your car."

"Oh, thanks Henry. There's no need. I'm just across the street." Nachelle's tiredness outweighed her common sense. All she wanted was to get home and soak in a tub of hot, scented water. Waiting for Henry would delay that pleasure. Exiting before the tenured guard made a federal case out of her decision, Nachelle snagged her keys from her bag and turned up the collar of her wool coat. The fierce wind sweeping around the corner of the Hayes Group building was unmerciful, and the temperature had already started its descent toward the thirties mark.

While her body carried out the mechanical motions of getting to her car, her thoughts returned to the dramatic day she'd had. The meeting with Nathaniel and Steven, Steven's willingness to let her drive the meeting, his offer last night of lovemaking and the subsequent withdrawal of that offer, his chameleon personality and her doomed attraction to him, all of these images blended together making her steps heavy. She was so engrossed in her review of the eventful day that the echoing footsteps following her didn't register until on some deep subconscious level a message of alert pierced her consciousness. She turned her head to see a man of medium build following her. Judging by his tall frame, it was not the building's security guard. Her heartbeat faltered, then started thudding faster as she increased the speed of her steps. *Why didn't I wait for Henry?* she thought. Fear thundered through her veins. *I promise if I get out of this situation alive, I'll never do anything this stupid ever again.* Forcing herself to think rationally, she remembered the small can of Mace she had attached to her keys. She quickly measured the remaining distance to her car and risked a look back to see if he had narrowed the gap between them. He had. Still, she was not close enough to the car to allow sufficient time to unlock the door, get in and drive off. Deciding the best defense was a good offense, she turned with the can held out and a finger on the button. "Hold it right there."

"No, Nachelle, don't! It's me, Harlan."

Several things dropped at once: Nachelle's mouth, the can of Mace, and her heartbeat.

"Harlan!" Nachelle screeched. Harlan was there in front of her, in the flesh! She was flabbergasted.

Harlan laughed and moved into the light. "Nachelle!" His rich, full laughter carried on the blustery wind. "Have you registered those moves with the police department? Boy, I thought I was a goner."

Nachelle bobbed her head first up and down then from side to side, letting his presence sink in. "I can't believe you're here." Nachelle said the first thing that popped into her head.

"I got your message. So, here I am." Harlan completed the few steps which brought him to her. Stooping, he picked up the keys and Mace.

"I hope my message didn't lead you to believe you had to . . ." Nachelle's eyes were large with inquiry.

"I know I could have handled this by mail, but that's so impersonal, and if I'm understanding everything correctly, this is a big damn deal." Harlan looked deep into her brown eyes. "Besides, when I ran away I left a lot of unfinished business. I thought this would be a good time to come back and resolve some of those issues." Harlan smiled. "Your phone call was the impetus I needed."

Nachelle was still slightly dazed. In the past few years, she'd tried to anticipate what she would do if or when Harlan ever returned to Fort Worth. The moment was here and she wasn't reacting in any of the ways she'd visualized. The surprise was too great.

Harlan exaggerated a shiver in the leather bomber jacket he wore. "Listen, it's pretty cold out. Can we go somewhere and talk?"

It was on Nachelle's mind to tell him she was tired and just wanted to go home when she took inventory and realized the fright and surprise he'd given her had knocked fatigue out of first place. "Well, how about a bite to eat? I'm starved."

"Sounds great." Her suggestion lit Harlan's handsome features. "Do you mind driving though? Believe it or not, I got lost on the way to mom and dad's. Fort Worth sure has changed."

"No problem. I'm right here." Nachelle turned and walked the remaining few steps to her car. Throwing her things in the back seat, she slid under the wheel and gave her passenger a sidelong glance. *He looks great,* she thought. *He doesn't look as if he's strung out or, for that matter, that he suffered any kind of hard day.* And, indeed he was every bit as handsome as the day she'd first met him. His olive-colored eyes still had that permanent twinkle of merriment, his mustache was neatly trimmed, his full, sensual lips were curved in a seemingly perpetual smile. His six foot, two-inch frame, which appeared hard and muscular under the jeans and sweater, forced him to slide the front seat back.

During their time at school, he'd been the dream man of every woman—old and young—around. His stunning good looks coupled with his charming personality, jovial sense of humor, and wealthy background made him ideal husband material. Nachelle had been flattered when he'd pursued her.

"Actually, I was thinking on the plane about Drake's. If it's still in business, let's go there. Phoenix has a couple of places that claim to be soul food restaurants, but if they were in the south, they'd be run out of town."

Nachelle chuckled. Now that the surprise of his return had worn off, she found herself full of questions. Concentrating on the dwindling traffic jam, she asked, "So, you got here, when . . . this afternoon?"

"Yeah, the plane landed, oh, around 3:00. I was anxious to see mom and dad so I went straight there, only I was the one surprised. Juanita met me at the door with a look you couldn't have dynamited off her face. Boy, it felt like old times with Juanita in the housekeeper uniform opening the door for me. I was reminded of my school days. She told me my parents went with your parents to the deer lease."

"Yeah, I . . . um . . . talked to them a few days ago. They're just relaxing, catching up on some reading, doing a little hunting, playing a lot of cards."

"Good. I'm glad. They deserve some peace and quiet." Harlan was reflective in his speech.

Nachelle carefully listened to his words and agreed. Adele and Ralph were indeed deserving of living the rest of their lives as stress free as possible. Even though she hated to admit it, Ralph *needed* to relinquish the responsibilities of the Hayes

Group. His doctors had told him years ago to reduce his stress level or be prepared for a third stroke. Nachelle's only regrets were that she didn't have the money to take over the company herself and that Harlan hadn't been responsible or strong enough to handle the pressures of running a large company.

Harlan's voice brought her back to the present. "Anyway, Juanita helped me get settled in my old room. I started to call and tell them I was here, but changed my mind. I don't want them to rush back on my account. I'll still be here when they get back this weekend."

Harlan turned in his seat so he could have a better view of her. "You haven't changed. You're as gorgeous as ever."

"Thank you." Nachelle replied, somewhat self-consciously. Sparing him a quick confirming glance, she spoke truthfully, "You look good, too. Phoenix seems to be treating you well."

"Thanks for being nice enough to ignore the extra twenty pounds I'm carrying." That famous Harlan smile showed. "The downfall to kicking a drug habit is gaining weight. I've been eating any and everything I can get my hands on. Fortunately, I've lost most of what I gained, but these last few pounds aren't budging." Harlan patted his mid-section and laughed, "And, something tells me my time in Fort Worth won't help the situation. After I unpacked, Juanita had a plate ready for me, and now Drake's."

"Wanna go someplace else? I don't want it to be said I contributed to your battle of the bulge." Nachelle smiled, tentatively testing old waters.

"No. Take me to Drake's or I'll have to hijack your car and find my way there the best way I can." They laughed at Harlan's determination to get his point across. "I can almost taste those barbecue spare ribs."

In a hop, skip, and a jump, they were at Drake's Cafeteria. As usual, there was a crowd. They made quick decisions at the buffet line, both deciding on spare ribs swimming in barbecue sauce, greens, candied yams, hot water cornbread, and for dessert, sweet potato pie. With trays in hand, they jostled around the hungry group finally locating and securing a fairly private table where they could talk and enjoy their food.

Considering they hadn't exchanged a word in months and that their last conversation had ended on a sour note, they chatted non-stop during dinner like old college chums recently reunited. Nachelle filled in Harlan's knowledge of people, places and things. Conversely, Harlan kept Nachelle laughing about his experiences living in Phoenix.

When the last piece of pie disappeared into Harlan's mouth, they pushed their empty dishes aside and enjoyed a cup of strong black coffee.

"That was good." Harlan edged his chair away from the table and patted his stomach. "Maybe I should have let you take us somewhere else . . . like Soup and Salad or some such place."

"Too late now." Nachelle kidded, wanting desperately to take off her pantyhose which now felt restricting. Her initial jitters at being in Harlan's company were still waiting in the wings, yet she had enjoyed their dinner together. But then, Harlan had always been one of those people who made others feel instantly at ease. It was one of the skills in his charm bag which had drawn her to him.

"Time's been good to you, Nachelle. I meant it earlier when I said you look great."

Nachelle smiled. "Thank you, Harlan." Memories of them during the happy times floated to the surface of her mind. They were as vivid as a clown's makeup, and just as jolly. Her smile grew, but she felt a little uncomfortable by Harlan's praise. Changing the subject she said, "Ralph and Adele will be so thrilled to see you."

"I have to admit that I'm anxious to see them, too." A comfortable moment of silence lingered before Harlan continued, "What about you, Nachelle? Are you happy to see me?" On a few rare occasions in the past, Harlan had exchanged his playful demeanor for a serious one and she recognized now as such a time. His brows drew together, his olive eyes turned more brown in color, and he leaned forward, elbows on the table, surveying her flushed face.

"I have to honestly admit, Nachelle, the papers aren't the only reason for my coming here in person," Harlan finished.

Nachelle knew there would be no getting around the subject of their history tonight. She looked down into her empty coffee cup, staring at the sparse coffee grounds as if they held the answer to her future. "Harlan, I don't want to jump to conclusions. What specifically are you saying?"

Harlan leaned forward and cupped his coffee mug. "Two years ago, I left town without resolving our relationship. I mean, I was so high that night I can't remember half of what went on. I know we ended our engagement and I . . ." Harlan's face grew more cloudy, more troubled, ". . . caused Dad's stroke, but I guess we never really got the chance to talk things through. You know, how we got from being happy and in love one day to being miserable and out of love the next."

Nachelle stared into his ever-changing eyes and sighed. Quietly, she said, "Harlan, what's done is done." In a friendly, reassuring gesture, she covered his hand with one of her own. "Everything worked out fine."

"Did it, Nachelle? I'm not feeling that it did. I know I damaged a lot of relationships." Harlan removed his hands from hers and brushed them over his face. "Luckily, the family counseling and visits with mom and dad really helped put that relationship back on the right track. But when I think about our last evening together, I can just kick myself. One of the reasons why I didn't move back to Fort Worth after my release was because I felt awful about accusing you of trying to steal my parents' love and hitting you. My actions were atrocious and an apology over the phone wasn't good enough. Can you ever forgive me?" Harlan held his breath, hope made his eyes twinkle brightly. And even if Nachelle didn't forgive him, he couldn't, no wouldn't blame her. At least he'd leave Fort Worth knowing he'd done the right thing.

Nachelle lowered her head and brushed invisible crumbs

to the side, stalling for time. It would be easy for both of them if she told him what he wanted to hear, but it wouldn't be the truth. Forgiving someone, who supposedly loved you, for punching a hole in your dreams and heart was an act she could not easily perform. Not that she didn't want to forgive and forget, but the scars went levels deep. Her horrible experiences with Harlan still, years later, colored her decisions, steered her life. How could she forgive him? "Harlan, I wish I could." At his crestfallen expression, she hurried on, "I mean . . . well . . ." Taking a deep sigh, she continued. "I'm glad you're taking this first step to resolving the past, but as long as you continue this up and down battle with drugs, I don't know that I can. The last time we talked you were extremely rude to me. You called me names and told me all kinds of stories so you could cajole money out of me. How am I supposed to forget and forgive when you continue to display the same tendencies?"

"See, that's where you're wrong, Nachelle. After that last fight we had on the phone, I made the decision to quit using drugs." Harlan held up a hand and smiled crookedly. "Yeah, I know you've heard this before, but I *am* through with that stuff. After you hung up on me, I didn't run back to the rehab center like I usually do. I kicked the habit . . . cold turkey . . . with no one to rely on except me. No counselors, no buddy system, nothing, and I've been clean ever since." He grabbed her hands, his excitement transforming his face to a more youthful looking Harlan. "Now, that I know I can do something on my own without my father's money or name, I'm ready to set things right." Lifting her hands to his lips, he brushed a kiss across her knuckles.

Despite the trickle of doubt that ran through her mind, she smiled. Before she could congratulate Harlan on his achievement, she was interrupted by a familiar voice.

"Hello, Nachelle."

Nachelle's eyes zoomed from Harlan's greenish-brown eyes to the onyx orbs belonging to her boss—not that she needed to visually confirm who spoke her name. Even blindfolded, she'd be able to recognize his deep, Southern drawl anywhere, anytime. And, indeed, Steven stood at the edge of their table, looking regal and dangerously appealing. He'd swapped his tailored suit for Texas attire—jeans, a sweater, and cowboy boots. His intense, black eyes raked over hers and Harlan's joined hands.

Tremors of physical awareness passed through her slight body and she flushed when she realized Steven must have seen Harlan's display of affection. Awkwardly, she disengaged her hand from Harlan's and replied, "Steven, hi." Strangely, she felt like a child caught in the act of stealing cookies.

Steven stood silent and unmoving.

"I'd like to introduce you to Harlan Hayes. Harlan, this is Steven DuCloux."

While the men exchanged the proper phrases and handshakes, Nachelle tried to ignore the tenseness creeping through her body, settling in her shoulders. The switch from the uncensored casual air she was sharing with Harlan to the taut, be-on-your-Ps-and-Qs feeling with Steven's predatory arrival was subtle. As Harlan reclaimed his seat, Nachelle donned her protective, professional cloak.

Harlan smiled. Nachelle noticed it was not sincere. "Dad speaks highly of you."

Steven nodded and although a dimple showed in his cheek, a smile didn't quite curve his lips. "Ralph has spoken of you often." Turning his attention to Nachelle, he said, "You don't waste any time, do you?"

Although a number of different scenarios crossed her mind—some good, some bad—Nachelle didn't know what specifically Steven was referring to. Her confusion must have showed on her face, for Steven quickly added, including more background in his response for Harlan's sake, "This morning I asked Nachelle to close out all pending paperwork regarding the buy-out. And here it is . . ." Steven consulted the silver watch on his dark arm, "less than twelve hours later and you're here in person to conclude the deal." His face was an unreadable mask when he continued, "Another example of your value to DuCloux Enterprises, Nachelle. Thank you."

The carved, professional smile on her face dropped when his complimentary remark settled in her mind as a stroke to her efficiency as an employee, reminding her of the rescinded sexual offer. Nachelle directed her eyes to her coffee cup. No way would she allow Steven an opportunity to see her dashed hopes; he would never know she preferred to be viewed as a desirous woman. Cupping and interlacing her fingers around the standard restaurant-issued china, she glanced at him briefly and murmured shallowly, "Actually, Harlan is the one you should thank. I simply made the call. He did the rest."

Harlan laughed, a jovial pleasant sound. "Nachelle doesn't give herself enough credit. What red-blooded man could refuse her anything?"

Nachelle managed a weak smile. Scanning their table, she added, in deference to her proper upraising, "Would you care to join us?" Silently, she begged for his refusal. She was too tired to monitor her every word and action.

"Thank you. But, the mayor is waiting for me across the room. I noticed you two over here and decided it would be rude not to speak." Steven turned to Harlan and stated, "I look forward to seeing you again." They shook hands a final time. Steven turned and took a couple of steps from their rickety table. "Oh, Nachelle . . ." He pivoted, ". . . don't forget our seven o'clock meeting in the morning."

Nachelle nodded her head, and quick as one-two-three Steven was gone.

Harlan shifted his gaze from Steven and gave Nachelle a guarded look. "When Dad called and told me he'd sold the company to DuCloux, I almost choked to death." Harlan sat back in his chair and discreetly eyed his old opponent. "As a matter of fact, I still can't believe Dad did this knowingly. He knows how cutthroat DuCloux is. Were you involved in this mess? Why didn't you stop it?"

A melee of emotions bombarded Nachelle. Anger, frustration, indignation all vied for first place in expression, indignation won out. Her words spewed forth like an uncapped geyser. "For your information, I didn't know what your father was up to. He and Adele made the decision and only included the lawyers in the negotiations." Nachelle stopped long enough for the manager to fill their cups and then resumed her tirade. "I asked your father why, and all he told me was 'it was time for a change.' But, maybe, just maybe Harlan, if you had been here none of this would be happening." As soon as the words were out, Nachelle regretted them, not the content, only her harsh tone of voice. One look at Harlan's face confirmed she had cut him to the quick.

Quietly, Harlan replied, "You're right, Nachelle. I shouldn't have blamed you, only myself. I'm their only child and I let them, you and me, down. From this point on, all I can do is try to make it up to everyone."

Nachelle placed her elbow on the table and cradled her forehead in her hand. The headache she'd been having off and on since Ralph told her the news resurfaced. "I'm sorry, Harlan. I shouldn't have been so cruel. I guess the merger and the uncertainty of the future is starting to get to me."

"No need to apologize." Harlan actually surprised her by chuckling, "If people had talked like that to me before, we wouldn't be in this mess." He sobered and captured one of her hands. "I'm worried about you though. He seems like a pretty uptight fellow. Are you going to be okay working for him?"

"I don't really have a choice," Nachelle murmured. "I made a commitment to Ralph to stay on until the road was clear for the Hayes Group employees." Since her heated outburst, she had not risked a look in Steven's direction. However, she felt certain that with the distance between them and the deafening background noise, he was ignorant to their discussion. Ever since he'd made his presence known though, she'd felt compelled to look his way. Even now she could feel the pull of his black-magic eyes. With false cheer, Nachelle clasped her hands together in her lap and finished, "I have a feeling that everything's going to be okay."

"I certainly hope so. He sure doesn't look like he knows what the word fun means."

"The success of his family's company is very important to him." Nachelle felt compelled to defend Steven. It occurred to her that Steven and Harlan were like night and day. Where Steven was indeed a very serious young man, Harlan was fun-loving and impulsive; Steven rarely smiled, while death couldn't wipe the habitual smile from Harlan's face; Steven was handsome, Harlan was downright cover-model beautiful. Nachelle was busy thinking these thoughts, staring into space, and missed the speculative look that crossed Harlan's face.

"Still, it's a wonder he hasn't let any of dad's staff go yet." Harlan pursued the subject.

"He appears to be truly committed to ensuring the merger is good for both sides. If there are to be layoffs, they won't happen for a while." A sixth sense or the pull of Steven's eyes caused Nachelle to look in Steven's direction. Her dark brown eyes collided with his. The contact held, and an invisible line seemed to draw them close so that no one outside them existed—just the two of them. Had it not been for a busboy carrying a loaded tub of plates and glasses, only God knew how long they would have continued to share that binding contact. With his passing, the spell had been broken; Nachelle was able to shift her eyes to Harlan.

". . . clear you're not to miss your meeting, so, I guess we'd better call it a night. He looks like he'd eat you alive if you were late."

"It has been a long day." She was grateful Harlan suggested that they wrap up the evening. She didn't think she could sit there another minute torn between Steven's assessing looks, Harlan's inquisitive questions, and her body's growing needs. *Damn, Steven DuCloux.* Nachelle thought. *If he hadn't said anything about sleeping with him, I wouldn't be so confused.*

Harlan helped her into her coat and as she turned to thank him, she surprised herself by saying, "If you'd like to come by around noon tomorrow to drop off the papers, maybe we could have lunch afterwards." She didn't stop to consider that her words may have been in defiance of her feelings toward Steven.

"Sounds great." Harlan smiled, and Nachelle noticed several women in the restaurant speculatively eyeing him. Smiling secretly to herself, she recalled the old adage: everything that looks good ain't good for you. Turning up her coat collar, she signaled her good-bye to Steven. Harlan captured her hand in a light hold and led her out into the winter night.

Nachelle backed out of the tight parking space and into the meager traffic. The wind was still high and occasionally rocked her Allante despite the solidness of the car. On the short drive back to the office, Harlan found a quiet jazz station on the radio and seemed content to settle back and enjoy the ride and the music. Nachelle took the opportunity to mentally review her agenda for the next day. Not surprisingly, that exercise propelled her thoughts back to the Silver Shark. She knew she would dream tonight of Steven's scorching looks and the fit of his faded jeans.

The street where the Hayes Group's building stood was deserted and dark. Thankfully, the floodlights in front of the building spotlit the visitor parking spaces on the street, making it easy for Nachelle to locate Ralph's gray Mercedes sedan. She pulled up to it and engaged the parking brake. Her sincere smile reflected in the light. "Thanks for dinner. Will you be able to find your way home or shall I lead you?"

"I'll do fine. Besides, you have an early meeting tomorrow morning and I've already kept you long enough."

Nachelle groaned playfully. "Don't remind me, but I thoroughly enjoyed dinner."

Harlan leaned forward and planted a soft, undemanding kiss on her parted lips. "I'll see you tomorrow. Goodnight, baby." Harlan smiled devastatingly and stepped out of the car.

Soon they were both zooming out of downtown to their respective homes.

Steven was ready to throttle someone. "Is she here yet?" He demanded into the phone receiver. He'd been waiting for Nachelle for almost twenty minutes, his patience had long since vanished. *Does she not think I have other things to do today? I'll bet it was that date with Harlan last night. Even though they left early, there's no telling what time she got to bed.* A visual image of Nachelle in bed with Harlan fueled his anger. It was enough to make him want to pick up the crystal blotter on his desk and throw it as hard as he could. Thankfully, he was not a violent man . . . and the blotter was a gift from his mother.

On the other end of the phone and unmoved by her boss' demanding tone, Dorrie replied, "No, she isn't."

It was a rare event when Steven blew up, but even in those instances when he did, such as now, she was not fazed. That characteristic plus the fact that she was efficient, independent, and knew the meaning of confidentiality made her priceless in Steven's book. Calmly, Dorrie replaced the receiver and returned to the spreadsheet she was working on. Hearing a slight rustle, she turned in time to see Nachelle round the corner, looking composed and very professional in a hunter green and black suit.

"I'm late for a meeting with Steven." Nachelle simply stated.

"Yes, you are." Dorrie unemotionally replied. She picked up the phone. "She's here." After a moment of silence, she hung up and nodded for Nachelle to enter the office.

The slight time lapse had given Steven the chance to stamp out the visual picture his wanderings had created and focus on the tactic he would use to find out the status of her and Harlan's previous affair. Although he had a planned lunch with Heather today, he had decided against asking Nachelle's best friend private questions about a previous love affair. Anyway, he would bet his life that Heather was protective and loyal to Nachelle. Instead, he planned to pump Heather for local charity opportunities and use his time with Nachelle to gather the information he needed to complete the personal background criteria on the checklist.

Coolly composed, Steven used his hand to direct her to the conference table which dominated one corner of his office and which at the moment held a modest continental breakfast. Picking up his coffee cup, Steven followed Nachelle to the table and sat down opposite her. He tried not to think about the short skirt she wore or the way her hips swayed suggestively when she walked or the way she crossed her fine legs or the full breasts that tugged at the frog closures on her suit or . . .

He changed the direction of his thoughts before his arousal was complete. As it was, he hoped he wouldn't have to stand or walk anytime soon. Gradually, he tuned in to whatever she was talking about.

". . . whole block. The electric company was hard at work on the problem when I left home."

"I see." Steven replied, somewhat enlightened by her last few words. Jumping right into his hidden agenda, Steven asked, "Why didn't you tell me he was in town? Our legal department has been trying to contact him for the past month."

"I presume the 'he' you're talking about is Harlan, and, if it is, he arrived just yesterday." She poured a cup of coffee from the carafe.

"Our attorneys left messages, sent certified letters and telegrams with no response. You make one call and he *flies* to town the same day. You must have some hold on him."

With Cross pen poised for calculating, note-taking, and doodling, Nachelle stared at her boss. She hadn't been sleeping well since she found out about the company changing hands, her bones were dead tired, and she wasn't up to lengthy explanations or dredging up the past.

As prim as a schoolmarm and with more patience than she thought she possessed, she answered, "Harlan has other business here. He's killing two birds with one stone." She hoped the tone of her voice conveyed to him that she wasn't up to answering any more questions about Harlan's impromptu appearance.

"I'd like to notify Legal of his whereabouts in case they need him for anything else. How long is he planning to stay in town?"

"I'm not sure." Nachelle drew her brows together and frowned. "Harlan's not one to make plans, but when he comes to pick me up for lunch, I'll ask him."

"You're going to lunch with him?" Steven jumped on her last comment, momentarily forgetting to hide his personal interest in her.

Nachelle apparently didn't notice the over-interest in his voice or chose to ignore it because she answered without missing a beat. "He's coming at 11:30 to sign the papers and then we're having lunch. Would you like to join us?"

"I have plans." Steven answered, but then thought, *is she inviting me to lunch because it's a strictly platonic business lunch? Maybe there's nothing remaining of their relationship except business, otherwise why would she invite me?* "If Harlan has any questions or concerns about the agreements we're asking him to sign, call me." Steven reached into the breast pocket of his charcoal gray suit and produced a business card. "Here's the cel phone number, hotel number, and both office numbers. I've already told you getting Harlan's signature is extremely important to DuCloux Enterprises' future. I want this matter finalized today."

Courageously, Nachelle stated, "You've made your position very clear." She recalled Steven's transformation to the Silver Shark at his hotel suite and knew he meant every word he said. Even though she and Harlan had not discussed the papers last night, she was sure Steven had nothing to worry about.

"Good. You may also want to confirm with Harlan if he received his invitation to his father's retirement party. That's not too far off," Steven added as an afterthought.

"It's in my purse. I'm planning to give it to him at lunch," Nachelle remarked dryly.

"Fine." Steven fixed her with a serious look. "Now that Harlan's in town, I hope he's not going to be a distraction for you."

Offended, Nachelle couldn't stop herself from attacking him, "Are you saying I'm incapable of separating my personal life from work? Do you think I have a one-track mind?"

Spreading his hands in defense, Steven apologized. "I'm sorry that didn't come out right. All I meant to say is you're doing a remarkable job with the merger and I don't want to lose you."

For the first time in a long while, she actually saw a flicker of humanness in the depths of his dark eyes. It produced a soft euphoric feeling within her.

Slightly breathless, Nachelle said, "You don't have to worry about me. My priorities are straight. I want this to be a successful merger for both companies. I want DuCloux Enterprises to be a success." Until she said it out loud, Nachelle didn't realize just how badly she wanted the statement to become reality. Even though she probably wouldn't be around after the merger was complete, she had a feeling the Hayes Group employees would be okay. She felt comfortable knowing she would meet her commitment to secure a safe future for the employees. As for her own future, she turned her back to the disappointing feeling that she wouldn't see Steven again after the merger. She told herself it would be for the best since her life without him would be more sane and less stressful.

"I'm glad to hear that." Although his cover-up line of questioning benefited him some, it was far from the monumental steps he had hoped for. He was antsy about Harlan's arrival and what it could do to his personal agenda. Before he spilled the beans or overreacted, he decided to retreat and then advance later.

Transferring his thoughts, actions, and words to business matters, he launched into a series of items needing her attention. By the time their meeting was over, Nachelle was left with a scant hour before Harlan was due to arrive.

Timeliness had never been one of Harlan's strong suits and in line with his character, he was nowhere in the building at the appointed time. Nachelle had waited for him for thirty minutes when she decided to call him at his parents' house. With her hand on the receiver, the phone rang before she could dial out.

"Hey, beautiful. I realize I'm late, I was talking to mom. Why don't you just meet me at Georgia's since I'm running behind?" Georgia's was a Cajun Creole restaurant nestled in Stop Six, a residential section of Fort Worth comprised of mostly African-American families with a sprinkling of Hispanics.

"Sure. Are you leaving the house now?"

"As we speak."

"Okay. See you shortly." Nachelle smiled and shook her head. *Harlan's still Harlan,* she thought with amusement, *some things about him will never change.* She chuckled because she knew she would still end up waiting for him at the restaurant.

To her surprise, Harlan was standing outside of Georgia's, watching and waiting for her. He smiled when he saw her approach. Slinging an arm across her shoulders, he kissed her cheek lightly and shepherded her inside. "I bet you thought I was going to be late again, huh?" he asked playfully.

"You're right. I would have lost that bet." Nachelle's smile matched Harlan's.

"I'm telling you, Nachelle, I'm trying to turn over a new leaf." Harlan pulled out her chair and then took a seat. "It's not been easy changing thirty-some years of bad habits. It's a continual battle." Harlan flipped open the menu and perused the offerings. "I'm starving. What about you?"

"I think I had too much coffee this morning. It killed my appetite. I'll just get something light." Closing her menu, she pushed it aside and clasped her hands together on the table.

Still reading the menu, Harlan looked up briefly to ask, "How did your meeting with the Shark go this morning?"

Nachelle grimaced, "Okay. It started shaky, but it was productive." She chuckled, "I can't be mad at you for running late since I was late for my meeting with him this morning."

"And you're still alive to talk about it?" Harlan asked, half-teasing, half-serious.

"Actually he didn't have anything to say about my being late. He was more interested in the merger progress and your papers." Nachelle opened her hands, palms up, on the table. "So while I'm thinking about it, why don't you hand them over now so I won't forget them later."

The waiter interrupted them to take their drink and food order. Harlan ordered the crawfish etoufée with a side order of New Orleans' crab cakes. Nachelle settled for gumbo and french bread.

"Your boss is not going to be happy with me, given the emphasis he's placing on those papers."

"What do you mean?" A feeling of panic started a slow boil within Nachelle.

"On the plane, I had the feeling I was forgetting something, but couldn't remember what . . ."

Nachelle started to groan before Harlan finished.

"That's when I remembered that I forgot to pack the papers."

Nachelle cradled her forehead in her hands and rocked her head slowly back and forth. "Oh, Harlan. Steven's going to hit the roof. He just mentioned not one . . . two . . ." Nachelle consulted her watch, ". . . three hours ago that getting those papers signed and submitted to Legal was the most important thing I had to do today."

"I'm sorry, Nachelle. I don't want to get you in trouble. Perhaps we can come up with a plan that'll satisfy everybody."

"Well, we'll have to do something. That's for sure!"

"I can call my landlord and have him FedEx the papers to me. I could have them to you tomorrow and you could deliver them to Legal early next week. That way it'll only be a few days late."

"Yeah we could do that or I could have Legal draw up another set."

"Which way is quicker?"

"I don't know." Nachelle blew out a deep breath and then looked at Harlan. "We don't even know if your landlord is willing to help and I don't know how long it would take Legal."

"Tell you what . . ." Harlan leaned forward with that cure-all sparkle in his olive eyes. "I'll pursue this from my end and you from yours and we'll keep the heat under them until it's a done deal. If we happen to get two sets of paperwork, so be it. At least we'll be doubly covered." Leaning back, he slapped the table. "Think that'll work?"

"Yeah." Nachelle responded slowly. As the seconds ticked off, the momentum of her head bobbing up and down increased. "Yeah. That's good. And, as you said, either way, papers will be signed." As an afterthought, Nachelle added, "Of course, I'll still have to tell Steven."

"Why, Nachelle?"

"Because he knows I'm meeting you for lunch today to pick up the papers. He'll probably be waiting for me at the door when I get back."

"Why don't you let me explain? It's my fault."

Nachelle was surprised. The old Harlan would have never admitted fault. He really was maturing. "Harlan, I'm proud of you." She couldn't stop herself from beaming. "Thank you for the offer but it's okay. I'll be fine." Nachelle laughed a good humored laugh. "As long as Steven gets all the legalities taken care of soon, he won't eat me alive." Nachelle sobered.

"He has a lot on his mind. He's moving forward with the merger, while running the original DuCloux Enterprises, and traveling between not only Fort Worth and Atlanta, but also meeting some of the Hayes Group's biggest clients around the region with Mike Adams in tow. He's making all these plans, doing all this work, when really, until we have your signature, nothing's final."

The waiter returned, delivering their scrumptious smelling meal. After ensuring everything was fine, he left them to pursue their conversation.

Harlan ventured a bite, smiled appreciatively, and asked, "So, if I'm understanding you, he's really strapped until I sign? Dad still owns the company?"

"Yes, and no. You and Ralph are majority holders in the business. Ralph's share has already been purchased by Steven, but there's a special clause in the documents that indicates Ralph will guarantee your cooperation. At this time, without those papers in house, legally, you and Steven have the same right to manage the Hayes Group." Nachelle sipped a spoonful of soup and added, "Once we complete the signature process and get it filed through Legal, Steven will 'own' everything." Nachelle put down her spoon and looked Harlan directly in the eyes. "Ralph did accept an extremely large sum of money from Steven. If everything's not finalized soon, it could be bad for Ralph. Steven's dead set on acquiring the Hayes Group and building his family's company into an empire."

"How does Dad really feel about this transaction? I mean . . . I know what he told me, but when we talked I didn't have the benefit of a face-to-face exchange."

"When Ralph called me into his office to tell me it was a done deal, I could tell he was torn in half." Nachelle spoke carefully, playing with her words so Harlan wouldn't feel blame. "He told me if he'd been just ten years younger, he wouldn't have called Steven. But, Adele had been riding him to quit and even his doctors were warning him regularly about his heart. So, one day he called Steven and asked him if he was still interested in acquiring the Hayes Group. The company means a lot to Ralph, but his health—and living—mean more."

"I see." Harlan spoke slowly, digesting all Nachelle told him. "Poor Dad. I know that must have been hard for him. He loves the Hayes Group company. When I was a small boy I sometimes thought he loved it more than me and Mom."

"Oh, don't be silly. He loves you guys more than anything." Nachelle shrugged her shoulders and in a matter-of-fact voice stated, "That's why he's giving it up. Now, he can spend more time with you and Adele."

"Of course you're right, but what I don't understand is why Steven? He was our fiercest competitor and I don't have to remind you about his questionable business practices."

"According to Ralph, he didn't want to sell his 'baby' to just anybody. He considered other individuals and companies. But, to tell you the truth, I think he wanted assurances that the company would continue to grow even if it was under a different name. And Steven's the guy for that. So, even as the combined companies expand and capture more market share, a little bit of the Hayes Group will always be around. Besides, a major point was the fact that Steven agreed to keep the Fort Worth office operational because of its central geographic location. That's a fact that's not common knowledge, but it was a big plus for DuCloux."

"I don't know about Steven though. Does the guy have any values? Can he be trusted?" A worried look marred Harlan's smooth features.

"All I can say is in the month I've been working with him, he has shown me none of the unscrupulous practices he's known for. Actually, just the opposite. He's let me lead the merger the way I see fit. He's agreed to fund your father's retirement party. He holds open forums with the employees every week. Now, don't get me wrong, he can be unyielding, presumptuous, and bull-headed, but he's also been fair and understanding."

"Sounds like you're becoming a Steven DuCloux fan club member."

"Hardly. I'm just there temporarily trying to do the right thing for our employees." *Liar,* an inner voice mocked her. *You dream about the man. You're angry with him and yourself because he appreciates your business acumen more than he values your femininity.*

Harlan finished the last of his lunch and thought about what Nachelle had told him. *I've got a lot to think about,* he thought as he pushed his plate aside. Signaling for the waiter, he asked, "Enough about business. Tell me about your love life? Are you dating anyone special?"

Nachelle almost choked on the last of her meal. *No, not dating, just lusting.* Gathering her scattered thoughts, she picked her words carefully. How did one tell one's ex-fiancé that he hurt her so badly that anything resembling love was a thing to be avoided like the plague? "I've been so busy with work, I've only had time to date sporadically."

"I thought I'd come back to find you married or at the least engaged. Even though I didn't appreciate you, there are plenty of other men looking for a good woman."

Nachelle stuck to the truth as she lived it. "You know how demanding this business is. The competition will eat you for lunch if you snooze. It doesn't leave a lot of time for a personal life."

"That's no reason to bury yourself. You're too young not to have fun, to enjoy life."

"I do manage to have fun. I don't sit at home on Saturday nights if that's any indication. And if I am at home on a Saturday, it's because mom and dad are in town for a visit or Vincent has flown down for a weekend."

"How is your family? Is everyone doing okay?" Harlan pulled his wallet out of his pants and placed the appropriate number of bills on the table.

"Yes, they're all doing okay. Vincent is still a confirmed bachelor. He says there are too many good-looking women in

D. C. to be tied down to just one. I don't think he's ever gotten over Julia's death. He denies it, yet whenever he goes home, he always puts flowers on her grave."

Vincent Oliver, Nachelle's senior by four years, had loved and lost early in life. In high school, he met and fell in love with Julia Montgomery. After graduation they got engaged and, although Julia had elected not to attend college, Vincent compromised by staying in their hometown and enrolling at the University of Texas at Austin. In his freshman year, he immediately joined a fraternity and at one of their frat parties, his brothers set him up with an exotic beauty. Julia had walked in on him in his dorm room with the other woman and upset, had run outside and into the street without looking. A semi-trailer, unable to stop quickly enough, met her halfway across the street. Only ten yards behind her, Vincent had watched as the love of his life died. He made it through college and went on to serve in the armed services and was now stationed at the Pentagon, but Nachelle suspected his heart hadn't made his career's forward journey.

"Mom and Dad bought a Winnebago several months ago and they've already gone to Yellowstone National Park and the Grand Canyon. They're thinking about selling their home in Austin since they're hardly ever there and now have the house on wheels." Nachelle felt a warm hand squeeze her heart whenever she thought about her family. Hers had been a happy, well-adjusted childhood in a middle-class setting. Her father, before his retirement, had been a successful commercial insurance agent, owning his own agency. Her mother had been the office manager, bookkeeper, receptionist, girl Friday; you name it she did it. Nachelle remembered spending many summers and after-school hours helping out in the business. Because they had conservatively and wisely saved money for early retirement and college educations, the Olivers sold their agency upon Nachelle's graduation from high school. When they had her safely ensconced in college and with Vincent off serving the country, they started living their dream—travelling wherever and whenever they wanted to. Still, even with all the globetrotting they did, they were never too busy to stay in touch with their two "babies."

Nachelle continued, "And, speaking of families, Heather told me to tell you hi."

Harlan exaggerated his response. "She did . . ."

"Yes." Nachelle playfully teased him. "She says she hopes to see you before you leave."

"I can't believe it. The great Heather Chadwick wants to see me."

Harlan knew he was not one of Heather's favorite people. Actually, he knew Heather despised him and thought he had been unworthy of Nachelle.

"Her business is doing quite well. She just signed a major contract with the Fort Worth school district and she produced a video. She's thinking about doing a Barney type of thing."

"Oooooh, soooo, she's shooting for the big time. What does the boyfriend or is it husband now, have to say about her success? Isn't that too many inflated egos in one house?" Sarcasm dripped from his words, his face twisted into an ironic expression.

"Harlan, be nice. Heather had only good things to say about you."

"Oh, really? Then it must have been a short conversation."

Nachelle shook her head. "I'm never going to get you two to like each other, am I?"

Harlan just shrugged his powerful shoulders and drained his tea glass.

"Okay, okay, I can take a hint. Enough about Heather. What about you? No special someone waiting for you in Phoenix?"

"I have been seeing a lady off and on for the past year but it's not serious. And, now seeing you again after all these months made me realize what a fool I've been." Harlan took her hand in his and stared deeply into her brown eyes. "Do you think there's a chance we could rekindle what we had? I mean before the bad stuff . . . the early times when we were totally devoted to each other with no family business, no drugs, no jealousy." Harlan caressed her palms. "I'd really like another opportunity to be with you, to really love you, Nachelle."

"Oh, Harlan, I'm flattered. Truly I am."

Harlan laughed lightly, "That doesn't answer my question."

Nachelle looked deep into his beautiful eyes and saw nothing but sincerity shining within them. She wanted to tell Harlan that if he'd asked her that same question two years ago, she might not be hesitating in her response. "I don't know, Harlan. I'm still getting used to the idea that you're really here and living a straight life."

"Yeah, I know this is out of the blue and you need time to think about it. After all, I surprise you by showing up unexpectedly, and now, I'm asking you to give me another chance." Harlan took her other hand and held them both close to his mouth. "Tell you what, it looks like I'll be here for awhile. Why don't we take time and get to know each other again? No pressure. I just want the chance to show you I've really changed." After a slight pause, Harlan continued, "I know things are hectic at the office right now, so we could just take it slow and easy and see what happens, okay?"

Nachelle was careful not to give him a sign that she was leaning one way or the other. Masking her feelings, she answered, "I do need some time to think things over."

"That's better than no." Pleasure immediately spread over Harlan's handsome features. "I promise you, Nachelle, if you give me a second chance, I won't let you down this time."

Nachelle returned his smile, but internally she was a ball of doubt. She didn't want to hurt his feelings, but she was fearful that this changed, drug-free Harlan who had returned to them would revert to the trouble-plagued Harlan who had caused her so many tears and so much heartache. After all, for Harlan, using drugs was only a symptom of a deeper problem that had to be excavated if he were serious about remaining drug-free. So far, he had yet to talk about the feelings of insecurity that had led to his drug use. Had he truly hit rock bottom and resolved all of his problems? Had he truly given up drugs altogether? Were the days of the 3:00 a.m. phone calls begging for money over? . . . and the cursing and name-calling and threats of violence? Could she risk opening herself up to him again, knowing that today he was on the wagon, but tomorrow he could fall off? Did she even want to risk going through that emotional see-saw with him again?

So many times in the past she had wondered what she would do if Harlan ever returned and asked to start things anew. She had always avoided answering that question. Her parents had taught her that it was possible for a person to turn over a new leaf. They had raised her to try not to judge others and allow people to grow and change. Did she owe him the opportunity to prove he was a different man? All of these questions buzzed dizzily through her mind. She could hardly focus on what Harlan was saying.

"I don't want to be pushy, but how about dinner tomorrow? I could come over and cook for you."

Nachelle's mouth dropped open in surprise. "What? You don't cook!"

Harlan released her hands and held up one finger. "Ah, but I do. I've learned how to do a lot of things like laundry, grocery shopping, you know . . . stuff like that."

Nachelle laughed despite her confusion. "Where's the real Harlan? What did you do with him?"

Harlan spread his hands wide. "Here I am, baby. You're looking at the new and improved model." Growing serious, Harlan asked, "So what about it, dinner at your place tomorrow night? Let me pamper you after a hard week at work."

Nachelle clarified his question, "Just dinner and talk?"

"Just dinner and talk." Harlan repeated.

"With an offer like that, how can I refuse? Besides, my curiosity about your cooking ability is killing me."

"Good. I'll come by Saturday afternoon. We can go grocery

shopping and hours later I will lay before you a spread fit for a princess."

Nachelle couldn't stop the laughter from bubbling up from within her. Still laughing and kidding Harlan about his new-found domestic abilities, they paid the bill and left the restaurant.

Nachelle returned to the office to discover Steven was called unexpectedly to Atlanta for business. He had caught the first flight after his lunch date. Firmly pushing away the feeling of abandonment, Nachelle attacked her work. She didn't allow herself to ponder the reason for her disappointment when she had learned he'd left town. Instead, she focused on how to tell him the legal documents would be delayed for a few more days. *At least I don't have to tell him face-to-face.* Picking up the phone, she dialed his personal voicemail box and left the bad news as a message.

The rest of the work day went as quickly as the previous days since the merger had been announced. Meetings, telephone calls, conferences, and paperwork kept Nachelle in a perpetual state of activity. When the six o'clock whistle sounded that evening, she packed some paperwork into her briefcase, packed her tired body into her coat, and headed for home.

Ten

The weekend arrived with a blast of freezing weather. Nachelle sorted through her personal mail lethargically. Her mind was full of thoughts of business, Steven, and uppermost, the request Harlan had made of her. She was no closer to an answer now than she was when she had had lunch with him. The confusion she felt had only magnified tenfold. She had even grown to regret her decision to allow him to cook for her tonight, but he'd already called to confirm. She boldly admitted Steven had a lot to do with her baffled state. He was still in Atlanta, but was due back Monday morning. Given his interest in the progress of the merger and the legal documents, she had expected to hear from him. He hadn't called—not once.

It was amazing to her that in the short time since he'd installed himself in Ralph's old office, it had already been stamped with Steven's own personality. Now, with him in Atlanta, it seemed like an empty hole existed not only at the office, but also within her. *How did he acquire such a major influence over my thoughts? How did I let this happen?* She miserably asked herself.

The phone rang and desperate for the distraction from her thoughts she answered it quickly. "Hello."

"Good morning. How about lending a friend a helping hand?" At 9:00 a.m., Heather sounded bright and cheery, a remarkable event since she was not a morning person and often didn't crawl out of bed until after ten. "I have a ton of repairs to do on the puppets and very little time before an afternoon performance."

Nachelle happily agreed. "I'm on the way." She hung up the phone and exchanged her sweats for wool pants and a heavy sweater. After brushing her hair into a ponytail and applying a light layer of makeup, she grabbed her purse and coat and headed out for the artsy section of town.

Within twenty minutes Nachelle was pulling into the parking lot of Heather's studio. She used her key to let herself in and marveled for perhaps the hundredth time at the transformation the cavernous building had gone through under Heather's guiding hand. Heather had literally taken an abandoned, yet solidly built warehouse and sectioned it into a theater, an office, and renovated the top floor into her private home. Nachelle walked through the lobby and circled behind the stage. She knew Heather would be backstage, surrounded by the lifeless, long limbed puppets that had already entertained numerous children.

"Heather, it's me."

"Hi, hey, follow my voice. I'm glad you're here. Boy, do I need help."

Nachelle rounded the corner to see Heather sitting cross-legged in the middle of the floor outfitting a male puppet with a black jacket, the size of which could have easily fit a twelve-month-old child.

"Help is here. Tell me what you need." Nachelle dropped her coat and purse on a nearby chair and plopped down on the floor.

Using her leg, Heather pushed the sewing kit and a pile of miniature clothes toward Nachelle. "The buttons are loose and some of the Velcro is pulling free." Nachelle had helped Heather with so many minor repairs she didn't need detailed instructions.

"No problem. What time is your performance?"

"At three. At the mall."

Nachelle ducked her head and began threading a needle. "So, how was your week? Did the final meeting with the school district go okay?"

"Better than okay. They agreed to all of my terms and I have their names on the dotted line. I'm really rolling now."

"That's great, Heather. Congratulations!"

"Thanks, and I appreciate the negotiation tips you gave me. It helped a lot."

Nachelle's exuberance at her best friend's success shone on her face. "Anything for a friend. We'll have to celebrate."

"Speaking of friends, guess who I had lunch with this week?" Heather's light, airy voice floated pleasantly around Nachelle.

Nachelle chuckled, glad to be around someone who didn't confuse the heck out of her. "I don't feel like guessing, just tell me."

"Okay, Miss Stick-in-the-Mud. Steven. I had lunch with your boss." Heather lowered her voice conspiratorially. "How can you concentrate at work with such a good-looking man around? That would drive me crazy."

It was on the tip of Nachelle's tongue to tell her it was driving her crazy, but she bit her tongue and focused on the meaning of Heather's words. Worry puckered her brow. "You had lunch with Steven? Whose idea was that?"

"His, and he was such a gentleman. *I* think you guys are unjustly giving him a bad rap. We had a pleasant time together. Did you know he has a sense of humor?"

A chill ripped down Nachelle's spine. "Forget a sense of humor! What do you mean we're judging him unfairly? What did you talk about?"

"Well, remember the night of the banquet . . . he told me then that when he got settled, he wanted to do lunch. Anyway, his secretary called about a week later. We had a great time just chatting."

"About what, Heather?" Nachelle's patience was evaporating.

In a sing-song voice, Heather answered, "Lots of things. But, mostly about him alternately living in Fort Worth and Atlanta. He knows I'm a native Fort Worthian and he wants to find a house here, so he was asking me about neighborhoods. Then, we talked about the nightlife. I gave him the names of a couple of black Catholic churches and we talked about appropriate charities or agencies that he might consider teaming up with and well . . ."

Nachelle could tell Heather was getting to the good part. "And . . ." she prompted.

Heather spoke rapidly, running her words together, taking only necessary pauses. "I asked him if he had been dating anyone since he's been here. He said no, and then I asked him about that woman in Atlanta that Mother dug up, and he said that relationship had ended months ago. He told me that since then he'd been concentrating on the Hayes Group and then I asked him why he was still single—with him being such a good catch and all—and he said his mother had the same question. We laughed and commiserated with each other about mothers and marriage. Then we talked about the ideal mate, you know, characteristics, attributes, etc. He actually has very simple needs. He wants someone who's supportive and understands the demands the business has on his time, someone who can stand up to the pressure of living life as a DuCloux and who fits in well with his family structure. The lucky woman must be a good communicator and somewhat independent and she can either work outside of the home or in the home, he doesn't care. And of course, they have to be sexually compatible." Heather drew a long breath and favored her friend with a quick glance. "He didn't mention your name and neither did I . . . even though I wanted to."

"Thank God!" Nachelle's head reeled with the information Heather had rattled off.

"I know you don't want to get involved in another work relationship, but I was really impressed with the guy and I think I'm pretty perceptive. As I said before, I think the guy's been given a bad rap and if you just share with him your past experience I'm sure you guys could work something out." Heather held up a hand to stop Nachelle from cutting her off. "Nachelle, people are not always what they seem and they're capable of changing just like situations change. That's all I'm going to say about the matter. Gerald told me to mind my own business so that's what I'm going to do."

Nachelle fixed her with a doubting stare. "Remind me to thank Gerald."

Heather laughed. "Now, tell me about Harlan. How was *your* lunch the other day?"

Mentally rewinding her memory tape, Nachelle thought again about their dinner plans this evening. Although he said he wouldn't pressure her, she knew Harlan would prod her for an answer and she wasn't prepared to tell him yes or no. *If only I could be certain he's honestly turned his back on drugs. Emotionally I'm not equipped to handle another disappointing relationship.* Yes, Harlan would definitely want an answer and she had no idea what she would say to him. Shaking her head as if that simple gesture would rid the confusion in her heart and mind, she picked up a toddler shirt with a button conspicuously missing.

"Earth to Nachelle. Earth to Nachelle." When she had her friend's attention, Heather quoted, "A penny for your thoughts."

"Lunch was fine, except Harlan wants us to get back together. He wants to start fresh."

It was Heather's turn to show surprise. "I hope you told him not only no, but *hell no*."

"I couldn't, Heather. He told me he'd kicked the habit forever and that he wanted to build a brand new future for himself, for us." The confusion resting within Nachelle was obvious to Heather.

Heather stopped fussing with the uncooperative puppet and begged earnestly, "Nachelle, don't fall for it. He's pulling your string. He's too weak to change."

"Why are you so willing to throw Steven at me with his unsavory reputation as a cutthroat and yet you won't believe Harlan's had a turnaround? Didn't you say earlier that people are capable of change?"

"Look, Nachelle, I've known Harlan longer than you. Don't forget we grew up in the same neighborhood, attended the same schools, had the same friends, were part of the same social clique. When he graduated, I was soooo glad to learn he had decided on Princeton instead of UT Austin where I was attending. If you know what's good for you, you'll ignore him and move forward not backward."

"What is it with you and Harlan? Why do I feel I'm always playing referee between you two?"

A troubled shadow landed on Heather's face. "If you care about yourself, drop his notion. Trust me, he won't quit until he destroys you." Heather's light-complexioned face grew red with the intense need to get her point across.

Nachelle laughed nervously. "Aren't you being a little melodramatic?"

"Drugs are a powerful force, Nachelle. And, when you add

that to a person who already has problems, it acquires even more power. Don't forget that." The silence after Heather's last statement was heavy. Neither woman said anything for a while, turning inward to their private thoughts and fears.

What Heather couldn't tell Nachelle, was that she knew the real Harlan better than anyone.

Their private high school had won a football game that night and to celebrate, a group of friends had ended up at one of the houses where the guy's parents were gone for the weekend. When the alcohol started flowing, things got rowdy quickly, and someone got the idea to play strip poker. Heather had refused to play, deciding someone needed to keep a cool head just in case. Even with all the commotion, she had ended up falling asleep on the couch and only awoke when she felt hands groping under her jumper. She had sat up quickly and was immediately imprisoned by Harlan and another boy. If it hadn't been for the fact that the boys were crazy drunk, and she had good aim in the appropriate places, she would have been a statistic in the police department's records. After fighting her way out of the house, she had run the few blocks to her parents' home. From that night forward, she no longer attended house parties, no longer hung with the same crowd, and grew to despise Harlan, who before the incident had supposedly been her friend. He had tried to apologize several times after the incident, claiming it was a joke, that they wouldn't have hurt her, but Heather had rebuked his efforts, the damage to her emotions and mind could not be erased by an apology. That had been the end of their friendship.

Being one year Nachelle's senior, Heather had already graduated from UT Austin and had returned to Fort Worth to work and live there by the time Harlan and Nachelle had become an item. As friends sometimes do, their telephone calls and letter writing had dwindled to almost nothing after Heather left campus. Nachelle became engrossed in school and social activities and Heather had become engrossed in living her life in Fort Worth. It had been a surprise and pure coincidence when Heather and Nachelle ran into each other at a local mall. The friendship had started anew and Heather soon learned of the pending marriage. She could have died! Especially seeing all the happiness and love shining from Nachelle's face. She closeted her feelings of doom and vowed to be the best friend Nachelle could have; she felt Nachelle would need one when Harlan ultimately showed his true colors. Although it took longer than Heather had anticipated, Nachelle *had* needed a good, trusted friend.

Although the air was heavy with unfinished business concerning Steven, the friends traded small talk on safe subjects, all the while working tirelessly until all the garments were mended and the puppets dressed. Two hours before the show was due to start, Heather's employees showed up and between the four of them they loaded the dolls, scenery, and accessories into Heather's van. The friends hugged, got into separate cars, and roared off in opposite directions.

Nachelle sat on her couch with her legs crossed under her. She could hear Harlan moving about noisily in the kitchen. Leaning forward, she picked up the glass of red wine Harlan had poured for her and took a tentative sip.

Wearing one of her pastel-colored aprons, Harlan entered the living room with a platter of cheese and crackers. Setting the tray down with a flourish, he bowed, and then used the remote to change CDs. The mellow sounds of Rachelle Farrell floated through the room.

"It smells wonderful," Nachelle remarked.

Imitating an Italian air kiss, Harlan brushed the tips of his fingers to his lips. "And, I promise it will taste every bit as wonderful as it smells.

"How about a dance while we wait for the oven to do the rest of the work?" Appropriately enough, Harlan opened his arms at the same time as Rachelle Farrell belted out the beginning words to "Welcome to My Love." Nachelle walked into his arms remembering the first time they had danced together. It seemed like ages ago. They had just gotten their grade on one of their graduate projects and it had been the highest in the class. Celebrating later at Harlan's off-campus house, he had taught her how to swingout Fort Worth style. The complex steps were hard to master then, but now she easily followed his lead.

"Break." Harlan demanded, slightly out of breath, after a couple of songs had passed. "I haven't done this since I left Fort Worth."

Laughing, Nachelle backed away from him and moved back onto the couch. As she turned to face the couch, her full, ankle-length skirt caught the wine glass she had placed too close to the edge of the low, glass and marble coffee table. Red wine splashed everywhere, but mostly on Nachelle's skirt and stockinged legs. "Doggonit." Nachelle swiped with her hands at the scattered red spots which made her brown and cream skirt even darker. Harlan raced for a kitchen towel to clean the coffee table. "That was really graceful, Nachelle," she muttered.

Harlan returned and wiped up the largest pool of liquid. "I'll take care of this if you want to change clothes."

"Thanks, Harlan."

The telephone rang as she walked towards her bedroom. "Do you mind getting that? I want to soak this skirt before the stain sets in."

"Sure." Harlan took a final, cleansing swipe at the spill and turned to answer the phone. "Hello."

A moment of silence passed during which the caller paused.

"Hello." Harlan repeated the salutation.

"Yes. Nachelle Oliver, please."

"I'm sorry she's not available at the moment. Would you like to leave a message?"

"This is Steven DuCloux. Please let her know I need to speak with her as soon as possible."

"Steven, this is Harlan. How's it going?"

Steven clipped out. "Fine, thank you, and you?"

"Good. Listen, Nachelle's changing clothes, but I'll have her call you after dinner. She has the number, right?"

"No, she doesn't. I'm at my parents' house in Atlanta." Steven rattled off the number and disconnected the call.

Harlan hung up with a thoughtful expression on his face. He'd never heard of a boss calling an employee at home on a Saturday night. Shrugging his shoulders, he headed for the kitchen to check on the lasagna.

Nachelle returned in time to sit down to a steaming-hot plate of pasta, salad and bread. Less than an hour later, they rubbed their stomachs and leaned back in their chairs, fully replete and happy. The kitchen was in shambles, but the food had been excellent and the company pleasant.

"Harlan, that was good." Nachelle let her head roll back against the chair's back. "I take back all my doubts."

"Thank you. I'm glad you enjoyed it. I didn't cook a dessert because I replaced my drug habit with a sweet tooth and now I'm fighting that sweet tooth."

Nachelle chuckled. "I wouldn't have had room for dessert anyway. I'm stuffed."

"How about coffee in the living room?"

"Sounds good. I'll get it since you did everything else." Nachelle bounced out of her chair before Harlan could argue. He had truly lived up to his pampering promise; she had not lifted a finger all evening.

In minutes, Nachelle placed a tray loaded with gourmet coffee, cups, and creamer on the sofa table.

"You may think I'm crazy when I say this, but, I'm almost glad I got hooked on drugs."

The cup Nachelle held dipped slightly. "You're right. I think that's crazy."

"Hear me out." Harlan put his cup down and sat on the edge of the couch. "Checking into the rehabilitation center and going through counseling forced me to realize I was my own worst enemy—not you, or dad, or mom, or the drugs, but me. They helped me understand how selfish, insecure, spoiled, and irresponsible I was and how unfairly I treated the people who love me."

Harlan stood and started pacing the length of the living room. He was talking with his hands as much as he was talking with his mouth. "I was afraid to return to Fort Worth because I wasn't sure if I was strong enough in my new life to withstand my old lifestyle, but these last few days haven't been bad. I've exorcised most of the ghosts, but the thing I was most afraid of was facing you. I really let you down and I regret it." Harlan stopped long enough to ensure his message was getting across. "Since we had lunch the other day, I've been thinking of ways that I could redeem myself. And, I was thinking . . ." He stopped and knelt in front of Nachelle. Earnest olive eyes met her brown ones and pleaded, ". . . wouldn't it be nice to reconstruct the past. You know . . . me, you, and Dad leading the Hayes Group, just like old times, but with the new Harlan." A vision of him and Nachelle running the company and engaged again filled his mind. He liked the picture and was pleased as punch with his plan. It would be the perfect opportunity to regain everyone's love and trust.

Surprise was not a strong enough word to record Nachelle's facial expression. With slack mouth, wide eyes, and raised eyebrows, her throat worked convulsively, yet the jumble of thoughts didn't readily work themselves into coherent words. "But . . . you can't be serious . . . there's . . . so much to . . . to . . . consider."

"Consider my foot! With me, you, and Dad in the game we can run DuCloux Enterprises right out of town." Exuberance oozed from Harlan's every word and action. "Listen, you said the other day that that deal wasn't final, so I say let's *not* make it final. We'll give Steven DuCloux his money back and thumb our nose at him. You don't have to work for such a hard-nosed cynic who expects you to drop everything when he calls."

It was Nachelle's turn to pace the living room floor, only she complemented her pacing with hand wringing. "Harlan, it's not that simple. A multitude of factors played into this major decision. A person can't just put the brakes on this deal and hope it will stop."

"But it's not impossible, is it? I mean, it would be sticky, but it can be managed, right?"

"Harlan, I can tell you've put a lot of thought into this idea . . ."

"But?"

Nachelle stopped treading a path in the carpet and said, "Okay, stop and think for a minute. Your Dad signed a legal document indicating he was basically vouching for your agreement to this deal. If we go back on that signature, Steven *could* and *would* sue. He wants the Hayes Group really bad."

"We'll hire the best legal mind in the state to fight him."

"That takes money and speaking of money, your Dad accepted a large sum of money from Steven. Ralph would have to pay him back every penny plus interest and in the short time I've worked for Steven, believe me he would want it back as quickly as he gave it to Ralph. That might be asking a bit much from Ralph, don't you think? We're talking about several million dollars." Nachelle put a hand under her chin and was suddenly quiet, one could almost see the wheels of her mind turning. "Come to think of it, this is a decision he really needs to be in on. It impacts him more than me or you."

Harlan stood up and crossed to where Nachelle stood, still deep in thought. Holding her arms, he acquiesced for the time being. "You're right, of course. I haven't spoken with Dad about this. They'll be back tomorrow afternoon and the three of us can sit down then. In the meantime, will you promise me you'll seriously think about it?"

"Yes, I'll give it some thought." Nachelle managed a weak, tremulous smile.

"Alright." Harlan moved his hands to snag her around the waist. Picking her up as if she weighed no more than a pound, he twirled her around, then put her down with a quick kiss on the cheek. "It's going to be great, Nachelle. Just you wait and see. Now, I'll go clean the kitchen while you call your temporary boss." Harlan broadly winked at her.

Looking confused, Nachelle said to Harlan's back. "Call Steven? Why?"

"Because he called while you were changing into those nice-fitting jeans. I forgot to mention it earlier and only just remembered when we started talking about the company. Sorry."

"Did he say what he wanted?"

"No. Just that he wanted you to call him as soon as possible." As an afterthought Harlan added, "He's in Atlanta. The number's by the phone."

Nachelle consulted her watch and sighed. She mentally calculated the time difference between Fort Worth and Atlanta. *It's already been over an hour, another thirty minutes won't hurt. It'll only be 10:30 there and Steven's already said he's a night owl.* "Harlan, considering the mess Chef Paul made in there, why don't we both clean the kitchen?"

"No, I told you I'm showcasing my domestic abilities."

"And don't think I don't appreciate it, but my ulterior motive is work. I brought work home from the office that I need to review."

"On a Saturday night! Why can't it wait until tomorrow?"

"It sounds to me like I'll be with you and Ralph tomorrow."

"Ah, yes. In that case . . ." Directing his hand toward the kitchen, Harlan said, "I'll wash. You dry."

In no time, the kitchen looked sparkling clean. The dishes were dry, the floor was swept clean, and all of the small appliances Harlan had used were back in their assigned spaces on the tiled countertop.

Harlan shrugged into his coat. "Thanks for a wonderful evening. Although we didn't talk specifically about us, perhaps we can tack that onto tomorrow's discussions?"

Nachelle accompanied Harlan to the door, murmuring noncommittally. Not that Harlan was really looking for a reply, his feet barely touched the floor.

Circling around him to straighten his coat collar, she playfully admitted. "I am thoroughly impressed with your domestic abilities."

Harlan roguishly replied, "Prove it." His eyes focused on her lips, making it clear he desired a kiss.

Shyly, Nachelle raised her hands and placed them lightly on his shoulders. Stretching on her tiptoes, she placed her lips softly on his. Instantly, Harlan pulled her close, wrapping his arms tightly around her waist. He kissed her with all the sensual energy he had. The kiss should have knocked her senseless, but when it ended, instead of trembling with desire or quaking with the need for more, she stood, almost unaffected.

"Thanks. That'll keep me warm." Harlan planted a quick kiss on her forehead and left.

Nachelle waited outside in the hallway until she could see him no more, then thoughtfully closed the door. She was only slightly surprised that her body hadn't responded to his kiss as it had in the past. In the heyday of their relationship, she would not have been able to stop at one kiss, but she supposed not only had time healed some of the damage to her heart and mind, but it also had extinguished the passion that his kisses used to kindle. As she walked to the phone to call Steven, she knew what her answer to Harlan would be.

Now, she thought, *dealing with Steven will be a totally different matter.* Donning her corporate hat, she dialed his number in Atlanta.

Steven's bass voice answered on the second ring.

"Good evening, Steven, sorry to be calling so late."

"It's not late at all. I should be apologizing for interrupting your evening, but I need to know the status of that paperwork."

Nachelle's grip on the phone tightened. She had had a long difficult week and was not up to engaging in a verbal fencing match with Steven. It was bad enough that whether they were in the same room or miles apart, she always felt vulnerable and on edge with him.

"I spoke with Harlan earlier. Was he there dropping off the

papers?" Steven had a legitimate business need to ask the question, but a personal need drove him to use a proprietary tone of voice.

"Actually, no."

The silence on the other end of the line was monumental. Nachelle continued, "The voicemail I left for you said the situation was under control. I realize I missed your deadline, but I'm working hard to get this resolved early next week." Nachelle's hands had grown clammy and she had long since sunk into the chair by the phone. Naming the feelings that made her body's temperature escalate, she felt embarrassed and incompetent at having missed a targeted date. She had always prided herself on exceeding, or at very least meeting deadlines. Searching deeper, she discovered she felt sick to her stomach knowing she had let Steven down. And now, with this extra twist Harlan had thrown into the mix, she didn't know if early next week would now be achievable. He was dead set on his plan to regain control of the Hayes Group. Nachelle knew without a doubt that he would push and push his father until he got what he wanted, but where would that leave Ralph? . . . Where would that leave her? She hadn't worked with Steven long enough to build the type of loyalty she had to Ralph. But right now, even though she was leading the merger team, she was still not guaranteed employment after the third quarter when the brand new, bigger DuCloux Enterprises was in place. Still, even with all the reasons she could think of for supporting Harlan's plan, she found that she was not in favor of reversing Steven's ownership. For the short time she had been with DuCloux Enterprises, she had learned some new skills to put in her professional bag of tricks. She appreciated the fierce loyalty he had to his family's company and it would be a challenge to work with such a competitive company. Plus, she was drawn to him, as a man. And, although she didn't understand the reason for her attraction to him, it was there, solid and unmovable as a concrete wall. Then there was Harlan's long-standing fight with drugs to consider; it couldn't be easily ignored. If only she had tangible proof that he had really kicked the habit forever, she could be more fair about her assessment of his idea.

A heavy sigh escaped as Steven spoke, slowly, "Do what you can, what you have to, to finalize this deal quickly." Steven paused to smooth his beard and then continued, "Nachelle, I know you're doing what you can, but I still have to ask . . . do I have anything to worry about?"

Nachelle closed her eyes, wondering what she should say. *Yes, Steven, you have a mutiny on your hands* or *no, Steven, I wouldn't worry about a thing* or *maybe, Steven, but I won't know until Ralph returns.* She had so many options to ponder, but a waiting, aggressive man was on the other end of the line. *Loyalty versus honesty,* she didn't like the choices. Refusing to choose, she hedged, "I won't know until Monday. Be assured, I'll keep you informed of my progress."

Her mind flitted to the meeting she would have with Harlan and Ralph tomorrow. She wanted the situation wrapped up, tied with a bow. She didn't like this dual role that she had inadvertently fallen into.

"Nachelle, I know we haven't worked together very long, but I do want you to know I have a great deal of faith in your abilities and I need you."

Nachelle's heart turned three flips upon hearing his deep voice caress those last three words. It pleased her and in turn made her feel worse than a liar. It was on the verge of her tongue to admit they might have problems with the contracts when Steven changed subjects.

"So, how's your weekend?"

With eyebrows raised, Nachelle was stumped momentarily. Steven was not a social chatterer. He said what he had to say, listened to the response, and then moved on. For him to ask her about her weekend was major . . . or maybe the Shark was taking on human characteristics. She wondered.

"It's been good. And, yours?"

"Hectic. We had a million kids at the house today. It was

my niece Jasmine's eighth birthday and she insisted on a party at Grandpa and Grandma's house. We're still trying to figure out how cake got into the drapes."

Laughing at the mental image his words painted, Nachelle spoke candidly, "An adult could only imagine."

"You have a nice laugh, Nachelle. We should hear it more often at the office." Steven's words fell softly against Nachelle's ears. They were like cool silk against soft, hot flesh. The beat of her heart increased and a warmth suffused her body from head to toe.

Shaken to the core, Nachelle murmured her thanks.

"One day I'd like you to meet my nieces and nephews. They're terrors, but they can also be sweet, little angels. Of course you'll meet my brothers, sisters-in-law, and parents at Ralph's retirement party."

"Yes, Dorrie told me they confirmed their attendance."

"And your parents will be there as well, right?" Steven held his breath, waiting for her answer. *The last item on the checklist—family suitability—could be determined in one night if all worked well,* Steven thought. And then he remembered his promise to Dorothy DuCloux.

Only hours ago as the DuCloux family had gathered in the den, awaiting the arrival of the birthday guests and the start of the party, Dorothy DuCloux had grabbed Steven's hand and pulled him into the family library.

"Come here. I want to talk with you." Dorothy had demanded. She was Steven's favorite sister-in-law and wasted no time getting to the issue. "What's wrong with you? You've been growling at everybody all day."

Steven had pulled out the worn checklist and showed her his lack of progress. "If I don't find a wife soon Mother's going to get me an 800 number and start doing phone interviews. I can't deal with that, especially when I've already got my eye on Nachelle Oliver. Everything about her tells me she's the one, but I can't get her to open up to me."

"Tell me what you're doing, but first of all why are you using the checklist before you know that you're even in love with this woman?"

"Because that's the way it's done. How do you think Donald got you?" Steven had joked with her, but Dorothy had not been amused. Even though she'd been married to Donald Du-Cloux, Steven's oldest brother, for ten years, the memory of Donald proposing to her with the checklist in his hand still irked her.

Placing her hands on her healthy hips, she read him the riot act. "First of all, Donald didn't even attempt to use the horrid list until he was already in love with me. It's a tool designed for follow-up, not execution. Secondly, no wonder the woman doesn't open up to you. I wouldn't either with that cold, calculated method you're using. She's a woman, Steven! A human being. You can't 'acquisition' her like you can a company."

Steven had paced the room, agitated. "Dorothy, this is important. I have to know this is the right woman and that the marriage is going to last. I have very strong traditions to uphold."

"Well, you're sure not going to uphold them by throwing this cruel method at the poor girl. Just what have you been doing?"

Dorothy had choked from anger when Steven shared with her the hiring of the private investigators and the sexual proposition. "Steven! How could you? You're such a warm, caring person. I can't believe you're being so stupid about this, and quite honestly, I can't believe she hasn't slapped your face."

After five minutes of ranting and raving, without letting Steven get a single word in, Dorothy had calmed down enough to give him some advice. "You throw that thing out and court her for real. If you're really serious about this being the woman, you need to treat her with kindness. Throw out that cold, corporate exterior and let her see the real Steven that we all love." After ending her speech, Dorothy took the paper from Steven and burned it in the fireplace. "Now, follow your heart and forget that damned paper. If it's meant to be, it'll work out." Dorothy had returned to the festivities, leaving Steven to think about her comments.

Because it had been a part of his life for so long, he had a difficult time thinking about a courtship outside of the confines of the checklist. It would not be easy to change his approach, but Dorothy had given him a perspective that he had not thought about. From Nachelle's angle, his methods must seem highly unorthodox. No wonder she was rigid around him. Agreeing with Dorothy, he decided he would use the checklist as an after-the-fact tool and let nature do the beforehand work. With that resolution firmly in place, he had rejoined Jasmine's birthday party with the plan to woo Nachelle starting that very evening.

Steven returned to the present conversation with a sexy smile on his face.

"Yes, my parents are coming," Nachelle answered.

"Good, it'll be nice to meet them."

Steven finished the call. "I've kept you long enough. I'm sorry to have interrupted your time with Harlan."

"Oh, no, he's gone. I was actually getting ready to do some work."

"On a Saturday night?" Steven exclaimed, gently. "Why, Miss Oliver, didn't anyone ever tell you all work and no play . . ."

"Yes, I've heard that a time or two, but there just aren't enough hours in a day. Surely, you've heard that one?" Nachelle cautiously picked up on his teasing manner.

Steven chuckled and replied, "I know how you feel." Settling down, he continued, "Don't forget we have that reception next week and a luncheon at the chamber."

"I haven't forgotten. It's on my calendar."

"Goodnight, Nachelle."

"Goodnight, Steven."

Sinking onto the couch, Nachelle grabbed a pillow and hugged it tight. The smile on her face spoke of the pleasure Steven's words had brought her. She had missed his presence in the office, and tonight he had seemed like a different man. Nachelle couldn't believe he had even laughed. She hoped when he returned Monday that he would be the same person he was tonight. It would help to lift some of the stress she was feeling, and make her remaining time at DuCloux more enjoyable.

Excitement brought her to her feet and she ran to her bedroom to find the right dress for the social events for the week—even though they were still days away.

Hundreds of miles away on the east coast, Steven maintained his seated pose in the darkened office at his parents' home and replayed the call he'd just had with Nachelle. Although he still didn't like the fact that Harlan had spent time with her this evening, knowing he would not be spending the night at her apartment was a relief. Jealousy had settled in and come to a full boil when the other man had casually answered her phone as if he had every right. And when Harlan had mentioned Nachelle was changing clothes, Steven had hit the roof. His mind had started building all kinds of intimate scenes between the two of them, egged on by their previous relationship. Forcing his mind from those unsettling images, Steven switched his thoughts to Harlan's return. He could not help but wonder what complications Harlan would bring into the picture, both personally and professionally, and why Harlan had decided to return after all these years. Even though Nachelle had forcefully told him her past with Harlan would not jeopardize DuCloux, the idea of Harlan returning bothered him. "I'll have to rely on Nachelle's honesty to provide the missing pieces to this puzzle," Steven told himself aloud.

Steven stood and stretched. Walking casually to the leather chair in front of the fireplace, he sat down and stared into the roaring fire. The intense feelings Nachelle drew from him were his primary concern. The connection between them was strong. He felt it and would bet his life that she felt it, too. Why she chose to ignore the invisible bond between them was beyond him. "There must be more to this broken engagement. Somehow I've got to find out what happened, but I'd stake my life on only three people knowing the entire truth—Harlan, Nachelle, and Heather." Steven got up and used the poker to shift the logs, making the fire blaze brighter. "Maybe I need to speak with Harlan man to man. His timing is too coincidental." A fierce desire sizzled through him. "I won't lose Nachelle. I'll think of something to combat Harlan's old hold on her." Steven stretched his long legs out in front of him, placed his hands behind his head, and envisioned a future with him and Nachelle in the leading roles.

Eleven

Nachelle drove through the open gates and parked in the circular drive in front of the Hayes's elegant white brick home. Before she made it to the double-front doors, Adele was standing in the open doorway, wearing a cotton apron on top of a silk dress. Her welcoming smile was brighter than the sun.

"Good afternoon, Adele. You look well rested." Nachelle moved the white box containing a bakery-bought cheesecake—Ralph's favorite dessert—to one hand and hugged Adele.

"Dearie, come in." Adele shut the door after Nachelle and placed a motherly arm around the younger woman's waist. "I feel great. I can't tell you what a great time we had at the cabin. Oh, before I forget, your parents send their love and they'll see you at Ralph's retirement party. Now, how are you doing? You look beautiful as usual."

They chatted like two old friends as they walked down the hallway to the kitchen. Even though the Hayes's had a formal dining room, they preferred to dine at the smaller, homier table in the kitchen. Harlan and Ralph were already seated, talking, when the women entered.

"Hi, everyone." Greetings, in the form of hugs, kisses, and kind words resounded throughout the room. When they were settled again, Adele wasted no time getting the food on the table.

While they ate, Ralph entertained them with stories of their vacation. And before long they were dishing out huge slabs of cheesecake and washing it down with coffee.

Harlan took the opportunity during the serving of dessert to turn the conversation to his idea. "Dad, I want to run something by you. Last night Nachelle and I were discussing the possibility of me not signing the papers and the three of us resuming the operations of the Hayes Group. We'd like to get your input, see how you feel about it."

Nachelle almost choked at Harlan's casual assumption that it was a joint idea and that she had agreed to it. She had told him last night that she would think about it and let him know. Now, he was lumping her in, one hundred percent, with his idea. She suppressed her anger until she could speak with him out of earshot of his parents.

"Son, I'm not sure what you're talking about. I signed a contract with Steven, selling the Hayes Group to him. All we need now is your signature."

"I know Dad and that's exactly what I'm saying. If I refuse to sign, the contract isn't valid, which leaves us wide open to continue as if this short period with DuCloux never existed."

Adele spoke up for the first time, worry filling her voice. "Harlan, it's time for your father to retire."

Harlan smiled charmingly. "Oh Mom, what do you mean? Dad's not an old man. You guys are only in your fifties. Plus, he's got the mind of a genius."

Ralph put his fork down. The gleam in his eyes told Nachelle, Harlan's idea had piqued his interest. "Go on son, finish your thoughts."

"Well, it's quite simple, all we do is meet with Steven and

tell him we won't be following through. We'll rescind all contracts, pay him back the money he gave you, and then me, you, and Nachelle will run the company, just like in the old days." Harlan spread his hands wide, depicting the ease of his plan.

Leaning back in his chair, Ralph crossed his arm over his rotund belly and rubbed his chin. He was silent for a few moments as he considered Harlan's idea. "You know . . . I believe there's some merit to that plan. Hummmm . . ."

It was no secret to anyone sitting around that table that Ralph had had plans for the Hayes Group to be jointly owned and controlled by father and son. It was a dream he had cherished and polished every day since Harlan's birth. Now, he was thinking he would have another opportunity to see that dream become a reality.

"Honey, aren't you forgetting what the doctors told you?" Adele didn't like the look in Ralph's eyes. Her husband's health was more important to her than anything else on earth. Her sense of peace was at stake. She was determined to prevent it from completely unraveling.

Nachelle sat quietly, opposite the table from Harlan. She held her breath, waiting for Ralph to make a decision. If he sided with Harlan she didn't know what she would do, she only knew she didn't want to go back to the way things were. Heather was right, it was time to move forward.

"No, honey, I'm not forgetting." Ralph turned to Nachelle. "What do you think?"

Darting a glance in Harlan's direction, Nachelle felt torn in two. She wanted to support Harlan. She felt like this was an important step for him, but she had to be true to her feelings and her gut told her it was a bad idea. She realized that part of her decision stemmed from the attraction she had for Steven, but now was not the time to examine how big a part that played in her response. "Legally, Ralph, it can be done, it would be a very tricky and highly explosive situation, but it can happen. However, ethically, morally, it's not a good

move. You have your word of honor to consider and Steven
has accepted that and . . . well . . . paid you based on your
word."

"Ethics, morals, what does Steven DuCloux care about
them? Have you forgotten the man has schemed to win contracts. The man simply buys up the companies that give him
grief. Why do you think he wants the Hayes Group?" Harlan's
voice escalated as he made his position and feelings about
Steven clear. His eyes narrowed and threw poisonous darts in
Nachelle's direction. He did not like it when he couldn't have
his way. "Whose side are you on anyway? Has Steven already
brainwashed you?"

Adele interrupted Harlan's outburst. "Harlan, calm down.
This is serious. We need to hear everyone's opinion."

"Your mother's right, son. Nachelle raises a very good
point." Ralph leaned forward and Nachelle could see her
words had dimmed some of his initial spark of interest. Ralph
picked up his fork and resumed eating. From past history,
everyone knew this was a sign that he was ready to move onto
the next subject. "Mother and I will discuss it some more and
we'll all sit back down in a couple of days and make a decision."

"There's just one more thing to consider . . ." Nachelle
spoke up. "Steven is expecting those papers by Tuesday at the
latest. He asks for a daily status."

Ralph offered, "I'll call him first thing tomorrow and tell
him we've had a little bit of a hiccup. Will that help?"

Nachelle raised her brows and shoulders, letting them both
drop dramatically. "It can't hurt."

Adele started clearing the table; Nachelle joined her.

"Nachelle, can I see you outside for a moment?" Harlan
was pushing his chair under the table, heading for the hallway.

Nachelle followed him, a deep sense of dread accompanying her. Even though she was angry with him for speaking
for her, she had no desire to discuss it right now. She needed
time to cool off. Besides, they had just started off on the right

foot again and she was determined that if nothing else she would do her part to keep their friendship alive. Even though they had not been discussing Harlan at the time, she recalled Heather's words about people changing. It was quite possible he'd misunderstood her last night.

The door had barely shut behind her when Harlan jumped in her face. "I thought you were going to back me! This should have been a five minute decision, but no! You had to go and stab me in the back like you've always done."

In the face of such an uncalled for, vicious attack, the dam she had built to house her anger burst. Heather's words flew right out the window. She retorted, matching his fierce whisper, "Harlan, I never agreed to back you. I told you last night all I would do is think about it. *You* were wrong for telling them it was *our* decision. I told you last night, it was Ralph's decision—not yours and certainly not mine."

"I never could trust you. You were, and still are, scheming to turn my family against me." Harlan spat out the hurtful, vindictive words, then pivoted sharply. Yanking his coat off the hook, he picked up a set of keys from the side table and exited through the front door, slamming it hard.

With her head hanging low, Nachelle thought about following him, but changed her mind just as quickly. When Harlan acted so vehemently it was best to let him cool off. Thinking of the past, Nachelle only hoped he didn't turn to his old habits. She prayed that he turned instead to the things he had learned in counseling. Turning, she faced the door to the kitchen and was about to enter when Adele walked out. "Was that Harlan slamming my door?"

"I'm afraid we had a disagreement. He's angry with me."

Perceptively, Adele put her arm around Nachelle's shoulder and ushered her into the kitchen. "He's angry with a lot of people. Come. Ralph's upstairs taking a nap. Let's you and I sit, drink some tea, and worry about Harlan together."

* * *

Late the next day Nachelle found herself sitting in her office, staring out her window with unseeing eyes into the black night. What did permeate her senses was the scarce downtown traffic. With a sigh, she realized this was one of many times in the last month that she'd witnessed the transformation of the downtown Fort Worth area from a thriving, many-headed animal during the day to a slumberous, lazy giant at night. She'd known in January that the merger would take all her time. And, indeed, between the demands that the merger placed on her and Steven's high expectations, it seemed that her every waking and sleeping moment had been monopolized.

To add to her overloaded mind, she'd had to deal with Harlan's return and the resulting complications. Yesterday at the Hayes's home she'd acquired yet another snag. Harlan had not returned home yet, and more than twenty-four hours had passed. The Hayes's were in a panic, especially after calls to his old friends and visits to his old haunts had not uncovered his whereabouts. If he didn't return by ten o'clock tonight, they would have to relive the nightmare of filing a missing person's report. Although none of them spoke the words, they all remembered the last time Harlan had been reported missing.

With a heavy sigh, Nachelle turned away from the dark and plopped down into her seat, kicking off her shoes. She thought briefly about shedding her pantyhose, but discarded the idea. Even though the city was having the usual mild mid-February weather, most of the employees were already gone and the building's heat system would soon knock down a few degrees for overnight efficiency.

Flipping open a report, Nachelle tried to concentrate on the figures in front of her. She couldn't. Too many thoughts jumbled around in her head, fighting for first place recognition. Thoughts of Steven won out.

Steven had been held up in Atlanta and according to Dorrie would not be back in town until Wednesday. Nachelle had experienced a bittersweet feeling. She was glad he hadn't returned since she was still no closer to producing the signed documents that would make the Hayes Group legally his. Although he had told her time and time again that he was pleased with her work on the merger, she felt badly that this one simple task was proving to be more challenging than merging two giant companies. On the other hand, she missed him. The office seemed dead without him. Nachelle admitted his proposition to sleep with him had acted as a catalyst, forcing her to confess to herself that he made her feel light-headed and sexually alive. It made her give him more mind play than she wanted to. The strong urgings she felt for him terrified her. She could not put aside her fear of office romances yet she could not put him or his offer out of her mind.

"Enough of this!" Nachelle turned to the next page of the report. "Steven closed that door and I can't afford to open it."

With strong determination, she'd tried to follow Steven's lead. But, the feeling of disappointment became a living, breathing organism. It reminded her of how his hand had stroked her cheek, her legs, her feet; how his eyes came alive whenever he looked at her in after-five attire; and how utterly attractive and sexy he was.

Nachelle had tried to choke the seed that Steven had unknowingly planted. She'd played mind games, focusing on his "bad" personality traits—he was intolerant of mistakes, wanted everything yesterday, and she'd already witnessed the transformation to the Silver Shark when a financial report was late reaching him. A review of his flaws kept her on track for awhile, but inevitably a positive trait reared its head to refute the negatives.

With her own eyes, she'd witnessed his commitment to the community. On more than one occasion, she'd seen him write a sizable personal check to a non-profit organization. She'd also learned from Dorrie that he personally financed the educational dreams of several students at black colleges. At meetings with employee groups, he was patient and candid.

The more she learned about him and the more time she spent with him, the more she found herself thinking about things that crossed the professional boundary. Things like why he wasn't married, why he never took a date to the social functions they attended, and . . . what would have happened if she had taken him up on his offer for a night of love? Would it have been another regretful experience or a night of new tomorrows?

Her daytime imaginings ran wild in her sleep. She dreamt of his strong, sculpted body, his plans and dreams for Du-Cloux Enterprises, and his multi-dimensional personality. She woke from those dreams with a heavy feeling in her loins and an even heavier feeling in her heart.

Between musings, Nachelle managed to read half the page, but her devilish subconscious challenged the accuracy of her statements. *How do you know a relationship with Steven will mirror the relationship you had with Harlan?*

I don't, she thought. With a resigned sigh, she closed the report. There was no sense in trying to read it. Her mind was too focused now on Steven.

The phone rang, giving her a reprieve from her disturbing thoughts.

"Nachelle Oliver."

"Oh, Nachelle, I'm so glad I got you. I tried to reach you at home and got the answering machine so just ignore that message when you get home, okay?" Sheila Whisenhunt, a friend from her college days, spoke in a rush.

The image of the young, pretty redhead with a face full of freckles who Nachelle had shared a dorm room with for four years, came quickly to mind. "Hi, Sheila. It's good to hear your voice. How are things going?"

"Terrible, just terrible. My work situation is getting no better. In fact it's gotten worse. Do you have a few moments to talk?"

Nachelle looked at her watch and then looked at the work on her desk. She had two hours to kill before she went with the Hayes's to file the missing person's report and since she wasn't getting any work done anyway, she gave Sheila her undivided attention. "Go ahead, Sheila."

"My boss did it to me again today. Can you believe it?" The young woman rushed ahead, jumbling her words together. "I don't remember how much I told you last time, but they're gonna get caught and when they do I don't want any part of it. They're all going to be fined or worse, go to jail. These executives have absolutely no ethics."

Knowing Sheila's flair for jumping to conclusions, a trait that most accountants—excepting Sheila—didn't usually harbor, Nachelle stopped herself from being overly concerned before she had all the facts. "Slow down, Sheila. Catch your breath."

Over the last few months, Sheila's calls to her had been growing in frequency, all due to a change in management at the company she worked for. Sheila was the Director of Accounting for Computermation, a major computer company, specializing in computer hardware and located in Reston, Virginia, Sheila's hometown. Sheila had been with Computermation since graduating college, and although she loved her job, she was not happy with the new management who had assumed control two years ago. According to Sheila's disjointed conversations, the new President and Vice President were running the business into the ground and only looking to feather their own beds.

When Nachelle probed her for specific information to support her accusations, Sheila would only say their practices were deceitful and unethical. She had never given Nachelle a full understanding of the situation. So Nachelle did what any good friend would do—just sat and listened. Nachelle didn't expect tonight's conversation would be any different.

"Nachelle, it's just awful! I can't believe they think they're going to get away with this. And, to have the gall to try to include me in their little scheme, why it's ludicrous! I took an oath as a CPA that I would uphold full disclosure. They're asking me to turn my head. Can you believe it?"

"Just what exactly is going on? What are they asking you to do?"

"Lie! They want me to lie and steal. I can't do that!"

Nachelle's patience should have expired minutes ago, but she was used to Sheila's method of starting a conversation in the middle instead of at the beginning like most people. She knew Sheila would eventually get around to telling her what she needed from her besides a sympathetic ear. "How? I don't understand. Are you talking about inventory, cost of goods and services, what?"

"Oh, Nachelle, I wish I could tell you more, but there's no need in getting you involved. I called you to see if you could send me some information. You all have federal contracts, right?"

"Yes, but not many."

"Boy, oh, boy, if I could say the same. We've got tons of them. Being so close to D. C. and all, we get so many federal contracts for repair and maintenance of government computer systems. Speaking of D. C., how's that good-looking brother of yours? Is he ready to get married yet? Tell him I'm still single." Sheila chuckled. "Do you remember that night he took me, you, and Heather out to dinner on Sixth Street? He really had that waitress thinking he was married to all three of us. Remember Heather slipping me one of her diamond rings to put on my finger. Gosh, what a riot."

Nachelle laughed with Sheila. From the sounds of it, even though Sheila appeared to be in deep trouble, she still had time to reminisce and ask about Vincent. Yep, Sheila was a bit of a scatterbrain, but not too much of one not to take notice of a good man. Nachelle replied, "College was a good time. And, Vincent's doing fine. He's still single, so yes, I'll pass the message on to him."

". . . Anyway Nachelle I need federal financial reporting files. I'd like to see the format the Hayes Group uses." In a conspiratorial tone, Sheila continued, "See, I was thinking that if I showed them a different format, they might think it's what they want and that'll get those big boys off my back until I can decide what action to take, do you follow me?"

Honestly, Nachelle didn't, but she let Sheila go on.

"So, can you fax me a copy of a federal report you guys have filed? I promise to keep it confidential."

Happy to finally find out what Sheila needed, Nachelle eagerly wrote herself a reminder note. "Sheila, I have someplace I have to be tonight, so is it okay if I fax it first thing in the morning?"

"Yes. That's fine, but I'd rather you fax it to my home. I don't want them to have a trace of it and since I live so close to work I can run home at lunch and grab it off my machine. Thank you so much, Nachelle. You're a life saver. I'll talk to you later."

Nachelle hung up the phone and finished her note to herself. Determined to get through at least one report tonight, she re-checked her watch and saw thirty minutes had passed. Within the next one and a half hours, she hoped to get a call from the Hayes's saying Harlan had returned . . . and that he wasn't strung out. Nachelle prayed for the best.

Turning back to the front of the report, she started over, determined to give her work her full attention.

Steven, on his way to his office, saw the light spilling from Nachelle's slightly ajar door. It was the only illumination in the dark hallway.

What's she still doing here? It's too dangerous for her to be here this late at night.

Deciding to forgo a knock, he pushed through the door and stopped in his tracks. What he saw made his American male blood sizzle. Nachelle was leaning back in her chair, with her shapely legs crossed at the ankles and propped on the desk.

Her head was thrown back exposing her lovely throat. She was sound asleep.

Desire ignited and spread throughout his body like a fire in the middle of a drought. *My God,* he thought as he walked forward. *I must be in heaven.*

Soundlessly, Steven placed his briefcase in the cloth chair facing her desk. He placed his hands on her desk and leaned forward to drink in his fill. His eyes traveled from the tips of her red-painted toenails, past her full thighs outlined under the camel-colored wool skirt, to the enticing rise and fall of her breasts hidden beneath a cream-colored silk blouse, underneath of which he could just make out the outline of lacy undergarments.

It had been two weeks since he'd propositioned her. Then, he'd been upset that she had unwittingly set his plan back. Now, with some time and new information under his belt, he appreciated her decision, but was angry with himself for not thinking about her feelings.

Since his talk with Dorothy, his interest in the checklist had diminished to a behind the scenes activity. Yes, it still held importance for him, but he knew what was of the utmost importance to him—and that was Nachelle. He'd had all day Sunday to think about her. She was the perfect woman—well-versed in the inner workings of a boardroom, yet feminine, gentle, and loving. He didn't need a checklist to tell him he wanted her physically, emotionally, and mentally. Still, he knew it wasn't a good time to make his true intentions known. First he had to overcome the resistance she'd shown the night he'd propositioned her, then he could show her his true self. Steven took a deep breath. This would be a new experience for him. He always had a plan, was always in control. But with Nachelle, he would have to hand the steering wheel to her.

When his eyes could take no more without touching her, he whispered, "Nachelle."

Nachelle's eyes popped open like a jack-in-the-box. She stopped short of screaming and falling backward in her chair.

Steven was around the desk in a split second with an apology on his lips. "I'm sorry. I didn't mean to scare you." He put out a hand to help her to her feet. "I was on my way to my office and saw that your door was open."

"It's okay. I thought everyone was gone. I . . . How long have you . . . I didn't hear you enter." Nachelle knew she was babbling. Adrenaline pumped through her, making her heart race. She couldn't believe he was there in front of her. He'd just been in her dreams, but she definitely preferred the real thing. Straightening her clothes and patting her hair, she remarked, "I thought you were in Atlanta."

"I was, but the meetings there didn't take as long as I thought. I decided to catch a late flight back tonight."

The word late caught her attention. "Oh, my God!" Nachelle fumbled for her watch; it wasn't on her arm. "What time do you have?" She grabbed Steven's arm and started wrenching his shirt sleeve up. "Oh my. Excuse me, please, for a moment." It was straight up ten o'clock. She hurriedly called the Hayes's house.

"Hi, Ralph, it's me. Any word?"

"No, and we were just about to call you. We've already talked to the police and filed the report. We just need to take them a picture. It's not necessary that you come." Ralph's voice sounded strained.

"Are you sure? It's no bother, really. I can be there in no time." Nachelle's heart ached for the older couple. She knew they were reliving the nightmare of a few years ago. She wanted to be there for them.

"No dear, you've always done our dirty work. Adele and I will handle this one. We realize he is the way he is because of us. We'll call you if anything changes. Goodnight."

Ralph hung up before Nachelle could plead once more. She replaced the receiver, looking thoughtful and worried.

"Nachelle, is everything okay?" Steven moved closer to her. "You look worried. Is Ralph okay?"

"Ralph's fine, but . . ." Nachelle took a deep breath and turned to face Steven. "Steven, did Ralph by chance call you today?"

Steven half-sat on the edge of her desk. A feeling of dread started stirring in his body. It warned him he would not like this conversation. "No, he didn't." Steven looked at the worry lines covering Nachelle's face and her subdued, almost beaten, body language. He had a sudden need for a drink. Combating that urge, he spoke calmly, softly, "This has something to do with the papers, doesn't it?"

Nachelle couldn't maintain eye contact. She dropped her eyes to the financial report she should have been reading. "Yes . . ."

"Harlan's not going to sign them, is he?" Steven's voice, although soft, had taken on a layer of steel.

Meeting his eyes, Nachelle knew she wouldn't be able to hide the truth when the police report hit the airwaves so she decided to come clean and ignore the traitorous feelings surging through her body. *Ralph and Adele will understand,* she told herself. "No, he's missing. No one's seen him since yesterday evening. The Hayes's are on the way to the police station to file a missing person's report."

"I see." Steven eyed her thoroughly, not saying a word. After a while, he stood up and slowly rounded the corner of her desk. With briefcase and coat in hand, he commanded, "Get your coat and purse. Let's go."

Wide-eyed, Nachelle stared at him. She had expected an explosion, she had expected to be fired, she had expected anything except this cool demeanor. She managed to repeat his last word. "Go?"

"Yes, to dinner. I'm hungry, and judging by the look on your face, you need a drink."

Nachelle didn't say a thing. Perplexed by his calmness, she didn't even straighten her desk, rather, she eased into her coat and, after slinging her purse on her shoulder, followed Steven out the door.

Within minutes they were bracing themselves against the cold, stiff winds rushing around the walls of the Hayes Group building. Moments later, she was ensconced in Steven's Lotus.

"Dorrie told me about some Cajun restaurant not too far from here. Can you lead the way?"

"Georgia's, yes." Nachelle thought about the irony of his request. *He would probably hit the roof if he knew that was the same restaurant Harlan and I had lunch at on the original due date for the papers.* Earlier today, she had received the second set of papers from the Legal Department in Atlanta, but now Harlan was missing. If it wasn't one thing, it was another. The whole situation was fraught with irony. Nachelle wanted to cry.

They rode in silence, each deep in thought. Steven was not surprised that Harlan had not signed the papers. There was no way a man would come hundreds of miles for a simply transaction unless he had an ulterior motive. He just wished Nachelle would come clean with him and tell him if Harlan planned an attempt to recapture the Hayes Group. If that were the case, and Steven would bet his life on it, then he had a serious fight on his hands. Of course, that didn't explain Harlan's disappearing act. The lost look on her face and the fear in her eyes were not feigned expressions. There was definitely more to this story. He sincerely liked Ralph and had faith this could still be a win-win for all concerned, but somebody—Ralph, Adele, or Nachelle—was going to have to ante up.

Following Nachelle's instructions, Steven reached the restaurant and pulled into the parking lot. Georgia's was as crowded as usual, but given the late hour, they didn't have to wait for a table.

"Well, well, well. Look who's here for more." Georgia herself greeted them, smiling. She had beautiful honey-colored skin which belied her age and her silver gray hair was pulled tight in a bun. Her Louisiana accent was thick.

"Hi, Georgia." Nachelle returned the greeting. As the "mother" in the community, Georgia made it her business to know everything and everybody. "How are you?"

"Fine, baby, can't you tell?" Georgia put her hands on her hips and laughed. She enjoyed her cooking as much as her patrons, and it showed. "And, who's this pretty man?"

"Aunt Georgia meet Steven DuCloux. Steven, this is Aunt Georgia."

"Oh, you the man bought Ralph's company. Welcome to Fort Worth! Since this is your first time to Georgia's, we'll have to treat you extra nice."

Georgia led them to a small table in one corner of the L-shaped room.

Without preface she rattled off the menu from memory. They made their selections, placing their drink and meal orders. Aunt Georgia smiled, and without writing one thing down, ambled off.

Nachelle surveyed her surroundings, anything to avoid Steven's piercing eyes. She noticed there wasn't a dress code. She saw everything from jeans to sequined evening attire. Upon further inspection, she recognized pictures of Negro baseball teams, fish frys on church grounds, and crab boils by the beach. The lighting in the restaurant was indirect, giving the place a secluded feel. Many couples were on the dance floor, swinging to the rhythms of the band.

A young man in his teens brought them bread, honey butter, and their drinks.

Steven took a swig of beer and leaned forward. The table was large enough for two plates, two glasses, and condiments, but not much else. His action brought him closer to her.

"So, are you going to tell me the real deal or what?"

Steven had been right in her office. She did need the Long Island Iced Tea. She was wound tighter than a ball of string. "I'm sorry, Steven."

"I'm sure it's not your fault. Harlan's a grown man capable

of making and enacting his own decisions. What I want to know is what I can do to get this situation resolved?"

Nachelle stared at him as if he had two horns growing out of his head. "I . . . You want to help?"

"Of course." Steven sat back and took another swallow of beer. "The papers aren't signed and Harlan's missing. *Something* has to be done." He paused to ensure she heard his next words. "I may be difficult to work with at times, but I'm not inhuman. If Ralph and Adele are having a problem, I'd like to help. I like Ralph and have a lot of respect for him. I sense there's a lot more at stake here than just my family's future."

"I didn't think you'd be interested in helping the Hayes's." Nachelle stared into her glass, wondering if she could really trust her boss with the ugly truth.

"Why not?"

Nachelle decided to put some of the truth on the line. "Your reputation for one . . . and your one-track focus on winning for another." Nachelle couldn't be sure, but she thought she saw a flash of hurt cross his face.

Steven finished his beer, signaled for another, and then sunk down in his chair so that he was partially sitting on his spine. The movement caused his long legs to straddle her chair underneath the small table. He leaned one elbow on the table and gave her his sizing up look. "What's my reputation? What have you been hearing?"

She couldn't pull back now. She'd opened this can of worms and now it was up to her to close it. "In the industry, you're referred to as the Silver Shark because you're reputed to be ruthless and heartless when it comes to acquiring and staying in business." Nachelle decided to leave off the attachment to his hair. It wasn't as important as the makeup of his character. "Many people say you deal underhandedly and will stop at nothing, even bribery and hiring key employees from competitors, to win a bid. Many years ago, the Hayes Group was a shoo-in for a multi-million dollar contract. DuCloux Enterprises stepped in and walked away with the deal using an identical, but more refined product. That left a bitter taste in a lot of people's mouths. And, it's been said you give directives that cross legal lines."

"What do *you* think, Nachelle? Do you think I'm capable of those things? Do you think I'm the kind of person who condones that sort of behavior?" Steven held his breath. Her answer held the key to a bright or dark future.

Nachelle met his eyes for the first time since opening the floodgates of truth. She saw within those black depths the need to know, the need for understanding. She responded to that need, honestly, "I think a sore loser started a very vicious lie and it grew as your company grew. I think it's sometimes easier to blame someone else than look internally."

Steven raked a hand over his thick, wavy hair. It wasn't exactly what he wanted to hear, but it at least was a good foundation to build on. "I haven't told anyone, besides my father and Nathaniel, what I'm about to tell you." Steven sat up straight and drank from his refilled glass. His broad shoulders blocked her view of the rest of the restaurant. "When my father was transitioning the controls of the company to me, we were in the middle of a fierce battle with the Hayes Group for Health Management Association's business. It was an international contract worth millions of dollars. And, yes, Du-Cloux walked away with that contract, but it wasn't until months later that even I, as the head of the company, discovered that one of our top level executives had paid one of your employees handsomely for the Hayes Group plans. With those plans, our design team was able to perfect the software and have it customer-presentable by our show date. Believe me as soon as I found out, I fired that man. Unfortunately, the damage had already been done. I felt badly and tried to offer Ralph joint custody of the contract without going into details, but he refused. And, I don't blame him. No man wants another man's crumbs." Steven reflexively smoothed his beard and mustache. "I'm not proud of that piece of history, but I'm glad to say that nothing like that has ever happened again."

Nachelle's heart flip-flopped in delight. She was glad to know the man she was attracted to was not an ogre. Of course, she could have listened to Mike and Heather and Ralph. They had defended Steven's character all along.

He continued, "So, suffice it to say, the rumors weren't totally wrong. And, it's quite easy to believe that's a normal operating procedure at DuCloux if you're not aware of the other 99.9 percent of the time we win contracts because we *are* the best. As for hiring—or stealing talent—as others would call it. Yes, DuCloux aggressively recruits. We want the cream of the crop and if that means we pull from our competitors, then so be it. As a matter of fact, the same design engineer involved in the Hayes-related scandal wound up coming to work for DuCloux. When I found out who he was, I personally terminated him. Despite the fact that he was super-talented, I don't want that type of person associated with DuCloux Enterprises." Steven spread his hands. "As for illegal directives I may have handed down . . . I would rather cut my hand off than jeopardize my company's future by blatantly ignoring the law. I have a whole staff of lawyers who ensure we operate above board. So what else besides my focus on finalizing this deal?"

Nachelle shook her head negatively.

"I do have a single-minded purpose to get this deal finalized. To DuCloux Enterprises, this represents our future. Hell, you've been leading the merger. You know the positioning we've established for the company. With the combined strength of both companies, we're set for an unlimited future. That means more jobs, more community reinvestment, and the opportunity to dictate *what* the future will be. With the Hayes Group's stellar performance in software and the strong focus of DuCloux on peripherals and hardware, we'll be an unstoppable team. This is like a dream come true for us."

"I understand." Watching Steven defend his actions, one could not help but admire his dedication to his goals. Nachelle was swayed by his enthusiastic response.

"Now, getting back to the Hayeses . . . how do we resolve this?"

"I should tell you Harlan doesn't want to sign the papers."

"I figured as much." At Nachelle's surprised look, he continued, "If our situations were reversed, it would kill me to sign away my family's company."

"With Harlan things are a little different." She thought about the contrast between the sons of two strong men. Harlan didn't give a hoot about his family's legacy, and Steven's focus on his family's legacy was paramount. She knew the pressures Ralph put on Harlan to manage the business and eventually lead it, but she imagined Steven's charge was no less easier. So, what then made one man weak and another strong? Nachelle shook her head. She guessed it boiled down to upbringing and a roll of the dice.

The innocuous tasting drink was beginning to give her a slight buzz. She pushed the drink aside. Now, of all times, she needed her senses about her.

Steven asked, "I'm interested in knowing where you stand in all this? How are you truly feeling about this situation?"

Good question, she thought to herself. And, while she had the answer, she wasn't sure that she wanted to share it yet with Steven, not right now when she was still a bundle of raw nerve endings. She was worried about Harlan, worried about Ralph and Adele, and concerned about an ugly past that may be awakening from sleep.

"You can answer that question later. I can only imagine the divided loyalties you must be struggling with. Just know this . . ." Steven pinned her with his serious eyes. "I enjoy having you on my team and think we can take this company far." Steven toyed with the idea of laying his cards on the table and expressing his personal interest in her, but he changed his mind. He didn't want to make another error with her, and although it had not been easy to lay the checklist aside, he was determined to approach her without a hidden agenda when the time was right. "Nachelle, I'd really like for us to be friends. I know I've screwed up in the past, but I'd really appreciate the opportunity to get to know you. I was hoping we could start over again? What do you say? Friends?"

He was truly a chameleon, complicated, unreadable, unpredictable. Recognizing the peace offering he held out to her, she accepted in good faith. With a timid smile, she said, "I'd like that Steven." They shook on it and Nachelle thought she would sprout wings and fly. Even with the uphill battle they faced, she felt good about their new status. She would deal with her attraction to him later. For now, she was happy.

"Good, then if you don't mind, I'd like to get my new friend on the dance floor and relieve a little stress. Join me in the Electric Slide?" Steven stood and held his hand out.

Aunt Georgia walked by with hands full of piled-high plates. "Go on, girl. The boys will be upset if you don't dance to their music. They practice long and hard every day." She grinned and with large hips swaying, walked on.

Steven prodded her. "You heard Aunt Georgia. The boys will be upset."

Nachelle quickly observed the band and the packed dance floor. For just this minute amount of time, she wanted to forget the troubles that would plague her when she returned home. She wanted to be carefree and relaxed for just a sliver of time.

Standing up, she inserted her hand into Steven's and followed him to the crowded dance floor. They easily fell in with the crowd and before long, the music crept into her bones and soul. Her mind relaxed and as she cut a corner step with the group, she met Steven's gaze and smiled. He returned the gesture.

Nachelle felt her heart lift higher and her insides turn to jelly. She noticed how his eyes crinkled at the sides and how his dimples became more pronounced. She liked his smile. It made her want to laugh and laugh and laugh until all the fears, the pain, the uncertainty was exorcised, but she didn't. She merely let the music and the good times carry her away.

Before long, the song ended and the band switched

smoothly to a slow tune. Nachelle attempted to walk off the dance floor, but Steven captured her hand and pulled her to him.

Nachelle went rigid. The childlike mood she'd allowed herself to indulge in vanished as she felt the hard planes of his body closing in on her. He placed one of her hands on his shoulder and took the other in his hand. His body picked up the sensuous beats of the Toni Braxton hit and they began swaying in time to the music.

A sliver of space separated their lean bodies but occasionally the jostling crowd pushed them into each other so that they were pressed—breast to chest, thigh to thigh—together. Nachelle's body heat rose, she could hardly breathe.

"Relax, Nachelle. It's just a dance." His chin rested on top of her head.

His words did little to help her adjust to the feel of him. With a little more imagination it would be too easy to pretend they were a couple in love, sharing the bliss of a slow dance.

At the office, whenever they had accidental physical contact, she always felt a heated reaction that she could only imagine resembled a nuclear meltdown. This touch, this intimate feeling was different. This felt like returning home after a lengthy absence. Or, like the satisfied feeling one got from snuggling under cozy bed covers on a cold winter day. It was comfort and seduction combined. She closed her eyes and let the heady combination of music, sweet lyrics, and Steven's strong heartbeat make way for the precious warmth she experienced being in Steven's arms.

All too soon, Steven pulled away and sought her eyes. "Our food is here." Steven's deep voice sounded thicker.

Nachelle tried to return to earth in time to prevent Steven from seeing the dreamy pleasure in her eyes, but she failed. She would consider the consequences later . . . much later.

With hands clasped, Steven guided her to the table. Nachelle felt like she was floating on a cloud way above earth, watching herself as she started her evening meal. A companionable silence surrounded their table.

"How you like it?" Georgia appeared like the mist, grinning, beefy hands on her hips.

Nachelle nodded her appreciation. A full mouth prevented her from responding.

"It's superb, Georgia. Better than my mama's, but don't tell her I said it."

Georgia walked away laughing, pleased that she had two satisfied customers.

Conversation held at a minimum as they devoured their delicious, filling dinner. They both declined dessert, electing to finish off the evening with coffee instead.

Steven sat back in his chair and stretched his long legs out in front of him. "That was great. Thanks for coming with me."

"I enjoyed it."

"I'd like to meet with Ralph, Adele, and you in the morning if they're up to it. I'll call you after I speak with Ralph."

Nachelle nodded her head in agreement. *He's serious about wanting to help resolve this mess.*

"Are you ready?" Steven asked, as he opened his wallet and laid some bills on the table.

Nachelle allowed Steven to help her into her coat.

Georgia guided them outdoors into the cold night. "Don't be strangers now," she said to them both. She stood outside waving to them as Steven started the Lotus and roared off down the street.

At the downtown parking garage, Steven pulled up to her car. "Thanks again for joining me. That hotel room gets lonely at times, and a person can only eat so many hotel meals regardless of how good the food is."

Smiling, Nachelle agreed, and thanked him for dinner.

Steven got out of his car and escorted her to her own. Unlocking the door and ensuring she was safely inside, he spoke through the open car door.

"I'll call you to make sure you arrived home safely."

Nachelle nodded and shut and locked the car door. Filled with a tingling warmth, she started the motor. She appreciated his protective nature.

She pulled out of her parking space and the Lotus followed her out of the garage. At the deserted downtown side street, they turned in the same direction. Steven's ride was only five minutes away, hers was twenty. She didn't care, she needed the time to sort through the events of the day.

Safely away from Steven's perceptive gaze, she allowed her thoughts to dwell on the evening. Despite a few brief, tense moments, she had enjoyed the ability to really open up to him. She hadn't realized how much she had needed to do that. Some of the tension in her shoulders had eased and she was surprised to discover that she had even managed to put Harlan and his disappearance out of her mind for a short time. Being with Steven in such a harmonious environment made her forget, almost, that she'd sworn to have nothing but a strictly professional relationship with him. Her soul clamored for many repeat evenings without the restrictions she'd so far rigidly enforced.

After tonight, Nachelle knew she would have difficulty seeing him as only a boss. She had eagerly accepted his offer of friendship since it would take the edge off working with him and be more in line with the type of working, productive relationship she'd enjoyed with Ralph. "I should have asked him about his past on day one," she reflected. "It would have cleared up a lot." Of course, the big difference between the two boss-to-employee relationships was the physical attraction she felt for Steven. She recalled the erotic dreams she'd been having about him. Remembering her pledge, she dredged up the painful past with Harlan to remind herself why she needed to keep the friendship strictly that and not cross the line into anything more sizzling. She was amazed that the pain now seemed less significant, the memories dimmer.

* * *

Steven was waiting in her office the next morning when she arrived. "Good morning, Steven."

He turned from the window and watched her deposit her things on her desk. She looked good enough to eat. She wore a one piece, fitted black dress of worsted wool. Two rows of black and gold buttons snaked enticingly from her chest to waist. The dress flared at the waist and ended below the knees. Steven's desire to follow the trail of buttons with his lips and fingers was halted by the remembrance of Dorothy's voice. "Don't push her, court her, show her the Steven we all love." So, instead of Nachelle for breakfast, he turned his thoughts to the meeting with Ralph and Adele at the Hayes's home. And, rightly so, he was more worried after the brief conversation he'd had with Ralph this morning.

"Same to you. Don't get too comfortable." Steven met her on the opposite side of the desk. "We have a meeting with the Hayes's this morning. I'm sure you've heard Harlan has not returned."

"Yes, I know. What time is the meeting?" Nachelle had spoken with Ralph last night. Despite the late hour of her call, he had been wide awake. She could imagine him walking the floor, worried to death. This morning when she called, she had spoken with Adele who confirmed that Harlan was still missing. Nachelle felt badly. She had wanted to believe Harlan had become more responsible, become more mature in his dealings with people, especially with his parents. She only hoped he was safe somewhere and would return home soon.

"Now. Let's go." Steven picked up his things and led her from the room. He was anxious to get over to the Hayes's and get this thing settled.

The drive was completed in relative silence with Nachelle giving directions and Steven following them. They talked sparsely, in generalities, about the weather, the basketball team, Gerald's chances for being named MVP of the league again, safe, harmless subjects that masked the unease in both their minds and hearts.

As had happened only two days ago, Adele met her at the door with a hug and a kiss. Even though she didn't know Steven, she gave him the same greeting. "Come on into the kitchen. I've cooked a big country breakfast and coffee's on the stove." They hung their coats up and followed her single file to the yellow-and-white decorated kitchen. Ralph sat at his usual seat at the table. He looked haggard, dark circles under his eyes proclaimed he hadn't slept a wink.

He rose to shake Steven's hand and hug Nachelle. "Steven, I'm glad you called. Thanks for coming."

"Anytime. I felt like we needed to have a heart-to-heart."

Ralph released his grip on Nachelle and spoke slowly as he recovered his seat. "You're right of course, and I should have been the one to initiate this meeting but . . . well . . ." Ralph stopped and turned to Nachelle who had secured a seat on his left. Steven sat opposite Ralph. "Have you told him anything about the past?"

"No, Ralph. It didn't seem appropriate coming from me. I did tell Steven that Harlan didn't want to sign the papers."

Adele set a turkey-size platter of breakfast foods in the middle of the table. Out of courtesy for her time, they filled their plates, but everyone, including Ralph who usually had a very healthy appetite, only picked at their food.

Ralph ran a hand down his face and toyed with his coffee cup as he launched into a brief but succinct history of Harlan's battle with drugs. He even shared the events leading up to his last stroke and the activity that followed. Oftentimes during his recourse, Ralph and Adele would hold hands as if they were each other's lifeline, and Nachelle supposed after thirty years of marriage, they were. When he wrapped up, the only thing Ralph hadn't covered was the breakup of Harlan and Nachelle's engagement.

"We talked about rescinding your offer." Ralph recaptured his wife's hand. "Harlan had this grandiose plan to not sign the papers, pay you back the money, and then we would resume running the company together. I have to honestly admit that for a moment I was swept up in the dream. The thought of my boy, back and healthy, with an interest in leading the company, it felt good." After squeezing Adele's hand, he raised her hand to his lips and kissed it. "You know, Steven, if it wasn't for this woman I wouldn't be nothing. You've heard the song, he's my rock and my salvation. Well, she's that for me. We talked Sunday night and decided we wanted to enjoy our early retirement." Ralph actually chuckled, "Heck, we were so jealous of Nachelle's parents for being able to pick up and go when they wanted to, not having to deal with meetings and faxes and attorneys and priority mail and competition that I'm surprised I even thought about rejoining the rat race."

"Besides . . ." Ralph turned to Nachelle and squeezed her hand affectionately, ". . . this young lady needs an unencumbered future, free from the harsh past."

"Thanks, Ralph, I appreciate that." Nachelle spoke from the heart.

"So, Steven, now that you know about the skeletons in our closet, if you still want the Hayes Group, I'll stick by my original agreement and somehow get Harlan, when he shows up, to sign those papers."

"Yes, I'm still very interested." Steven's face was carved of granite; it gave nothing away in regards to how he felt about Ralph's story.

"Good, then you go on and do what you've been doing. I'll make sure those papers get signed and back to you."

Nachelle pulled the set of papers she had received from Legal from her briefcase.

Steven spoke in his usual professional tone, "When Harlan returns he can sign these. They read the same as the last set, but, please, read them and get back to me if you have any questions."

Shortly afterwards, Nachelle and Steven left. Thoughts ran

deep on the return drive, the radio playing softly providing the only noise.

Nachelle knew she should make some attempt at conversation, but she just wasn't up to it. Her anxieties surrounding Harlan's disappearance were transforming into anger. And seeing Ralph and Adele again scared to death for their son made her even angrier. *He could at least have the decency to call his parents and tell them that he's shacking up with some bimbo he just met or he's higher than a kite or God willing, that he's okay,* she thought. Anything except this blasted silence and constant flip-flop between worry and anger. Nachelle also knew it had taken a great deal out of Ralph to admit his son's weaknesses. He had had such high expectations for Harlan, but Harlan hadn't been able to meet them. And, to admit that in front of a man who you really didn't know except in terms of a business deal must have been hard. Her heart bled for the couple.

Steven's thoughts were more focused on Nachelle. He trusted Ralph and had no doubt the man would meet his agreement. He was glad Ralph had trusted him enough to be completely honest. He had felt when he had talked to Ralph on the phone earlier this morning that Ralph had more on his mind than an early morning chat, and boy, did he. Now, he had an inkling for the reason Nachelle kept a wall between them. With the hell Harlan put his parents through, he could just imagine what Nachelle had had to endure. *Hell, I wouldn't blame her if she didn't trust another man as long as she lives,* he thought. Even though the story behind Nachelle and Harlan's relationship had been conspicuously left out, he felt Harlan's drug use had a lot to do with Nachelle's desire to keep a shell around her. Now, he felt even worse about the way he'd approached her. Steven continued to berate himself silently, *why couldn't I have been upfront and said to her, "Hey, I like you, I'd like to get to know you better, can we date and see if a long-term commitment can come from this?" But, oh no, I*

*had to follow that checklist to the highest degree. I've got some
ground to make up, but at least I've already started.*

They reached the building and walked in continued silence
until they got to her office. Steven opened the door and followed her in. He knew she needed some time to herself, but
he had to get something off his chest. "Nachelle, I hope you
know I won't repeat anything Ralph told me this morning to
anyone. I appreciate his honesty. It goes a long way towards
understanding."

"Thank you for not pressuring him. I'm so afraid for
Ralph's health, and now with Harlan missing I don't know
what that's going to do to him—to either of them."

"My respect for him just blew through the roof. And Adele
is obviously devoted to Ralph. It's good to see love hail so
strong in such a long-term marriage."

Nachelle smiled. "Yes, they do give you hope for the
world."

Steven looked thoughtfully at Nachelle. "Well, I'll let you
start your day." With his hand on the knob, he turned back to
her, and asked, "If you're free for lunch, I'd like to see you. We
can order lunch in or eat out—whatever you're in the mood for."

Nachelle identified the sincerity in his eyes and realized
something about him was different. Physically he looked the
same, but that granite edge seemed to have melted away.
"Thank you, Steven. I'd like that." She remembered the "different" man she had spoken to on Saturday night and that he'd
asked for her friendship last night. *What change is this that's
come over him,* she wondered. Whatever it was, she liked it.

"Good, then I'll see you around lunchtime."

At the appointed hour, Nachelle walked to Steven's office
and into a pleasant surprise. Steven had arranged for an indoor
picnic.

"Oh, Steven, how wonderful." Her eyes lit up in delight.

Laying in the middle of his floor on a red-and-white-
checked tablecloth was a spread to behold—roast beef with
Kaiser rolls and spicy brown mustard, pasta and potato salad,

a fresh garden salad with romaine lettuce and cherry tomatoes, strawberry shortcake, coffee and tea.

"I decided you'd had enough decisions to make over the past few years, I took this one out of your hands. Kick off your shoes and dig in." Steven had not only shucked his jacket, but also his shoes. His tie was loosened.

That was one command Nachelle had no trouble following. She shed her black designer pumps and plopped down on the cloth. Nachelle fixed her plate and chowed down. During lunch, Steven entertained her with tales about his nieces and nephews. He even pulled out pictures he kept in his briefcase. Nachelle was able to match faces to stories and it was evident that Steven loved kids. They went on to talk about a variety of subjects ranging from the Bosnian war to asbestos, from reincarnation to capital punishment, from the black political agenda to the ozone layer. Nachelle could have sat on his floor for the rest of the afternoon talking to him, but it was not to be. Dorrie interrupted them.

"Steven, Nathaniel's on the line. He says it's extremely important."

While Steven went to retrieve the call, Nachelle packed up their remains and slid into her shoes. The time on her watch told her she should be back at work anyway, two hours had passed. It had been a long time since she had had a two-hour lunch.

Steven reluctantly let her leave. The problem he and Nathaniel were discussing was something which needed all his attention. Fun was over for today, but happily there was always tomorrow.

For the next four weeks, Nachelle spent more time in Steven's company than she had dreamed possible. They attended social affairs as company representatives, they lunched sometimes alone, sometimes with some of the other executives, they even left work early one day to see the newest Spike

Lee movie after they had discovered they were both Spike Lee fans. And, as their time together grew, their comfort and respect for each other grew proportionately.

During that time, they still kept a close ear to any information leading to Harlan's whereabouts. Nachelle maintained daily contact with Adele and Ralph, but still no word. The police in Phoenix had been to Harlan's home several times, but there was no sign of occupancy. According to the local police, the longer his disappearance, the more likely he would not be found alive. But the police could not be certain of anything and nerves were being stretched to the limit. Ralph and Adele were becoming so frazzled that Nachelle's parents had canceled their trip to Florida to come to Fort Worth to stay with their friends. She was extremely glad for Steven's company as he became her diversion from troubled thoughts. He tried hard to keep her mind off Harlan. Nachelle recognized and appreciated his effort.

He'd even become a sounding board for Nachelle to discuss Sheila's job problems. Although the work situation Sheila dealt with was still hazy, she and Sheila had begun to call each other at work every day. It seemed to Nachelle that Sheila just needed a friend to unload on. Sometimes their calls would only last a few seconds, and at other times, the calls would go for thirty minutes or more. Nachelle didn't mind since it seemed to help them both. It gave Sheila the opportunity to vent and release and, for as long as the call lasted, it cleared Nachelle's mind of Harlan and the growing affection she was developing for Steven.

Nachelle's feelings for Steven were growing more precious and entering that territory she had previously walled off. But even while knowing she was playing in a mine field, she couldn't stop. The private section he had closed off initially was an open book to her which made it more difficult to focus on her personal pledge. She knew she needed to step back from him, but he was like an aphrodisiac. She enjoyed his company and he became the friend she leaned on when her problems beat her down.

Once, he had even accompanied her and Heather to one of Gerald's basketball games. After the game, Nachelle had side-stepped Heather's probing questions with noncommittal shrugs, but Heather knew Nachelle as well as she knew herself. Something was up, the signs were glowing like a naked, 100-watt bulb. Nachelle smiled more frequently, she and Steven touched far too casually to be strictly coworkers, and they occasionally communicated without words—a sure sign they were dating according to Heather's books. But, true to her promise to Gerald, she stepped out of Nachelle's business—even though it was killing her.

Steven stuck to his plans to win her first as a friend before pushing her into a serious commitment. He still craved her soft flesh, but the greater need to make her a mate for life won out. He took his time and woke up one day to discover that she had completely snatched his heart.

Twelve

Steven perched on the edge of the couch in the suite of rooms he occupied at the Worthington, rolling an empty hi-ball glass between his hands. In less than an hour, they would be officially retiring Ralph Hayes and for someone who should have been as excited as the Superbowl champs, Steven sat as still as a statue, looking into the bottom of his glass. His mind, usually fully occupied, was even more so tonight. And, as it had been for the past several weeks, the primary thoughts were focused on a certain female vice president who oozed intelligence, femininity, and good character; a woman who exhibited everything he wanted in a mate, but one who was afraid of love. *Doesn't she see I'm not Harlan, that I would never treat our commitment to each other so callously?* Steven was at his wit's end on how to proceed with Nachelle.

He knew he was in love with her but he had no idea how she felt about him. He wanted Nachelle to be Mrs. Steven Du-Cloux. He wanted her to forsake all others and be as devoted to him as he was to her. He wanted to rise in the morning with her in his bed and retire in the evening with her at his side. He wanted them to share the joys and heartache of parenthood together. He had visions of them leading DuCloux Enterprises to Fortune 100 status. *God, I love her so much! If she'd just give me a chance. I know I can make her happy. I would make it my job to treat her like a princess.* Steven groaned and it was only the sound of the elevator bell, announcing someone's arrival, that stopped him from throwing his glass in frustration.

Dorothy DuCloux walked through the open door. "Hi, love. Were you expecting . . ." She stopped both in stride and in speech. Her mouth fell open, and after a stunned moment passed, she rushed forward, a look of concern etching lines in her beautiful mocha-colored face. "What's wrong, Steven? You look awful."

"Thanks, Dorothy. I can always depend on you to tell me the truth," Steven murmured sarcastically.

"And I, you. Now, what's up? You look like you've lost your best friend." Dorothy placed an arm around Steven's waist and guided him back to the couch.

Steven sat down, stretching one arm along the back of the furniture and using the other hand to prop up his head. "I'm lost, Dorothy. I don't know what to do."

"You're kidding. You! Lost!" Dorothy's facial expression changed from concern to disbelief. Ever since she had married into the family ten years ago, she'd only known Steven to be self-assured, focused, and unwavering in his successes. Something must *really* be wrong with him.

At Steven's disgruntled look, she hurriedly explained, while patting his knee, "Honey, you know I'm teasing. I just . . . I've never seen you like this before."

"I've never been in love before." Steven leaned forward,

placing elbows on his knees and cupping his hands under his chin.

"I can't believe it, Steven, you're in love!" Dorothy, his favorite sister-in-law, suddenly changed her worried expression to relief, clapping her hands in glee. "How delightful! I'm so excited!" Dorothy bounced off the couch. "Where's the phone? I wanna call and tell mom."

Steven grabbed her hand before she shot out of reach. "I said, I'm in love, not I'm getting married. There's a difference."

Dorothy looked down and saw that same dejected look on Steven's face. "Okay honey, you're going to have to help me with this one. I'm not following you." Reclaiming her seat beside Steven, she gently placed a comforting hand over one of his.

"She's the one I told you about a while back. You know, Nachelle Oliver, one of the VPs from the Hayes Group."

Dorothy knew exactly who he was talking about. She nodded.

Steven stood up and started wearing out the carpet. "I mean, I knew this woman stirred my blood like no other. Hell, I knew that after the New Year's Eve party. Then, when we started working together closely, spending a lot of time together, I saw other qualities I admired." Steven stopped in front of Dorothy who sat amused, but sympathetic on the sofa. "You know this is all your fault. I was doing just fine with that checklist."

"Seems to me I remember you doing nothing more than offending her with that checklist." Dorothy held up a perfectly manicured hand in a boy scout manner. "But, if it makes you feel better to blame your current love problems on me then by all means do so. I have broad shoulders." Dorothy could no longer contain her laughter. "Oh, this is rich, Steven, just rich. The great Steven DuCloux beaten by love. Gosh, I can't wait to meet her."

Steven smiled a killer smile.

It didn't stop Dorothy from finishing her laugh. "I'm sorry, love. I'm just . . . You caught me totally off guard." Sobering, she stood up and put her arm around his waist. "Tell me more."

"I don't know how Nachelle feels."

"I see."

"She's been hurt in the past, and, well . . . you know what they say . . . once burned, twice shy. Somehow I've got to make her understand how I feel, without scaring her off." Steven opened his hands in a pleading gesture. His frustration was evident.

"Look, I know you didn't ask my opinion, but when has that ever stopped me."

Steven rolled his eyes and said, "Never."

"Right, so from a woman's point of view, let me offer this piece of advice. Lay your cards on the table. Tell her you love her, that you want to marry her, but you understand she's scared. She needs to know you'll help her work through her fears, that you'll be supportive. Talk to her soon, tonight, after the party, if you can." Dorothy inserted her hand into his. "Or, you can just plant a wicked, wet kiss on her lips and if the girl's got any sense, she'll follow you wherever you lead." Dorothy wiped her hands as if she had just finished feeding her kids a snack, then sashayed off to look at some artwork she spied on the walls.

"You know, Dorothy, I don't know why I listen to you. You've gotten me into more trouble . . ."

Dorothy threw a glance over her shoulder. "You'll be thanking me at the wedding reception."

"Yeah, yeah." Steven didn't let Dorothy see his smile. He loved Dorothy and allowed her to say and get away with things most people wouldn't dream of saying or doing to Steven. They had a special relationship that Steven cherished.

Steven checked his watch. "I don't want to rush you after you've been such a big help, but I need to finish dressing before Nachelle gets here."

"No problem," Dorothy said. "I'm going to look around this lovely suite for a few minutes."

Steven started toward the master bedroom, then stopped and turned back to Dorothy. Stooping, he kissed her smooth cheek. "Does my brother know how lucky he is?"

With a precocious smile on her face, Dorothy stated, "Why don't you remind him tonight?"

"Consider it done." Steven squeezed her shoulders, then released her.

The Worthington Hotel loomed ahead. It looked regal and resplendent.

Nachelle smiled, *We couldn't have picked a better place to have Ralph's retirement party. Everything will be wonderful.*

As she pulled her car into a parking space, she couldn't believe it had been ten weeks since Ralph had relegated the reins to Steven.

It's amazing how quickly things change. The thought came with a mixture of melancholy and excitement.

In addition to the multitude of changes at the office, she herself had experienced a turnabout.

No longer did she consider Steven the enemy raider. They'd managed to build a comfortable, complementary working relationship. She'd developed a great deal of respect for his business acumen and high ethical standards. He cared about his employees, but it was also widely observed that DuCloux Enterprises was his baby and as such, always won hands down. On top of it all, he'd proven to be a very trustworthy friend.

Nachelle stepped into the elevator and rode the express to the penthouse. She and Steven had agreed to meet before the party to settle the bills with the hotel manager. She glanced at the slim silver and diamond watch on her wrist.

Right on time.

Her thoughts returned to her most monopolizing subject of late—her and Steven. Somehow, she had let Steven get under her skin. It only took one memo with his signature, the mention of his name by an employee, or one whiff of his cologne lingering in the hallway, to bring him to mind. His attentiveness, concern, and gentlemanly ways had worked to undermine her personal commitment to avoid office romances. She now viewed Steven as a direct threat to her heart.

In the beginning, to remind her she was treading into dangerous territory, she had relied on her memories of her failed relationship with Harlan and the resulting office gossip. But now, when Steven walked into her office, looking supremely confident, she couldn't stop the racing of her heart nor a smile from gracing her face. With no conscious effort on her part, the past had slipped to the back of her mind.

The elevator door parted and pulled her from the past to the present. She stepped into the dimly lit foyer and pulled up short when she spotted a woman standing in the doorway leading to the expansive suite of rooms. Judging by her attire and air of sophistication, Nachelle guessed she was a cultured socialite, someone who had probably never worked a day in her life.

"Please, do come in." The lady smiled and opened the door wide, gesturing for Nachelle to enter. "I've been dying to meet you." Her drawl was more pronounced than Steven's, and it made Nachelle think immediately of Georgia peaches.

Nachelle entered the room, looking at the lady speculatively. She knew the hotel manager was a man, so who was this woman? And, why was she so comfortable in Steven's rooms? She was certainly beautiful, and had a crown of hair that Nachelle had always wanted—thick and mink brown.

From an interior room, Steven bellowed, "Dorothy, come tie this blasted thing."

The lady named Dorothy grimaced and remarked, "He's such a bully. I don't know how you stand him." She yelled back. "Handle it yourself, big boy. I'm entertaining." Turning to Nachelle, she held out her hand. "I'm Dorothy DuCloux, Steven's sister-in-law, and one of the many family members you'll meet tonight."

Relief washed over Nachelle like a brush on canvas. She was glad to know the other lady wasn't Steven's date. "It's nice to meet you, Dorothy." She sincerely meant what she said. Her greatest fear about tonight was meeting Steven's family, especially Adolphus, the patriarch of the DuCloux clan.

Steven entered the room, fighting his satin bow tie. His silver and black head was bent and a frown darkened his face. "This damn thing is broken." He looked up from fidgeting with the frustrating slip of fabric and stopped dead in his tracks. Once-busy hands fell to his side.

"Nachelle." He walked forward. His eyes, as slow and penetrating as his steps, traveled the length of her body which was encased in a form-fitting, red and silver-sequined, floor-length dress with a thigh-high side slit. "You look . . ." He stopped, unable to think, act, or talk.

Nachelle's heart lifted at Steven's obvious approval. She admitted she'd bought the dress with Steven at the front of her mind. It had been a wild and reckless choice, but seeing the look on Steven's face, she was glad she'd decided to wear it.

"Wonderful, absolutely wonderful." Dorothy completed Steven's sentence. "While he finishes gaping, let me tell you that I'm available tonight if you need help with anything."

"Thank you. I appreciate the offer."

Dorothy patted Nachelle's arm. "I think he's finally coming to, so I'll leave now and go check on my own man. I'm sure you can handle it from here." With a friendly, Miss America wave, she left.

Steven cleared his throat. "I'm sorry. I didn't mean to stare." He could have kicked himself for being so obvious! It was very important to him that Nachelle feel comfortable around him, trust him. A stupid mistake, like the one he'd just made, could set her running.

He rushed on in an effort to regain control of the situation and his hormones. "The hotel manager already dropped the statements off."

Steven walked to the desk situated by the open French

doors. The white, sheer curtains on the doors billowed inward in response to the premature winds of spring. He opened a manila folder and stated, "I've already signed. They just need your signature."

Nachelle followed him to the desk and sat down. There was no need for her to review every charge; however, there *was a great need for her to compose herself.* The figures gave her the time and opportunity to do so.

Steven moved away. The more space he put between them, the greater his chances of staying focused on his and Dorothy's plan to lay it on the line. Already, without even touching her, the blood was rushing to every potent part of his body.

Finally, Nachelle signed the statements and stood. "I'll have Accounts Payable cut a check on Monday."

"Fine. Leave them here and you can pick them up after the party." Although his eyes wanted to roam freely over her seductively clad body, Steven forced himself to meet her eyes. "Are you ready to go down?"

"I am, but you're not." Nachelle walked to Steven. When she was face to face, she reached up to knot his bow tie. "When I was in high school, I always tied my Dad's ties. It was our special time together in the morning."

Steven was incapable of responding. He stood rigid and tall, trying not to inhale her scent or focus on her red-colored lips which were pursed ever so slightly as she concentrated on the tie. He rammed his hands in his pockets to keep from pulling her to him. He summoned all of his self-control and endured the temptation she posed. Thankfully, the tie cooperated this time.

"There. Go see if you like it."

"I'm sure it's fine." Steven didn't want to do anything except get down to a crowd of people as soon as possible. "Let's go," he stated gruffly.

Nachelle preceded Steven to the elevator. He had hoped the short walk to the elevator would allow him enough time to regroup. Unfortunately, he soon realized the sight of Nachelle from the back was no less exciting than the front.

Her rear view is sweeter than divinity. I'd better watch myself. It's going to be hard to remember I'm practicing a hands-off policy—at least until after we talk.

He was still somewhat dazed and surprised about his feelings for Nachelle. It had not been easy to admit that his professional agenda to acquire a suitable, criteria-driven "partner" had been usurped by the personal affections he'd developed for Nachelle. He was in love with his bewitching and aloof vice president.

His first waking thoughts were of her. And, when he slept, he dreamt about the minutes they'd spent together. His consuming infatuation intruded on his work hours. He would find his attention span wavering and finally disintegrating whenever they happened to be in meetings together or if he caught a glimpse of her in the hallway or heard her voice.

The validation of his love and affection for the brown-skinned beauty came when he'd tried to call Nachelle at home one evening and had been unable to reach her until after midnight. He'd had to stop himself from demanding where she'd been and with whom. He'd felt a degree of jealousy that he'd never experienced before . . . and he hadn't liked it. He knew then he was down for the count; he loved Nachelle and he didn't need a criterion list to tell him she was the woman for him. Fear of her reaction to his feelings had kept him from approaching her, but Dorothy's comments had made sense. He would just have to prove to Nachelle that his love for her would help her overcome her fear of involvement.

Nothing ventured, nothing gained. Steven quoted the familiar cliché and aimed to do just that—venture into Nachelle's world.

The elevator door opened and side by side, they walked to the grand ballroom. A small group of employees, community members, and dignitaries had already arrived. Dorrie and Millie were running around with small clipboards checking and double-checking the minute details. Nachelle and Steven split up to assist the secretaries, greet the guests, and generally mingle.

At the appointed hour, the ballroom was filled with well-wishers waiting for Ralph's arrival. The lights were doused and silence descended. Moments later, Ralph and Adele, escorted by Ray and Sharlet Oliver, entered the room and a chorus of "For He's a Jolly Good Fellow" broke out. The look of rapture on Ralph's face was worth the long hours of planning. The party was under way!

For the first hour, Nachelle concentrated on playing the perfect hostess. She circulated, mingled, and ensured the supply of food, drink, and music remained plentiful. During one of her trips to the stage where a band played a variety of hits, she was stopped by an older lady who had familiar-looking features.

"Are you Nachelle Oliver?" The lady spoke with a Southern drawl. Nachelle knew instinctively she was looking at Steven's mother. Her stomach dipped and twisted like it was on a roller-coaster.

"Yes, ma'am. I am."

"I'm Nadine DuCloux, Steven's mother. If you have a few minutes, I'd like to introduce you to his family." Nadine turned and led Nachelle to a group of ten people sitting around a table. Nachelle scanned the table and recognized only two of the people. Nathaniel Johnson was seated next to a man who was an older version of Steven, and Dorothy was seated two seats away from Nathaniel. She winked when Nachelle met her eyes, and Nachelle felt some of her nervousness ease.

Nadine performed the introductions, and if Nachelle's life had depended on repeating the names of Steven's brothers and sisters-in-law, she would have quit breathing that night.

With introductions out of the way, Adolphus DuCloux spoke, "Nathaniel tells me the merger is going slowly. Why is that?" His rock-hard, intense black eyes, so similar to Steven's, unnerved her. She looked at Nathaniel and thought she saw a wicked grin before he replaced it with a bland expression. "You do realize we have millions of dollars tied to this venture?"

Heavy hands descended on her shoulders. Nachelle knew,

without turning her head, that Steven was the owner of those hands. She could feel her body responding to his contact.

"Dad, I hope you're not talking business." Steven spoke, beating Nachelle out of the opportunity.

"I was merely asking a question."

"A question that can no doubt wait until Monday." Steven removed his hands from Nachelle's shoulders and moved to stand by her side. He kept one hand on the small of her back.

"Nathaniel, I expect you to keep Dad focused on having fun, okay?"

Nathaniel politely nodded his head, but didn't speak.

Steven turned to Nachelle. "If you're ready, we should start the program."

Nachelle was thankful for Steven's intervention. She knew she could have handled both men, but not as pleasantly as Steven had. It was obvious Nathaniel had not been kind to her or her work performance in his reports to Adolphus.

"It was nice meeting you." Nachelle manufactured a smile. "Mr. DuCloux, I'll be happy to meet with you Monday, if you would like." She turned and joined Steven on the raised dais in the front of the room.

Shortly afterward, she and Steven kicked off the program recognizing one of Fort Worth's pioneers in commerce.

Two hours later, with Ralph juggling an armload of gifts and fighting back tears, the formal part of the evening ended. Ralph took his seat at the VIP table, along with Adolphus and Nadine DuCloux, the mayor of Fort Worth and her guest, Ray and Sharlet Oliver, Adele, Steven, and Nachelle. The partying then began in earnest.

Steven performed his gentlemanly duties, but not expertly enough. Although he enjoyed dancing with the other ladies at the table, it was Nachelle he wanted in his arms. So far, she'd spent the better part of the evening in the arms of various older men.

During one dance, as Steven twirled Adele around the dance floor, she provided him with the opening he needed.

"Do you mind if I dance with my husband?" Adele looked up at Steven.

Steven glanced around the dance floor and spotted Ralph and Nachelle dancing. His smile was genuine when he replied, "Don't mind at all."

He guided them to the couple. Adele left his strong arms and placed a stopping hand on Ralph and Nachelle's waists. Steven positioned himself out of Nachelle's view, as silent and watchful as a sentinel.

"Ralph, dance with me." Adele delicately demanded of her husband.

Two pairs of shining eyes turned in Adele's direction.

"Of course, honey. I'd love to." Ralph relinquished his hold on Nachelle and his smile broadened when he realized to whom he'd relinquished Nachelle. After a nod to Steven, Ralph pulled his wife into his arms and whisked her off.

Nachelle watched as the husband and wife team, smiling deep into each other's eyes, drifted off.

She sighed and wondered if she'd ever be as happy as Adele and Ralph were that night. Adele literally beamed knowing her husband no longer had the stress of running a multi-million dollar company and Ralph was floored at the respect and admiration heaped on him.

"Seems we're left without dance partners." Steven bent and whispered in Nachelle's ear, reminding her that she stood in the middle of the dance floor with a huge smile on her face.

Nachelle turned to face him and was again rendered breathless at how devastatingly handsome he looked. Sexuality oozed from him, making her susceptible to his deep voice, his physical touches, the smoldering promises hidden in the depth of his sexy eyes. She wondered, looking at him, how she had ever likened him to a shark. He was a man to be reckoned with sure enough, but he was also one of the most caring, intelligent, and honest men she'd ever met. At Steven's guiding insistence, she found herself pulled into his arms. The feel of him pressed against her was enough to rob her of her speech. She simply succumbed to his moves mindlessly, relishing the heavenly feeling of being in his arms.

"Have I told you you look very beautiful tonight?" Steven's breath fell softly on her temple, arousing the fine tendrils there.

"Yes. Several times."

"You don't mind if I say it again, do you?" His voice was low and sensuous, causing ripples of sensation along her spine.

"I don't know any woman who gets tired of hearing compliments." Despite her best intentions to stay uninvolved, Nachelle found herself hanging onto Steven's every word and move. She knew she shouldn't play with fire, but for just once, she wanted to imagine what Ralph and Adele, what her parents felt for each other.

Steven shifted his head so that his spoken words caressed her ears. "You are the most beautiful woman here tonight."

Nachelle couldn't stop the trembles that coursed through her body. She knew that Steven must be feeling her reaction to his words, but there was nothing she could do to stop it.

Nachelle lifted her head and met his eyes. "Thank you," she whispered.

A look of desire flamed in his coal black eyes. His hand tightened on her back, pulling her closer still. When she felt a responding tremor shake his body and seconds later felt the overwhelming, unmistakable evidence of his desire, she knew the power of her womanhood.

"We have to talk. Tonight." Steven's tone was deep and husky.

Applause, directed at the band, disrupted the sensual mood that the slow dance had created. Reluctantly, slowly, Steven relaxed his physical grip on her, but the connection between soul, mind, and body was still intact.

Nachelle nodded, wrapped up in their corresponding feelings.

They came apart and followed the other couples off the floor.

For the rest of the night, duty prevented them from seeking each other's arms, although the need for both of them was suffocatingly great.

Three hours later, a tired but happy crowd of people began drifting to the front lobby, bidding final farewells to Ralph and Adele as they departed.

Finally, with all their guests gone, Adele, Ray, and Sharlet gathered their things to leave. Steven and Ralph were absently huddled somewhere together.

Sharlet Oliver, a caramel-colored woman with strong features and long, baby-fine hair like her daughter's, cupped her daughter's face in her hands. "Everything was beautiful, Nachelle." She lowered her voice and whispered in her daughter's ear. "Ralph needed this. He needed the mental break from worrying about Harlan."

Adele piped in, "Yes, Nachelle. The party was lovely." A dark shadow crossed her face. "I just wish Harlan had been . . . well, that he was here." Sharlet placed a supportive arm around Adele.

Nachelle's father spoke up. "Are you going to be here much longer? They're expecting a storm to blow through town around 3:00 a.m." Even retired, her father, a tall man with chiseled features and dark chocolate skin, which his children had inherited, kept track of weather conditions. Paying off hail, tornado, and other natural disaster claims had been a part of his life for too many years to stop noticing. "With that skimpy outfit, you don't want to get caught in the storm."

Nachelle chuckled at the typical fatherly statement. The other women clucked.

"Thank you for your concern Daddy. I'm just staying long enough to ensure everything's wrapped up."

"Well, I hope that's not too long, dear, you need your rest." Adele reached up and patted Nachelle on the cheek.

Nachelle placed a kiss on Adele's wrinkle-free cheek.

"Thank you, Adele. You know I think the world of you and Ralph."

Ralph, laughing and looking twenty years younger, joined them in time to hear Nachelle's last remark. Steven trailed behind the man of honor.

"And we feel the same way about you." Emotionally and physically exhausted, Ralph was ready to leave. "Thank you, dear, for arranging everything. We'll see you two for dinner tomorrow, right?" Adele was hosting a big after church dinner for the DuCloux family at the Hayes's house. It was their way of saying thanks.

Steven and Nachelle's eyes collided in a heated exchange. Nachelle felt her body throb in desire. Although she loved her parents and the Hayes's, she wished them gone so she and Steven could talk.

Simultaneously, they both answered Adele. "Yes, 2:00 sharp."

Adele looped her arm through Ralph's, leading him to the door. "I'm really tired, Ralph. Let's go." Steven fell in step beside the couple and the threesome left the ballroom. Nachelle hugged and kissed her parents and they too followed the retiring couple.

Humming a song from the party, she walked around the ballroom thinking about the direction in which Fate led her human charges. Satisfied that no one had left any personal belongings, she backed out of the room and into the hotel manager.

"Oh, sorry."

"Mr. DuCloux asked me to give you this."

Nachelle took the envelope and opened it. She saw the pass key to his suite and a note which read: *Please meet me upstairs.*

Nachelle faltered for a second, then remembered the passion-filled dance they'd shared and the promise of a private conversation. She entered the penthouse elevator and pushed the button for the suite.

I can handle this, she thought bravely as the elevator whisked her upward.

She entered the elegant suite and not seeing Steven, figured he was detained downstairs. She walked around, touching, but not really seeing the beautiful artifacts that graced the walls and furniture. She remembered that weeks earlier, she had spent time alone with Steven, late at night, in this very room. Their relationship had evolved quite a lot since then—she just wasn't sure to what level. She wondered if that was what Steven wanted to talk to her about. Had she read his expression correctly while she danced so responsively in his arms? Was Steven interested in a personal relationship, and if so, was she willing or ready to be involved at that level?

Steven's arrival into the room stopped the tide of thoughts. Her body acted like a metal detector, able to hone in on his very presence. With critical eyes, she searched his face for a clue to his mood or thoughts.

"Thanks for staying. Would you like a drink?"

"No, thanks."

Steven poured a whiskey for himself and took a seat on the couch. "Come here." He patted a cushion next to him in invitation.

Nachelle replaced the crystal figurine she'd been holding and joined him on the couch. Steven shifted so that barely three inches separated them.

"I asked you up here because I want to talk about the future, our future." Steven took one drink from the high-ball and placed the glass on the coffee table. "I don't know the details of yours and Harlan's relationship, but I figure with his drug use it must not have been a very fulfilling experience for you."

Nachelle nodded, unable to speak or break eye contact with Steven.

"I know this is going to be difficult for you. You've been through a lot in the name of love. But, I . . ." Steven paused, his voice softened and poured like melted butter over her heart and mind. "Nachelle, I need for you to trust me. Trust us."

Nachelle was mute. A jumbled mass of thoughts, feelings, and emotions crowded her mind, impeding her ability to connect thoughts to speech.

Steven trailed a teasing finger down one side of her face. His eyes dropped to her parted lips. Unknowingly, they sent a message her voice couldn't.

"I can't deny this any longer." Steven spoke in a whisper. He framed her face in his hands and placed his lips softly on hers. With his tongue he traced the outline of her lips and then quickly darted his tongue into her mouth, then out. Nachelle trembled from head to toe and covered his hands with her own.

"Steven," she whispered. Nachelle could no more stop what was happening than she could stop a freight train. The trusting, enamored feeling she had for him was rooted in her heart. Because of that feeling, she wanted to share with Steven her most precious gift—herself.

"I know," he said.

With those final words, he began to fulfill both of their desires.

The kiss started as a slow exploration. They nipped, teased, and touched until the heated core in the pits of their stomachs demanded more. Then, as the vibrant display of fireworks grew in intensity, Nachelle opened her mouth to fully receive his kiss. He willingly, eagerly accepted her invitation. A sweetness she'd never experienced filled her head, body, mind, and soul. She knew she would never be the same.

As the kiss deepened, Steven gathered Nachelle to his chest. The action gave him further access to her mouth.

She gave, he took; he gave, she took, until they trembled violently in each other's arms. Moaning, Steven tore his mouth from hers to trail tiny, moist kisses down her throat and to the scooped neckline of her dress. He followed up with small kisses placed here and there on her face. Finally, no longer able to stand their separation, he reclaimed her full lips for another mind-altering kiss.

Blood thundered in Nachelle's ears. She ached to get closer
to Steven. Both of her hands slid between their torsos and
moved up and over his shoulders. His jacket came off easily.
Before she could start on the buttons of his shirt, Steven surprised and pleased her by running a caressing hand under the
thigh-high slit in her dress. She gasped and dug her nails into
his shoulders.

Steven whispered into her mouth, "I've wanted this for so
long, Nachelle. God, how I adore you." He stood up to discard
his cummerbund, tie and shoes. He never broke eye contact.
Disheveled, she was equally appealing.

"I'm going to enjoy making love to you, Nachelle." He
stooped and picked her up, sitting her on his lap as if she
weighed no more than a feather. Before his head dipped to
claim her lips yet again, his eyes searched hers for any contrary sign of what they were about to do. Seeing none, he
visually caressed her from head to toe then took her mouth
in a kiss that promised a lifetime of love. She returned his
promise kiss for kiss, glorying in the hardness of his shoulders, his chest, his arms. Her need to be one with him consumed her.

Laying her back on the sofa, Steven stretched his body half
over her, kissing her neck, throat, tracing the outline of her
ear, nibbling at her lobes, while his fingers played gently with
the nipples pressing against her sequined gown. Their passion
exploded until any barrier between them became too restric-
tive.

Steven rolled Nachelle onto her stomach with her body
between his heavily muscled legs. He leaned forward and un-
zipped her dress. His tongue followed the zipper, trailing her
spine, nipping her shoulder blades, and leaving her squirming
in ecstasy.

The dress slid from her body to his hand to the floor. He
then slid his hands into the waistband of her pantyhose and
pulled them down. His tongue caressed where nylon once
was.

Nachelle rolled over, unable to stand his assault, ready for their complete joining. She lay in her scant undergarments before Steven. The pins in her hair had long since been lost and her curls fell in tantalizing spirals.

"So beautiful." Steven touched, kissed her where his eyes feasted—legs, arms, stomach, face, hair.

His caresses were driving her over the edge. "Now, Steven, now," she pleaded.

Steven shed his garments faster than an eye blink and brought her to him. Passionately, their lips met and clung as if they were breathing life into each other.

"Nachelle," Steven breathed. "I can't tell you the number of times I've dreamed of this."

He covered her face and throat with kisses. Moving downward, he unclasped her lacy bra and, with his tongue, circled and captured the erect point of her breast. His hand gently cupped and caressed the other soft mound.

Nachelle arched upward and her hands tangled in his thick, wavy hair. Her breath was ragged and she saw black-and-white psychedelic designs behind her closed eyes. She never knew pleasure could cause a person to totter on the edge of consciousness.

Steven released his captivating hold and burned a path to her stomach. Long, shocking sensations shot outward from her core when he traveled lower still to the edge of her wispy panties. His breath, hot and sweet, teased her core. With deft hands, he removed the last article of clothing separating them and touched her intimately. She writhed and trembled in satisfying pleasure. Steven drove his finger deeper and deeper until she was sure she would splinter into a thousand pieces.

It was Nachelle who pulled him upward. He continued the assault on her fevered body by taking full possession of her lips, her tongue, her mouth. Just when she thought she could take no more, Steven made them one.

He entered her, slowly moving in, then out, in long, smooth

strokes. Nachelle cried out and held on for dear life. Together they moved in an age-old rhythm.

Steven covered her mouth hungrily, taking kisses as if he was a starved man. Her name, intermingled with his own, resounded throughout the room.

Slowly, together, they traveled to the pinnacle of joy, and once there, culminated their journey simultaneously with a long, deep release. Their hot, moist bodies trembled and their jagged breaths mixed in the heated air, their names spewed from their throats and reverberated off the walls.

The return to earth was slow. Neither was willing to release the pleasure each had given. Finally, the need to know drove Steven to lift his head and search Nachelle's eyes. No regrets, no sadness was found. He kissed her thoroughly and laid beside her, pulling her limp body into his arms.

Neither was willing to disrupt their tenured hold with words; their bodies had already done the communicating.

Thirteen

The sound of deep, steady breathing penetrated Nachelle's senses, and woke her from a peaceful sleep. Her eyes opened and as she focused on the handsome face sharing her pillow, memories of the previous night swiftly returned.

She and Steven had shared a night of love that had fulfilled her like nothing else she'd ever experienced. Several times throughout the night, Steven had awakened her, and each time it had been worth the lost sleep. She vaguely remembered him carrying her into the bedroom after one of their interludes. This morning, she felt vibrant, very alive and so very satisfied.

Nachelle stirred with the intention of easing out of the bed. Steven's arm, thrown haphazardly around her waist, tightened, holding her in place.

Groggily, he asked, "Where're you going?"

"To the bathroom," she whispered.

"Hurry back. I'm not through with you."

Nachelle smiled and scurried out of bed to attend to her morning routine.

The bathroom in the master suite of the penthouse was larger than Nachelle's living room and kitchen combined. The entire room gleamed like a freshly waxed floor and smelt faintly of Steven's male scent.

Nachelle turned on the taps and lathered her face. Even the insignificant actions made muscles she hadn't used in a while moan in protest.

Standing tall, she looked at her reflection as her soapy fingers coated her face. Her thoughts returned to Steven who waited for her in the next room.

They had just moved their relationship to another level, a place she never dreamed possible, but where would it take them? The merger plans were zipping along faster than they had anticipated. In another three months all would be finalized and what would happen to her then? Steven had not discussed any future plans, leaving her to assume she would be looking for employment within a couple of months.

Nachelle stooped and vigorously rinsed the soap off her face. *I can't begin to imagine a future without Steven,* she thought. She had come to depend on him more than Heather or even her own mother. Nachelle stood up quickly as the truth hit her. She was in love with Steven. She loved being near him, loved the attention and respect he gave her, and hated the idea of ever separating from him. It was also clear to her now why she had not been able to uphold her personal pledge. Steven had gotten beneath her skin and now possessed her heart. A moan of confusion exited her body as she slid onto the bath bench. She was happy, and yet she was sad too.

I'm not ready to announce to the world that we're more than co-workers. What if Steven doesn't want to plan our personal future just like he's not making commitments for the future at work? What if Steven doesn't feel the same way about

*me as I feel for him? Not once last night did he say he loved
me. Neither did you say it, Nachelle,* her inner voice taunted.
Questions and thoughts circled around her mind, waiting for
a place to land, leaving room for the old doubts and insecurities from her previous office affair to creep up. A feeling of
déjà-vu seduced her and an invisible hand squeezed her heart
as the full implications of her actions from the previous night
dawned. Her heart sank to her toes.

A sudden desire to speak to Steven about her fears and the
future assaulted her. Putting actions to her thoughts, she patted
her face dry, quickly brushed her teeth using an extra toothbrush, took a speedy shower, and wrapped a huge terry robe
around her.

The first thing she noticed upon entering the bedroom was
that Steven was not in bed. After a quick scan of the room,
she realized he was nowhere to be seen.

*At least I don't have to deal with the temptation of jumping
into bed with him,* she thought with relief. *His potent lovemaking can easily make me lose my mind and it's more important that we talk.*

A wave of aromas—the smell of coffee, bacon, and fresh
pastries—gave her a hint of where he might be. Her mouth
watered as she followed her nose to the living room where a
breakfast buffet was laid out on the glass-topped table in the
small alcove near the patio doors. Steven was already seated
at the table, reading the newspaper.

The rustle of her robe tipped him off to her presence. He
looked up and smiled. "Good morning, beautiful."

Nachelle felt a sense of calm flow through her. Everything
was going to be alright as long as he continued to smile at her
like that.

"Good morning," she returned with an answering smile of
her own. She noticed that he'd taken advantage of the other
bathroom. Water droplets still glistened in his silver hair.

Steven helped her into a chair and poured a cup of coffee.

He placed the cup in front of her and planted a kiss on the top of her head.

"As badly as I want to make love to you, I think we first need to finish that talk we started last night."

"You must be a mind reader." Past ghosts or not, she was happy. It felt good being with him, uninhibited.

"No, I'm not, but I do want you to be happy." Steven reached across the table and framed her face. He drew her near and they shared a tender kiss that made its own promises, and that set her pulses tripping. She was on the brink of booting their talk to hell when he withdrew.

"That'll have to last us until we've settled some things." Steven leaned back in his chair and prayed for self-control. He had intentionally gotten out of bed so they could plan their future. And if they had a future, he had to know where she stood emotionally and mentally. It was important to him that she understand what he wanted from her and that he learn what she needed, expected.

Nachelle was glad she was seated, otherwise his combination of virility and affection would have knocked her cold off her feet. It was bad enough that that one kiss already had her passions stoked.

Steven speared a bite of cantaloupe and fed it to her. "Last night was wonderful, Nachelle. I don't think there's any doubt that we don't appreciate each other's body . . ." Steven put his fork down and enclosed both of her hands in his own. ". . . but it goes deeper than that for me. I think I fell in love with you the moment I met you on paper. Your intelligence, your work performance, your loyalty to the Hayes Group, everything about you seemed to jump off the page and scream: here I am. Your search for love is over."

Nachelle's mind went numb. She couldn't believe Steven had actually spoken words of love. Disjointedly, she parroted his words. "You're in love with me?"

"Yes. Oh, yes." Steven kissed her fingertips and continued. "At first I was hard-headed and refused to believe that true love could happen without the aid of a checksheet." At Nachelle's confused look, he explained in detail about the history and reason for the checklist. They both laughed when Steven explained he had been following the checklist when he first asked her to go to bed with him.

Nachelle shook her head slowly, smiling. She indeed remembered that night Steven had proposed a night of passion to her. It dawned on her that the following work day he'd handled the situation like a business transaction. Ironically enough, his proposal was the catalyst that moved her from thinking of Steven as a cardboard cutout to a real, flesh and blood man with the power to stir her blood.

"I'm truly sorry about that, honey." Steven kissed the palms of her hands and continued, "Then, Harlan returned. I almost hit the roof the night I saw you with him at Drake's. I didn't care about him forgetting those blasted papers! I could easily have killed him for kissing you."

Nachelle smiled. "You had nothing to worry about. By that time, I was already under your spell."

"Good, I'm glad to hear that because if any man ever kisses you again, I won't be responsible for my actions." A dark look crossed Steven's face. In the past, Nachelle would have winced at that look. Today, it was just the fierce look of a man who was serious about protecting his own. It made Nachelle glow as if she'd swallowed the sun.

Getting back on track, Steven spoke, "My sister-in-law, Dorothy, the lady you met last night, helped me realize that I was miserable because I was putting too much stock in that checklist and not enough into the natural attraction we felt for each other. I realized I was in love with you and wanted you to be my wife. No rating on a list could reverse the decision my heart had already made." Steven paused, searching her face. "What's wrong, Nachelle? Please tell me those are happy tears." He was worried that he had frightened her or assumed too much regarding their new relationship.

Nachelle swiped at the tears cascading down her cheeks. "Oh, Steven. I never thought I could feel this good, this alive again." It was slowly piercing Nachelle's senses that happiness *was* within reach. She vaguely listened to Steven, but who could hear over the sweet song her heartstrings were playing? "I never thought I would hear those loving words again. I'm so happy." She half-stood and half-leaned over the small round table to wrap her arms around his neck. She kissed him tenderly and then pulled back.

Steven smiled and kissed her lightly on either side of her mouth. "From now on, those are the only tears I ever want you to shed—tears of joy."

She rewarded him with a deep, passionate kiss.

Steven moaned. Eager to be physically close to her, he stood up and inched around the two-person table. Bodies pressed close, they delved into each other's soul with their lips, tongues, and hands.

Holding her tight, Steven whispered in her hair. "Does this mean you love me?"

"More than you know," she whispered back against his lips.

They shared a long, satisfying kiss.

"Baby, you're testing my self-control."

Nachelle smiled and rubbed their noses together. "You're right, of course. There is more we need to discuss."

Steven took her hand and led her to the sofa. He sat down and cradled her sideways in his lap. "So what do we do now? Do we tell our family, friends, the staff we're in love and plan to marry?"

At the mention of the word staff, Nachelle thumped down to earth and let the rest of Steven's comments float by without comprehension. That same uncomfortable feeling she'd had in the bathroom returned. She looked deep into Steven's open, honest eyes and was encouraged by what she saw. Sighing deeply, she stated, "Steven, please understand I am so very happy right now, but . . ." Nachelle stopped. How would

Steven react when he heard the full truth of the aftermath with Harlan? If she wanted the happy future he painted, she had to take the plunge and share all the details of her past.

Steven squeezed her and coaxed her to go on. "I'm here for you, baby."

"I know Ralph shared some of the difficulty we went through because of Harlan's addiction, but what he didn't tell you was the rigorous trials Harlan put me through. Compared to the ugliness I endured at the office during and after Harlan's disappearance, I got over Harlan relatively easy." Nachelle made to get up but Steven's viselike grip kept her locked in place. She looked at him and seeing his silent encouragement gave him a half-smile. "There were a lot of lies created and perpetrated against me at the office by people whose trust I thought I had earned. They turned on me because they thought *I* had destroyed the Hayes's seemingly happy home. They accused me of sleeping with Ralph, supplying Harlan with the drugs to string him out so I could get his job, they even said I was after the Hayes's money and wouldn't stop until I owned the company. All of these lies and more I had to combat and live through. Productivity fell, morale was awful, for the first time in a long time the Hayes Group posted a loss. I didn't know how to pull the troops back together to concentrate on business. And, as if that wasn't enough, I was worried about Ralph. His condition wasn't improving and the doctors weren't positive he'd recover. Then, there was the police. I had to stay in touch with them about Harlan's whereabouts. It was too much, I was on the verge of cracking up. I even had to leave town and go to Vegas for a week just to clear my head."

"Vegas?"

Nachelle laughed, "Yes, Vegas . . . the strip, no less. For me, it's the best town for getting back on track. I mean, it's kind of sick, but being around people who had more problems than me really helped me to focus on the fact that it wasn't the end of the world. I met people there who were using their last dollar to try and hit the jackpot. They had no way back home, no money for food or other resources. Facing that type of adversity compared to my problems really helped me re-group. Plus, I was lucky. I had good friends and family who were there for me. I'm sharing this with you so you can understand I need some time to get used to this love affair. I mean . . . we work together and I just don't want to deal with any more rumors and lies."

Nachelle didn't realize until she was through with her monologue that she had gripped the lapels of Steven's robe and had squeezed them into tight rolls. Such was the depth of her feelings about the matter.

The action had not escaped Steven's watchful eye. Despite the desire to shout to the world his love for Nachelle, he was willing, knowing he had her heart, to grant her her small wish for some time.

Nachelle gave Steven a half-smile and finished. "I'd rather not announce anything right now. I don't want anything to taint me, you, or what we have together. Can we keep it our secret until I'm more secure? I just need some time."

"Honey, I'll do whatever you want as long as you know I'm here for you—always. Whatever problems we encounter in the future we'll tackle them together, you won't have to go through any trial alone." Steven pecked her on the nose. "But, I do have to warn you that I don't think we can keep this a secret for too long. Mother and Dorothy already have a big clue." Steven smiled and Nachelle wondered how she ever thought he was the Silver Shark. He was Steven DuCloux. The man of her dreams.

"You can add Heather to the list." Nachelle smiled and placed her hands on either side of his face. "Thank you for being so understanding."

"I know a better way you can thank me." Steven gave her a lustful look.

Nachelle kissed him softly on the lips. Standing, she pulled him up with her and led him back to the king-size bed.

The young couple added a new meaning to the term "a lazy Sunday morning."

Fourteen

By the time Nachelle arrived at the Hayes's house, all of the other invitees to Sunday dinner had arrived. Muttering to herself, as she walked around all the cars parked in the drive, she blamed Steven for her tardiness. "If he had let me out of the bedroom sooner, I would have had more time to get home and get dressed." Nachelle smiled to herself. "Of course, I was a *very* willing partner. I guess I'll take some of the blame."

Deciding to forego the usual formalities, Nachelle entered without knocking and had hung her coat up in the closet before anyone spied her. She should have known the first person to see her would be Steven. "Welcome." His deep voice reached over and caressed her from the opening of the living room.

Nachelle spun around, almost dropping the cheesecake she held, and smiled broadly. "Hello. How are you?"

Steven walked to her and with a devilish grin said, "Hungry."

Looking at the gleam in his eye, Nachelle knew he wasn't referring to food. "Straighten up. There are a house full of people here."

"You're telling me." The look in his eyes conveyed his unhappiness with the amount of people present. He would have been happy with just two people—him and her.

"Nachelle, we were just getting ready to send out a search party." Sharlet looped her arm through her daughter's and Steven's arms and pulled them into the living room where the other guests sat talking, laughing, and generally having a good time.

After hellos and how you dos were concluded, Adele shepherded everyone into the dining room for dinner. The meal was divine and the company even better. Steven's mother turned out to be a terrific joke teller. It was such a surprise considering her standoffish appearance. Adolphus DuCloux, on the other hand, was the most solemn man Nachelle had ever met. Nachelle knew after spending a couple of hours in his company where Steven inherited his drive for success and his serious, life-or-death outlook concerning the operation of DuCloux Enterprises. Steven's three brothers, Donald, the oldest, Anthony, the next in line, and John delighted in picking on the youngest son, even though the "baby," Steven, was the tallest and most muscular of the bunch. Nachelle learned that Steven was a good sport and did indeed, as Heather had reported, have a sense of humor. Steven's three sisters-in-law, Dorothy, Morgana, and Shelby, all beauties, ranged in personality from quiet to lively, with Dorothy being the most rambunctious. Based on the joviality around the table, Nachelle decided Steven must have had a well-balanced, well-adjusted childhood.

Nachelle was in the kitchen helping Adele with dessert when Sharlet and Nadine DuCloux walked in.

"Can we help?" Both ladies asked in unison.

Adele responded brightly, "No, I think we have everything under control."

Sharlet sidled up to her daughter and asked, "Then, you don't mind if we ask Nachelle when she and Steven plan to get married."

Nachelle dropped the knife she had been using to slice the cheesecake and turned wide-eyed to her mother. "Mother, how did you know?"

"We knew last night. So, why are y'all trying to keep it a secret?" Nadine closed in on the other side of Nachelle. She was trapped. "Weddings require a lot of planning and we need as much notice as possible."

"Dear, haven't you learned by now that mothers know

everything?" Adele piped in. "Now, give, when's the big day so I'll know when to start dieting?"

Before Nachelle could clear the fuzz from her brain to answer them, Steven burst through the doors. "I kinda thought you all would be double-teaming on my lady. When I saw you ladies heading in here, I figured an ambush was in the works." Steven smiled despite the seriousness of his charge.

"You're not to old to be spanked, young man. Now get over here and let your mama give you a big congratulatory hug and kiss."

A new round of hugging, kissing, and exclaiming went on until Donald DuCloux, Steven's oldest brother, walked in rubbing his stomach. "I've got a little more room in my stomach for . . ." Donald, an engineer with the most logical, analytical brain of all the boys, stopped in mid-sentence. "What's going on?"

"A wedding would be my guess." Dorothy maneuvered around her husband and joined in the fray.

Within minutes, all fourteen people were standing in the kitchen, surrounding the happy couple and chatting happily about the proper season and best time of day for a wedding, the best place to honeymoon, what the name of the first child should be, and so on.

With a tight grip on Nachelle, Steven managed to whisper, "I'm sorry, Nachelle. This isn't what we agreed to."

A bright-eyed Nachelle responded, sincerely, "I don't mind. You were right. Surrounded by such happiness and love, I know we can conquer any and everything."

Steven kissed her on the cheek before he was pulled away by Dorothy for some merciless teasing.

The thank you dinner party turned into a celebration of love and got so loud Adele barely heard the doorbell when it rang. Regretfully leaving the rumpus, she floated to the door, her face a study of happiness. The smile on her face dropped when she opened the door to find two uniformed policemen standing at attention with their hats off.

The black officer spoke first. "Are you Mrs. Ralph Hayes?"

Adele's eyes grew wide with fear, and shaking her head affirmatively she stepped back and away from the officers. Instinctively, she knew.

". . . and you have a son named Harlan who you reported missing over a month ago?" Adele started screaming.

A mass of people rushed from the kitchen, spilling into the hallway. Ralph, Ray, and Steven were the first to reach Adele's hysterical side.

Fixing his eyes at a point on Ray's forehead, one of the cops, in a robot voice, designed to keep his emotions jailed, reported, "We're sorry to report that Harlan Hayes is . . . dead. His body was found and identified this morning. We're terribly sorry."

Adele's wailing reached an ear-splitting level. She fell back into Ray's waiting arms. Ralph stood in shocked stillness, numb and oblivious to his surroundings. Woodenly, he turned and walked into the living room.

"We're sorry to have to ask, but we need someone to come to the station to officially identify the body." The black cop finished the routine.

Nachelle took deep calming breaths, but everything went blurry, seconds later tears trailed a river down her cheeks. She cried for what could have been for her and Harlan. She cried for the Hayes's. She cried for Harlan.

Efficiently, the DuCloux family mobilized and dealt with the police, whisked Adele upstairs to her bedroom, cleaned the kitchen, and quietly left, leaving Ray, Sharlet, and Steven to console the Hayes's and Nachelle. Thirty minutes later, the family doctor arrived and sedated Adele. Steven and Nachelle followed the doctor out, heading for the police station. Upon arrival there, they learned Harlan had been murdered. The police suspected a drug deal gone bad based on the evidence at the crime scene. His body had been fished out of a local lake. At a crowded police station, in a crowded city where the good people were getting harder to find, Nachelle fell completely apart, leaving Steven to close one chapter in the Hayes's story.

The plane landed at exactly 8:00 on Tuesday morning at Hartsfield International Airport. Within fifteen minutes, Steven had disembarked and was comfortably ensconced in the back seat of the company limousine. Nathaniel, armed with a dour look and a briefcase full of papers, looked ill at ease.

"When were we notified?" Steven spoke sharply. He was worried, but his outward appearance reflected calm assurance.

"One hour ago." Nathaniel settled his glasses on the bridge of his nose. "I took the call since you were in-flight from Fort Worth. I tried calling you on the air phone, but the interference from the rainy weather prevented contact."

The news Nathaniel had shared with Steven when he walked off the plane left Steven feeling like he'd been socked in the stomach by Mike Tyson. He was sick, and for the first time in a long time, frightened.

Computermation, a Virginia-based computer and electronics firm, the second largest in the industry, had announced their intention to escalate payment of a sizable sum of money from DuCloux Enterprises. According to the press conference Computermation's executives had held this morning, the thirty million dollar accounts payable that DuCloux Enterprises owed to Computermation for computer hardware was being called in immediately. The Computermation executives had gone on to say DuCloux was behind in their payments and had not responded to previous attempts to settle the balance. DuCloux had ten days to cough up the entire sum or else . . .

The whole situation disgusted Steven since he personally had renegotiated the account with the President of Computermation not six months ago. Now, the man spoke as if their agreement had never been negotiated. Of course, it had been a gentleman's agreement, no written record existed. Steven was very upset.

"Does Dad know?" Steven narrowed his eyes. With each ticking second, his heart sank more and more.

"Yes, and he wants to see you before you go to the office."

Steven closed his intense black eyes and gave in to a moment of weakness. He knew his father was going to rant about the Hayes Group purchase and their weakened financial state because of the outlay of cash and stocks to acquire the Fort Worth company. Quite simply, DuCloux Enterprises didn't have thirty million dollars in liquid assets. No doubt Adolphus was going to huff and puff about the long-standing family decree requiring each heir to keep the business owned and controlled by a DuCloux.

Steven felt like an anvil had just dropped around his neck. Not only was he faced with defending his actions to family members, but he now had to fight the competition. And, he had deserted Nachelle at a time when she needed him.

His mind flitted to Nachelle. *And, I can forget about planning for the future for now.* He wanted, no needed, to conserve his mental, physical, and emotional faculties for the battle with Computermation. Steven had a feeling there was more to Computermation's request than met the eye. They had been trading partners for years and to suddenly call in a note with no warning and no reference to the renegotiated account was highly speculative and an unusual business practice. Optimistically, Steven promised silently to himself, *my wedding gift to Nachelle will be victory over Computermation and a secure future for us and our children.*

He smothered a feeling of fatality and braced himself for the onslaught. Now was a time for self-survival.

The limo driver pulled the long, sleek car into the curved, flagstone driveway of the DuCloux residence. Steven emerged and saw the cars belonging to his brothers. He passed a quick hand over his eyes, stiffened his backbone, and went in to control D-day. No matter how high the odds were stacked against him, he would give Computermation the fight they were looking for.

The DuCloux men were already circled around the massive cherrywood dining table. Nadine DuCloux hugged and kissed her youngest son before leaving to get him a cup of coffee. Subdued greetings from his father and brothers followed his arrival.

A natural born leader, Steven eased into his role and directed the creation of a strategy that would put an end to Computermation's threat. After several hours of huddling with his brothers, Adolphus and Nathaniel, a tentative plan was designed as well as an alternate plan. From his parents' house, Steven traveled to the Atlanta offices to meet with a battery of DuCloux lawyers. Although those meetings were more brief in time, they were no less consuming of Steven's mental abilities. A very tired and worn Steven entered the office of the CEO and President in late afternoon and proceeded from that point to discuss details of their own press conference and news release with Dorrie, his PR staff, and Nathaniel. He also tried to reach the President of Computermation; his call was never put through. In early evening, he was ready to hold a brief conference call with his executives in both Atlanta and Fort Worth. Aside from his early morning thoughts of Nachelle, it was during the arranging of the call that he remembered his love. The thought of her was the one thing that made him smile in the midst of all this trouble.

"I sure would like to know what you're smiling about," Nathaniel remarked as they were waiting for the operator to connect all the callers for the conference call. He, like most of the other Atlanta executives, were scattered around the oval pinewood conference table in the executive conference room. They were prepared for a long night and an even longer fight with Computermation.

"Love, Nathaniel, love," Steven remarked, still showing bright white teeth.

Nathaniel humphed and reviewed the detailed notes he'd been collecting all day.

Finally, with Nachelle and the Fort Worth executives on line, Steven recanted the bad news in more detail than the media had broadcast. Quickly, but with a great deal of defined strategy, Steven outlined the battleplan he and his family had developed. Once the question and answer period was over, he disconnected all the callers and cleared the room, sending everyone home to get a decent night of sleep.

Slouched in his chair, Steven delved into a few private moments of peace. His heart was still racing at the prospect of losing the company and his mind, taxed all day, was still running a mile a minute, creating and discarding alternate plans to rid the company of the imposing threat. It dawned on him that he hadn't eaten all day, save the breakfast his mother had pushed on him but which he had only picked over.

Even with the hunger pains that suddenly manifested and grew in strength, there was one need that was greater. Reaching forward, Steven picked up the phone and dialed Nachelle's telephone number at home.

She answered on the third ring, sounding breathless and as sexy as hell.

"Hi, sweetheart. How are you?"

Nachelle moved the files that had covered her lap and rushed into a lengthy dialogue. "Steven, thank God you called. I didn't want to say anything on the call with all the other people on line, but you remember my friend Sheila I was telling you about. Well, Computermation is the company she works for. I never mentioned it before because I didn't think it was important. I'll bet this move on their part has something to do with the trouble she's been having with the new President and Vice President."

"You're kidding me? She works for Computermation?" Steven sat up straight in his chair. Hope flamed bright.

"Yes, has been since we both graduated from college. She's

the Director of Accounting and she's alluded to some unethical practices going on there."

"Can you call her and see what you can find out?"

"I'm one step ahead of you. I left a message on her answering machine as soon as our conference call ended."

"Well keep trying to reach her and call me when you get something. Dorrie knows to put your calls through immediately."

"Will do. Now, tell me the truth, how are you doing? You sound tired."

"I am and I miss you, but for the time being there's not a thing I can do about either situation."

"You told us to go home and try to sleep. Why don't you take your own advice?" To lighten the situation, Nachelle added, "Do I need to call your mother and get her onto you?"

Steven laughed, despite all the hoopla of the day. "No, thank you! Consider me gone."

Once the light mood ended, Nachelle offered, "Steven, everything will work out just fine. Try not to worry."

"Thank you, baby. I needed to hear that." After a slight pause, Steven said, "I love you."

"I love you, too. Talk to you tomorrow."

They hung up the phone, each, although thousands of miles apart, with full hearts and a smile on their face.

The weather in Atlanta on Wednesday matched the mood in the DuCloux Enterprises offices. It was gray and overcast with scattered rains accompanied by loud clapping thunderbolts and quick-streaking lightning. Although last to leave the office the previous night, Steven was the first person in the office, arriving well before the sun rose. After a quick review of some previously neglected work, he turned on the television in his office, and unfolded several morning national and local newspapers. The news was no different today than it had been yesterday. Computermation was still a threat.

Steven laid the paper down and rubbed his forehead. By divine intervention, he had hoped his problem would have disappeared by morning. But, it stared at him in written form from *The Wall Street Journal, USA Today* and *The Atlanta Constitution*. Although the articles weren't as dominant as the day before, the small space given to the news today made Steven feel even more vulnerable. *Do they think it's a done deal? That we're going to automatically run to bankruptcy court? Do they honestly think we're going down without a fight?* The cuss words he spewed forth did nothing to lessen the feeling of foreboding. "There's no getting around it. I'll have to meet with Computermation as soon as possible."

Less than an hour later, Nathaniel walked into his office with a sour look on his face. "There's been new developments you need to know about before you attempt another meeting with Computermation."

Steven sat up straight and put down the newspapers he'd been reading for the third time. "What is it?"

"I think you ought to wait until the others arrive. They'll all want to hear the news."

Steven stood up with fists balled. He was in no mood for games. "Nathaniel, if you don't tell me now, I'll . . ."

A knock on the door interrupted Steven's threat. Before Steven could round the corner of his desk, Nathaniel was already at the door allowing some gentlemen from Corporate Security and Legal in. Adolphus DuCloux and Steven's brothers were thirty seconds behind the other men.

Steven asked, "Okay, Nathaniel. It seems you've got the audience you wanted. Spill it." Steven's patience had fled long ago and it was evident.

"I thought the timing of this announcement was very strange so I did some investigating and discovered that Computermation had some help in making its decision to bankrupt DE. What I found was that we have an inside informant feeding Computermation information about DE. Here are the reports Corporate Security put together. It clearly lists a connection between one of our Fort Worth executives and Computermation."

The silence in the room was intense.

All except Steven crowded around the hard evidence Nathaniel presented. Giving Nathaniel the coldest stare he had, Steven clipped his words. "Who, Nathaniel? Just give me a name."

"Nachelle Oliver. The person *you* selected to lead the merger."

Steven felt dizzy. He didn't know what type of sick little game Nathaniel was playing, but the other man didn't know how close he was getting to unemployment. Instinctively, he defended her. "It's not true. Nachelle's not capable of such a devious act."

"Look at the reports yourself. There are many calls from her office to the offices of Computermation. Coincidentally, the calls correspond to the first of January when we acquired the Hayes Group and are as recent as last week."

Steven's mind refused to believe the woman he loved could be involved in anything that would hurt him or his company. "I don't have to look at the report. I know Nachelle."

Adolphus spoke up. "Son, it shows right here she made several calls over the past few months to Computermation. These are authentic reports the boys pulled from the physical lines."

"But, there's a mistake. I'm telling you. Nachelle has a girlfriend that works for Computermation. They talk frequently."

Nathaniel pushed his viewpoint, "Well what about the faxes then? Why were so many lengthy faxes leaving her office in the late evening going to this private residence in Reston? Were they exchanging recipes or confidential information?"

"Nachelle would have told me if she were faxing any information to Sheila. These fax reports are wrong."

Silence followed Steven's outburst. The anguish on his face was enough to liquefy a stone statute.

"Son, I know you love her, but do you really *know* her? Face it, you've only known her for a few months. Maybe she's been toying with you." Adolphus, taking his lead from his trusted right-hand man Nathaniel, supported the second-in-command.

Donald spoke up, "Nachelle doesn't seem like the under-cover type. To destroy DE would mean destroying the Hayes Group and there's no doubt she's devoted to that company. Maybe she's being played by her girlfriend and doesn't know it."

"There's only one way to find out," Nathaniel broke in. "We'll have to question her . . . in person."

All agreed to Nathaniel's suggestion including Steven. He relished the chance to prove his Dad and Nathaniel wrong.

The men filed out of the CEO's office, all keeping their thoughts to themselves. Nathaniel and Adolphus were the last to leave. As he prepared to walk out the door, Nathaniel said, "Steven, I didn't want to do it, but it's the survival of DE I'm concerned about. And, don't forget she was on the conference call last night. It's probable Computermation now knows the plans we've developed."

The door closed, leaving Steven alone with his thoughts and the hardcore evidence of Nachelle's supposed betrayal.

Nachelle looked up from scanning the Thursday edition of *The Wall Street Journal* and glanced at her desk clock for the zillionth time.

9:45 a.m. He'll be here any minute.

Nachelle had learned from her daily, ritualistic call to Dorrie in Atlanta, that Steven was on his way to Fort Worth and was expected in the office around 10:00.

Although the news of the possible bankruptcy of DuCloux Enterprises was two days old, she had grown exceedingly anxious and worried during that short time frame. The last time she'd seen Steven was at the airport Tuesday morning. Then, they had been embraced in their own world and had had no clue to the adversity they would soon be facing. They had parted without a care in the world, save Harlan's death.

Forty-eight hours later, she had transformed from a happy, in-love woman to a short-tempered wreck. She had tried all day Wednesday to speak with Steven directly. Her call attempts were always intercepted and routed to Nathaniel, who provided meager information about the proceedings. Not that she had a lot to share with Steven. Sheila had yet to return her calls and could not be reached at work. Frustration and dread had crept into her heart and head.

With the advancement of time, so too did her need to hear Steven's voice increase. Her heart ached for him, and she wished fervently that he was physically near so she could wrap her arms around his neck and speak reassuring words in his ear. She knew exactly how he was feeling and the thoughts that were undoubtedly surfacing in his mind. After all, it wasn't too long ago that the employees of the Hayes Group had been subjected to stress due to the uncertainty of their futures.

The fancy black hands of Nachelle's quartz clock reflected 9:55 a.m.

"Five more minutes," she muttered.

Nachelle was excited about Steven's arrival. Even though they had separated only days ago, she felt like it had been years. She missed Steven and couldn't wait to feel his soothing, protecting arms around her. She knew the apprehension she'd been feeling about the announcement and what it would do to DuCloux Enterprises' future would melt away at his touch.

Honesty drove Nachelle to identify the additional, darker feelings that had cropped up over the past day. Feelings of hurt and rejection stemming from no contact with Steven in the past twenty-four hours were growing and steadily chipping away at her psyche. In her past relationship with Harlan, lack of communication had driven a wedge between them. She didn't want that problem repeated with Steven, but the newness of their relationship and her ignorance about why he hadn't *made* the time to return her calls ripped through her central nervous system. Nachelle didn't want to doubt her and Steven's ability to survive this major hurdle, but the insecurities brought on by his absence existed.

Nachelle stood and began pacing the room. She glanced at her wristwatch and clasped her hands behind her back.

Her pacing didn't last long.

Millie knocked on the door and poked her head through. "He's here and waiting for you in his office."

Nachelle almost ran Millie over in her haste to reunite with Steven. She walked briskly down the corridor and around the corner. She had to stop herself from running to meet him, otherwise, heads would surely turn.

Dorrie barely looked up when Nachelle appeared. She pointed at the door and continued addressing the red lights lit up like a Christmas tree on her phone.

With a sexually-charged flutter in her stomach, Nachelle opened the door and entered.

Steven was immaculately clothed in a deep charcoal suit with his usual white starched shirt and colorful tie. He stood behind his desk facing the door with his hands clasped behind him. The picture window acted as a backdrop to his drop-dead gorgeous looks.

"I'm glad you're back." Nachelle spoke from the heart, her eyes sparkling with love. She quickly closed the gap between them and was about to throw herself into his arms when an arresting voice stopped her.

"You may not be so glad when you read this." Nathaniel stepped forward from the shadows of the office and threw a bound report on Steven's desk. His voice was neutral, staid.

Nachelle turned to face the older man, momentarily startled and confused. "Oh, Nathaniel. I didn't know you were coming back with Steven."

"Considering the circumstances, we felt it would be better

if both of us were here." The fleeting smug look that crossed his face was unmistakable.

Struggling to understand Nathaniel's statements and covert body language, Nachelle turned to Steven with worry lines marring her forehead. "What circumstances? Has something else happened?" She placed a beseeching hand on his arm and waited for an answer.

Steven looked at the petite hand laying innocently on his arm. In an unsensitized, clinical mode, he had watched the play between Nachelle and Nathaniel. His thoughts, centered on the family's legacy in jeopardy, were eating him alive. The executives at Computermation had refused to meet with him, which further validated his idea that something more substantial was behind their attack. He just wished he knew what it was so he could defend DE properly. As it was, DE was fully exposed with no idea of when or where the next volley would come.

To add to his struggles, Steven didn't know what to make of the investigator's report that Nathaniel had so carelessly tossed on his desk. If one *were* to believe the report, one would think Nachelle guilty of releasing confidential financial reports regarding DuCloux Enterprises' performance to Sheila. But, Steven knew Nachelle would not under any circumstance release any confidential information to Sheila or anyone else. She knew the rules. Hell, she wrote them. But, right there in those unsolicited reports was proof that faxes had left Nachelle's office to Sheila's home in the late evenings and early mornings. The investigators, Nathaniel, and Adolphus believed she tipped them off to DuCloux Enterprises' weakened financial position.

In his heart, he knew Nachelle was not the saboteur and that there existed an innocent explanation behind the numerous faxes. Hence, his decision to bring Nathaniel to Fort Worth with him. Her innocent explanation could be witnessed by someone whose heart was not involved. But, to present an unbiased picture, he had shelved his emotions and with great difficulty chiseled a protective facade. He needed logic and a strong will to make it through this session.

"Nathaniel is referring to some disturbing news that has reached us." Steven reached across his desk and picked up the report. "This is a report Corporate Security pulled from your telephone and fax line. It appears a number of calls were made from your phone to Sheila at Computermation." Steven held out the report to her. "I know you were helping her with a problem, but your help was purely by listening to her vent, right?"

Shock reverberated throughout Nachelle's body. Her almond-shaped eyes grew larger with first surprise, then dawning knowledge. "Someone pulled my phone records? What in the world for?"

"For the protection of DE, that's why." Nathaniel's response was heated.

Nachelle was stunned at his outburst. She and Nathaniel had never hit it off, but he had never been so outright belligerent toward her. Turning to Steven, she continued with her own questions. "What's going on here, Steven? I need some answers."

"We came here to ask you the questions."

Sternly, Steven shushed the older man. "Nathaniel, please. Let me handle this."

"Handle what? Am I being accused of something?" Nachelle searched Steven's face and saw she had hit the mark. "What? Steven . . . you're scaring me. What is it?"

"Nachelle, please just answer my earlier question. You were merely a sounding board for Sheila. You never faxed any company records to her." For his own heart's sake, Steven posed the question as a statement. He wanted it to be so.

"Yes, I did." Nachelle answered truthfully. "A couple of times I faxed her financial reports but . . ."

Anger exploded within Steven like a bomb. He threw the report on his desk and stormed her. "Nachelle, why? Why did you do it?" He grabbed her upper arms in a viselike grip and shook her. "You know the rules for releasing confidential records to a competitor. Because of your actions, you opened up the floodgates for the destruction of DE. DE's been in my family for years and now with one stupid move, you just blew it all to hell. How could you do that to me? . . . To DE? . . . To us?" Steven released her. His breathing was ragged, his heart broken.

The tears didn't start immediately, but her throat suddenly grew a lump the size of a grapefruit. She wanted to tell Steven she was only helping a friend. She wanted to defend her actions by telling Steven the records reflected outdated information on the Hayes Group, not DE, but since DE had purchased the Hayes Group, Steven would probably see it as one and the same. Besides, with his reversion to the Silver Shark, there would be no getting through to him. He'd made it clear that she was a disappointment to him and that his company had first place in his heart.

Broken heart aside, her pride flared. *And why should I have to defend myself to the man who supposedly loves me? He should know me better than that,* she thought in retaliation. Boiling, contrasting emotions made her body tremble. She could feel herself splintering in two. One side was full of the hurt that he thought so little of her, of their love; the other side was angry that he so carelessly damaged her reputation, questioned her integrity, her loyalty. The anger replaced heartache for a split second before the grapefruit in her throat started a bobbing action. A sign she would soon be releasing tears.

Even knowing the tears were near, Nachelle had to make one last try. Ignoring Nathaniel's presence, Nachelle took a baby step toward Steven to fight for the love she'd been dreaming of.

"Steven," she whispered. "You can't possibly believe I'm capable of knowingly hurting you."

In response, he held up a stopping hand and turned his back to her.

She swallowed the lump in her throat and forced the tears

back. Gathering strength from the pain, she squared her shoulders. The knife causing her internal agony twisted another knot. The nightmare of a failed office affair was happening again, except this time it was more deadly than the first. This time, she had given her heart and soul to the Silver Shark. And, as rumors had indicated, he had chewed them up and spat them out.

Nathaniel stepped forward from his position by Steven's desk and as written in the corporate officer's handbook, released her of her duties. "Please return to your office and get your personal items. A security guard will meet you there and escort you out of the building."

With a last, lingering look at Steven's stiff back, Nachelle turned and with head held high walked out of Steven's door, out of his life. His door closed behind her with a lifeless, dull thud.

The protective dam she had built in Steven's office then crumbled. She ran to her office, swiping at tears. There, she gathered her personal belongings and left. The scalding tears kept her company on the drive home.

For the second time in two days, Steven felt like the wind had been knocked out of him. He had been prepared to laugh all the way back to Atlanta. To realize that the woman he loved was responsible for the possible end of DuCloux Enterprises made a part of him wither and die. The accompanying pain was unbearable. Rage, helplessness, and love mingled within him, making him clench and unclench his hands. The tears rolled down his face, his world became blurred.

Fifteen

Nachelle sat cross-legged on her couch. A box of Kleenex, a cup of once-hot tea, and a slightly used bottle of Jack Daniels littered the blanket that was tucked around her.

"Here. Eat it." Heather placed a tray containing a bowl of soup and crackers across Nachelle's legs. "You need to put something in your stomach." She propped her hands on her slight hips and adopted an intimidating stare.

Nachelle turned her nose up at the offering and mumbled, "I'm not hungry. You eat it."

"I'm not the one who hasn't eaten all day. The ten o'clock news will soon be on." Heather sat down on the couch beside her and picking up the spoon, placed it in Nachelle's hand. "At least a couple of spoonfuls just so my cooking effort won't go unappreciated."

That comment, more than any feeling of hunger, made Nachelle comply. Heather had been with her since lunchtime, holding her hand, stroking her hair, and speaking reassuring words. She didn't want Heather to think she was ungrateful, for indeed she was very appreciative of Heather's friendly, accommodating ear. Talking about the morning's unfortunate encounter had helped to ease some of the pain, but a wooden stake still felt lodged in her heart.

"Thank you, Heather, that was good." Nachelle lied. The soup had tasted like wood and it now settled in her stomach like a stone at the bottom of a river.

"Good. Now . . ." Heather removed the tray and set it on the coffee table. "Let's talk about the future. What are you going to do? Stay and fight or cut your losses and start fresh?"

Nachelle unfolded her sweatpants-clad legs and stretched them out on the coffee table beside the discarded, half-eaten tray of food. "I don't know Heather. Between this, and Harlan's funeral yesterday, I don't even want to think anymore. I just . . ." On the verge of tears again, she clamped down on the painful feelings.

"I know. I'm sorry I'm pushing you, but sometimes it's easier if you keep your mind and hands busy on other things or establish a plan."

"You're right, Heather. You're a dear friend. I don't know what I'd do without you." Nachelle grabbed and tightly held onto her friend's hand. "You were there for me during the breakup with Harlan and now with Steven." Nachelle attempted a laugh, which erupted as a disgruntled snort instead. "I guess I just don't have very good luck with men, do I?"

"Well, if you ask me I say it's not you who lost out." Heather laid her head against Nachelle's. "I'm sorry I pushed *him* on you. If I'd known he would have turned out to be such a horrible company man, I wouldn't have cheered for him."

Nachelle tried to laugh, but yet again it came out more as a gurgle. "In the end, it was my decision. I don't blame anyone but myself."

"You're a good woman, Nachelle, and one day you'll have it all—love, happiness, an unlimited career path, 2.5 children, the white-picket fence, a Volvo station wagon . . ."

Despite the pain, Nachelle smiled. "Okay, okay, I get the picture."

"I need to go and call Gerald so he'll know where I'll be tonight." Heather stood up and pointed at the food tray. "And don't touch those dishes. I'll get them later."

"Aye, aye captain." Nachelle soberly replied. She wrung the mangled tissue in her hand yet again. *Heather is right. I do need to make some plans. I can't go back to DuCloux Enterprises and even though I have savings, I refuse to deplete it. Maybe now is the time for a change of scenery. Maybe I could move back to Austin, get a job, and live in my parent's home.* The tissue got another wringing as Nachelle pondered the many directions her future could take.

When Heather returned from placing her call, Nachelle was nowhere nearer a decision. Her mind just wouldn't concentrate on anything except Steven DuCloux and the love they had found and lost. Her feelings and thought processes vacillated between denial, anger, fear, and love.

"Gerald sends his love."

"How is he? Fully recovered yet?"

"His knee is still sore, but he swears he's starting in Saturday's game. Hey . . ." Heather's animated face bloomed in excitement. "I'm flying to Portland for the game. Come with me. We'll have great fun."

"I don't know, Heather. I don't have a job anymore and plane tickets at the last minute are expensive."

"I'll pay. As you know, I just signed that big contract with the school district and I have a ton of mall engagements coming up for Easter. Consider it a loan, Ms. Independent."

Nachelle was pleased that Heather's puppet business was taking off and at any other time, she would have jumped at the opportunity to see Gerald play basketball, but a small voice inside her head reminded her that Steven *could* call and beg her forgiveness. Although the chance was slim, her heart told her it was possible. And, for all the bravado she showed Heather, she knew that if he called, she'd run to him in a minute—such was the depth of her love for him.

"Let me think about it. I'll let you know in the morning."

"Promise me you'll give it some serious thought. Portland has the exact scenery you need to clear your head."

"Alright already." Nachelle rolled her eyes heavenward and put out a detaining hand. "I said I'd let you know." Nachelle escaped while she could. "I'm going to take a bath and then go to bed. You know where everything is. Make yourself at home."

Less than an hour later, Nachelle pulled her bed covers up to her chin and stared at the designs created by the narrow strips of light seeping past her bedroom's blinds and curtains. Alone with an active mind and pained heart, Nachelle knew sleep was impossible. Her mind recounted the events in raw detail and, before long, the tears started anew. That was when she made up her mind to leave with Heather. *Anything to take my mind off Steven,* she thought, as she flipped on her side and watched with blurry vision as the digital clock impersonally ticked off the minutes of her life.

* * *

The boardroom at the DuCloux Enterprises' Atlanta office was stifling, and it looked like the ceiling had rained paper. Reports, ledgers, and memos were scattered everywhere— chairs, the credenza, the conference table, even the floor. The small but determined staff of executives scratched their heads, flipped through reports, and searched for the elusive, creative answer that would save the company. DE's bank was still reviewing their request for a loan, other banks had told them a flat out no based on the press releases, and there wasn't enough time to sell stock to raise the funds. Computermation knew what they were doing.

Steven sat at the head of the table. His eyes watched the frenzied activity going on about him, but his mind was far away.

It was Monday, four days since he and Nachelle had parted, and four days before the Computermation deadline. There hadn't been a minute within those past four days that Steven hadn't thought about her. His life had turned into a living hell due to one missing element—Nachelle.

He'd had hours and hours to think about their parting scene and with the benefit of hindsight, he knew he'd been wrong. Nachelle was no more capable of destroying DuCloux Enterprises than he was. Her final words—"You can't possible believe I'm capable of knowingly hurting you"—continued to circulate in his mind, causing him to wallow in regret and wishing he could unsay his condemning words and undo his damaging actions. He knew there was a reasonable explanation for her involvement. He regretted that he hadn't allowed her a chance to explain before his anger took control.

It had taken Steven all of one day to realize he had been wrong, and it had taken an even shorter time frame to act on his convictions. He'd tried calling her at the Fort Worth office, at her home, at the Hayes's, at her parents' home in Austin, and at Heather's work and home number—to no avail. His phone calls were always received, but no information regarding her whereabouts was ever released. He admitted he couldn't blame them for shielding her. Hell, he blamed himself for being the world's biggest, most misdirected fool.

Unwilling to let her walk out of his life, he had instigated a search for her. Just this morning, the private investigators had reported that they had staked out every location in Texas where she could possibly be hiding out—the same locations he had called—but had not seen her coming or going.

Steven pushed away from the table and walked to stand by the window, distancing himself from the present. The busy downtown movement on Peachtree wasn't enough to divert his mind from Nachelle. *Where could she possibly be,* he thought angrily. *I've got to find her and ask for her forgiveness. She needs to know that I need her in my life permanently.* Steven played back the memory tape in his mind of the telephone conversations he had had with her family and friends in Fort Worth. The only person he had not been able to personally talk to was Heather. One of her employees had informed him that she was in Portland, watching Gerald play and wasn't expected back for several days.

"Steven? Steven!" Nathaniel raised his voice, hoping to attract his boss's attention.

"I'm sorry." Steven rejoined the distressed employees at the table. He had no idea they had been waiting for an affirmative or negative reply.

"What do you think about . . ." Nathaniel delved into an explanation of the latest recommendation.

A knock on the door interrupted Nathaniel's narrative. Dorrie hovered near the door, looking anxious. "Steven, may I talk to you for a moment?" The expression on her face meant more than the usual disappointing midmorning report about Nachelle.

Steven jumped up and almost ran to the door. His heart thudded so heavily against his chest, he thought it would burst through the surrounding muscles, tissues, and bone. His palms shed a thin layer of moisture. "Excuse me," he murmured to the crowd in general before shutting the heavy glass door.

"More news?" Steven asked. His facial expression resembled a brewing thunderstorm.

Having been happily married for some thirty odd years, Dorrie could only imagine the heartache her boss was feeling. Even though he did not tell her what had happened, she had pieced together, from handling the important and confidential documents and telephone calls, the events. And, she had known, almost as soon as Steven, that he had fallen—hard— for his vice president. It was not a hard puzzle to fit together. "This package arrived just moments ago."

Steven grabbed the large manila envelope out of her hand and walked hurriedly to his office. He slammed the door shut, leaving the rest of the world outside. From the envelope, he withdrew a single sheet of paper.

He read silently:

Steven—

I never meant to hurt you or DE. In helping one friend, I hurt another more important friend. I'm sorry.

I finally heard from Sheila (her boss had forced her to take a personal leave of absence. She was staying with her parents in the country for a while, and just recently returned home hence her delay in getting back to me). She told me Computermation does not really want the thirty million dollars, they want DuCloux Enterprises, lock, stock, and barrel. Their plan is to force DE into bankruptcy and then step in and force you to sell all stock to them. Their goal is to be the number one company in our industry, and, as you can tell, they will stop at nothing to achieve that goal.

I spoke with Ralph and he is willing to loan you the money you paid him for the Hayes Group. Please call him. Also, Sheila is working on some things from her end. She'll call you when she has something concrete.

Good luck,
Nachelle

Steven re-read the note several times, trying desperately to keep his emotions at bay. He turned the envelope over, looking for a return address. None was indicated, however, the postmark declared Fort Worth.

"Dorrie! Come in here." Steven bellowed into the phone.

As soon as his secretary entered the room, he ground out the questions. "When did this arrive? The envelope was open. Was this all? Have you notified the investigators yet?"

Dorrie held up her hand. "Steven, calm down." She stepped closer and answered. "I opened the envelope this morning. What you have there is all that came." Looking at her boss, Dorrie could feel her own heart twisting in shared anguish. "I called the investigators and informed them about the package, that it didn't have an address, and was stamped three days ago. It's not much to go on without an address, but they promised to research it. She could be anywhere."

Hope fizzled like a wet match. Steven hung his head and re-read the brief message. No clues could be distinguished from the short lines, but one thing he did know and that was a person who cared had thrown out this lifeline. *Even though I hurt her, she's still willing to help me. This is just more proof that I'm the biggest fool in the world.*

Steven sighed. "I want the search intensified and I want hourly reports."

"I'll pass the instructions on."

"And Dorrie," Steven's dejected voice stopped her exit. "Thanks for not asking any questions." With his hand on the phone, Steven said, "After this call, I'm leaving the office. Tell Nathaniel I'll be back in a couple of hours."

Dorrie silently vacated her boss's office.

Steven's call to Ralph was brief. Ralph agreed to transfer the money within twenty-four hours. It was no surprise to

Steven that Ralph refused to release any information about Nachelle or her whereabouts.

Steven hung up the phone and slipped into his suit jacket. Even with Ralph's generous offer, they weren't out of the danger zone. He walked out of the building and across the street to a small pedestrian park. There was no point in pretending that he could concentrate on the work taking place in the boardroom. He sat down to think about "what ifs."

The next day dawned bright despite the weather reports from the previous night which had predicted rain, rain, and more rain.

In his bedroom, Steven brushed his black-tailored jacket with a lint brush. He could hear the stirrings of the servants as his parents' big colonial house came to life. The smells of a Southern breakfast wafted through the vents. It reminded him of the last breakfast he and Nachelle had shared. It reminded him of the one night of lovemaking they had shared. He felt like crying.

A knock on his bedroom door interrupted his thoughts. A servant announced through the closed door the arrival of the car and Nathaniel.

As Steven completed his morning routine, he operated on automatic pilot with his thoughts focused on the investigators' reports. So far, based on the new, measly information they had received the previous day, they had discovered nothing about Nachelle's whereabouts. In the meantime, his life and future hung in limbo.

Steven descended the stairs, reviewing the day's agenda in his mind: meetings, meetings, and more meetings. Today was day seven in the ten-day countdown. It would not do well to let his mind wander during the intense meetings. The future of many would rely on his performance today.

At the bottom of the stairs, just as he was about to enter

the dining room, it suddenly hit him where Nachelle was. He stopped dead in his tracks and a tremble shook his body.

"I know where she is," Steven whispered to the empty foyer. He had no proof he was right, only a gut instinct that was stronger than grain whiskey.

He ran to the dining room to tell his Dad and Nathaniel he was leaving town for a few days. Then he flew from the dining room, leaving both men staring after him in confusion. Steven started dialing the number for the airport, but Adolphus Du-Cloux depressed the receiver. "Just what the hell do you think you're doing?" The angry expression on his face would have felled a polar bear.

"Saving my life, Dad." Steven sighed, running a hand across his eyes. "I don't expect you to understand."

"Does this have anything to do with that woman?" Adolphus demanded.

"It has everything to do with Nachelle. I love her and I'm going to tell her so."

"How can you even think about bringing that woman back into our lives after what she's done to us? Have you lost your mind?"

"If I don't bring her back, I *will* lose my mind. I'm going to get her and she's going to sit by my side as we save the company. Now, if you'll excuse me, I need to call and arrange for a flight."

"Son, we're going through a crisis here and you're the leader. If you leave, you might as well not come back."

"Adolphus, you don't mean that!" Nadine DuCloux stood at the end of the hallway near the kitchen entrance. As she advanced, both men could see her nervously wringing her hands and see the tears glittering like diamonds in her eyes.

"Dad, if everything goes well, I'll only be a few days." Steven turned his back on his father and dialed the hanger at the airport. As he relayed the appropriate information, his mother and father hugged, banding together as if he was going away forever.

With the travel formalities out of the way, he turned back to his parents, and said in a much calmer voice, "Dad, you know I won't let you or DuCloux Enterprises down, but this is something I have got to do for me and Nachelle."

Adolphus didn't say anything. He simply turned and shuffled back to the dining room where Nathaniel sat, dumbfounded.

Nadine wrapped her arms around her youngest child and whispered tearfully. "Follow your heart son. Follow your heart."

He pulled his mother close and kissed her smooth cheek. "Thank you, Mother."

Within an hour, he was on the company's private jet bound for Las Vegas.

Sixteen

Steven stepped off the plane and wondered how in the heck he was going to find Nachelle. Even narrowing the choices down to the strip, Las Vegas had more hotels than a politician had lies. *I'll just have to check all of them,* he thought dismally. He was anxious to find Nachelle, apologize, and profess his love.

He struck out at the first, second, and third hotel. Although the employees were eager to help him find Nachelle after the semi-truthful story he fed them, she simply hadn't checked into their establishment. As he sat in the back of the taxi enroute to the next hotel, he rethought his plan, meager as it was. For the first time, he wondered if he was even on the right track. *I know I'm right. I know she's here.* Steven pounded his hand in his palm and replayed the Sunday they had shared in his hotel suite. It was hard to believe that it had been less than ten days ago. He felt liked he'd aged considerably since then.

That Sunday morning, as they had cuddled in the aftermath

of lovemaking, he distinctly remembered teasing her about Las Vegas being her "refresh and renew," "stop and regroup" city. They had laughed uproariously at his classifications and later had fallen back into each other's arms for another round of loving. If their recent predicament didn't qualify as a needed trip to Vegas, then he didn't know what would.

The heavily-accented foreign taxi cab driver stopped his car under the portico of the fourth hotel on the strip. Steven waved a fifty-dollar bill under the man's nose and instructed him, "Don't move until I return."

Smiling and nodding his head in agreement, the driver flashed Steven the thumbs up.

Strolling rapidly through the magnificent lobby of the hotel, Steven was oblivious to the eager stares of the single and married women and the cleverly concealed, but envious, looks of the men. He walked to the registration desk and demanded to see the manager. A few minutes passed before a short, balding man with a handlebar mustache and slightly pigeon-toed feet walked up to Steven.

After the man greeted Steven, Steven launched into the same white lie he had used at the other hotels. Manufacturing tears, which wasn't a great stretch, Steven told the man he and his wife had had a big fight and she had angrily left town without telling anybody where she was going. Steven went on to tell the man that they had honeymooned at his wonderful hotel and he was hoping he could check his registration records for Nachelle Oliver. The manager bought Steven's version of the truth—hook, line, and sinker—and retreated to his office to search their computer records for Nachelle's name. Just as Steven was about to lose his patience and barge through the office door, the manager returned with a smile, an apology for the delay, and a key to Nachelle's room.

Steven stopped just short of hugging the man. Reining in his excitement, he thanked the man and paid cash for an extra couple of nights, upgrading them to the honeymoon suite.

After dispatching the very happy taxi driver, Steven went

to the room Nachelle had been occupying for the past few days. Just outside the door, he paused, and thought about what he would say to her. He tossed around several ideas and finally decided he didn't like any of them. *When the time comes, I'll know what to say,* he concluded. Silently, he inserted the key and opened the door. A blast of air-conditioned air welcomed him and considering it was early afternoon, he was surprised at the darkness inside the room. Slowly, his eyes adjusted to the absence of light, and he moved forward with one hand slightly out in front of him, feeling his way into the interior of the room.

He spotted a lamp and snapped it on. The pool of light was limited, but it was enough to let him know that there was no one in the room. He scanned the adjoining bathroom and closets. Her clothes hung neatly in place; Nachelle had obviously gone out.

Disappointed, Steven sighed. *I'll wait all day . . . all night . . . all year if I have to. She's more than worth it.* He picked up the phone and called Dorrie to discontinue the hunt. His next call was to room service. He ordered a bottle of champagne and had it sent to the hotel manager with a note of thanks. Settling comfortably on the bed, he sat back to await Nachelle's return.

The hotel room was too cold! Nachelle realized she had forgotten to cut off the air conditioner on her way out to swim. Her wet body trembled as she closed the door. Half by feel, half by memory, she made her way through the box-shaped room in the dark, in search of the thermostat. "Why did they put the dumb thing way across the room," she chattered.

Raising the lever on the thermostat, she turned, and with her eyes now accustomed to the gloom, saw the outline of a large body on her bed. She choked back a scream. Her heart began a world record beat as she mentally calculated her chances of escape.

Before she could make a move, the body swung long legs off the bed and clicked on the bedside lamp.

"Hello, Nachelle. You're looking . . . beautiful." Steven's hungry eyes feasted on her skimpily-clad body. "I've missed you." It took a truckload of restraint to keep from showing her just how much he truly missed her. He'd hurt her tremendously and knew he'd have a lot of talking and apologizing to do before he could sample her intimate gifts. *We'll have a whole lifetime to make love,* he promised. *This time will be reserved for talking.*

Nachelle would have fainted if she hadn't been so relieved. Her physical relief was short-lived as the full impact of his presence set in. "What are you doing here? How did you find me?" Her heart slammed against her ribs. She was so shocked and surprised to see him there, she didn't feel the duffel bag slide from her shoulder.

Over the last few days, since she had parted with Heather and Gerald in Portland after the basketball game, she'd had nothing but time to think about the direction her life had taken. Her mind had refused to think about anything or anyone except her failed relationship with Steven. Her mind had conjured his presence so many times that she thought she might be hallucinating now. His image, his smell, his body, his mannerisms had become ingrained in her mind, and it had become impossible for her to complete a twenty-four hour period without thinking about him or yearning for his touch.

She had resigned herself to believe the fact that she would never see him again, that she would have to work through the pain and anger she had suffered at his hands. Even when Heather had informed her that he was calling all over Fort Worth and Texas—daily—looking for her, she had refused to listen to her heart, but rather to her head. She had convinced herself that he was only interested in tying up the loose ends by officially ending their brief love affair. She hadn't allowed her heart to believe that he would ride up on a white charger and sweep her off to his castle. That was a fairy tale dream and she was through believing in fairy tales.

Still . . . at the rate her heart was pounding and with the wild dips her stomach was taking, she admitted she hadn't schooled her heart enough. Despite the pain and disappointment, she loved him, and it was bittersweet poison being so close to him.

Slowly, as if awaking from a deep sleep, she roused herself and repeated her question. "How did you find me?"

Steven walked toward her. His intense black eyes scanned her from head to toe. In a deep, husky voice he stated. "You told me." The blood roared in his body and his heart nearly burst in its hyperactivity.

It took all of his self-control to keep from crushing her to him and slathering kisses all over her. She was salve to his broken heart and looked so tempting in her one-piece swimsuit covered only by a gauzy white cover-up. He ached to claim her, but he had an agenda that needed to be resolved. He couldn't give in to his desires . . . not yet.

Steven stopped one foot from her and continued. "The Sunday before Computermation had their press conference, the Sunday we stayed in bed all morning and sealed our love for each other, you mentioned this town was your hide-from-the-world place. You told me that this city, with all its millions of troubled visitors, made your problems seem less significant. I teased you about it, remember?"

Nachelle closed her eyes as the scene unfolded behind her lids. Yes, she remembered. She remembered all too clearly the lovemaking they had shared that day, the pillow talk that had dominated the morning hours. At that time, she'd had no idea the love wouldn't last or that any of their conversation would lead to a monumental crossroad.

"I can tell by your face you remember." Steven took another step toward her. "As for finding *this* hotel, well, if I had to spend the next half of my life searching every hotel in Vegas to find you, I would have. I've missed you, Nachelle, you don't know how sorry I am for losing my cool. I should have listened to you. I should have given you the opportunity to talk." His voice was soft, longing.

Nachelle felt herself swaying toward his deep-timbered caressing voice. She opened her eyes and forced herself to remember that this was the man who had trampled on her heart. And remembering brought back her anger. She ground out, "How can you miss someone who's responsible for jeopardizing your precious company?"

Steven spread his hands in a pleading gesture. Now that he had the good fortune to see her again, he was anxious to prove his love. "Nachelle, you and I both know you didn't set Du-Cloux Enterprises up for the kill. I blamed you because I was angry, but I didn't . . . don't mean it. I honestly believe you were helping a friend and just . . . I don't know . . . forgot about the confidentiality of some things. But, it's okay, honey. Together, we can work it out."

"You sure didn't think that a week ago," Nachelle accused, trying hard to stay focused on the issue and not the longings of her heart. Nachelle knew he was right for being disappointed in her for sharing confidential information with Sheila. She knew better, she just hadn't been thinking, but she could have explained all that if he'd just given her the chance. "You turned your back on me and accused me of . . . of . . ." Even though the pain was still real, she knew that she would always love Steven.

"You're right." Steven ran a hand through his wavy hair and begged for her understanding. "There is no excuse for laying the blame at your feet. You're not the one who created the thirty-million dollar debt." Steven placed his hands on his waist and said, "The only excuse I can offer is that I was under a great deal of stress. I wasn't thinking straight, and when I finally did come to my senses, I knew that I had screwed up royally. I'm afraid my fear of losing the company overrode my better sense and my heart."

"So you sacrificed me for the company?" Nachelle asked.

"Yes, I did," Steven answered bluntly, staring deep into her eyes. "But, not having you in my life this past week has made me realize that I'm more afraid of losing you. I can always start another company, but there's only one Nachelle."

Steven stretched out a tentative hand and stroked her face. "I'm sorry I destroyed your faith in me. Believe me, I have suffered for it too."

Nachelle read the corresponding pain reflected in his eyes and felt a glimmer of hope rise from her mire of despair. *Dare I trust his words? Can I afford to believe in him, and in love, a third time?* Nachelle honestly admitted to herself she was afraid to dare.

On a breath, she asked, "What do you want now?"

"To apologize and ask for your forgiveness. I need you in my life, Nachelle. I love you."

She heard the plea in his voice and listened carefully to the words he spoke. In the depths of his black eyes, she read everything his voice projected: love, pain, regret. Still, the past haunted her, she saw images of Harlan floating through her mind.

"How do I know, what guarantees do I have that you won't sacrifice me again? What happens the next time we fight or the company's in jeopardy? Are you going to listen to me then or are you going to turn away from me?"

"I'm only human, Nachelle. I'm sure I'll make more mistakes before my life is over. The only thing I can promise is that my priorities are in order and you're number one, not DE."

"You promised me you wouldn't treat me like Harlan did, yet you broke that promise before it was five days old. How can I believe you, Steven?"

The comparison to Harlan cut through him like a machete. Steven spoke softly, "All I can give you is my word that it won't happen again." Steven turned and walked away from her. Picking up the two keys to the honeymoon suite, Steven threw one on the bed. "Believe that I love you, Nachelle, and

I will try my hardest never to disappoint you again. I'm sorry."
Steven walked out her door.

Nachelle walked slowly to the door and rested her head
against it. Within seconds, the muffled sound of his footsteps
faded. Turning around, she pressed flat against the door and
took deep puffs of air. That exercise didn't stop the tears from
rolling down her face. Deciding she needed to get out of the
room, Nachelle peeled off her swimsuit and stepped under
the tepid shower stream. Within minutes, she had donned a
denim dress and joined the throng of pedestrians travelling
up and down the strip. Thankfully, Las Vegas was a twenty-
four hour town and although she was alone in heart and mind,
she was not alone in strange company. On this trip, she didn't
wonder about the magnitude of others' problems; she concentrated only on her own.

Instead of seeing the brightly colored neon lights blink enticingly at her, she saw Steven's image. She recalled the fear
and pain reflected in his eyes; the same emotions she now
fought. She knew he suffered as she did, still, she couldn't
risk a ride on another emotional roller-coaster. She'd had
enough of that with Harlan. Heather's words branded her
thoughts: "Steven is not Harlan. You can't compare the two."
She remembered her answer to Heather had been: "No, but
there are enough similarities to concern me." She had made
that remark only days after the buy-out had been announced.
Now, months later, she knew that remark to be untrue. The
only comparison between the two was that they were both
black men. Steven was as different from Harlan as salt was
to pepper. Separating Steven from his predecessor, Nachelle's
mind cleared and she knew Steven would indeed live up to
his promises. Then she recalled what her mother had told her
at Harlan's funeral: "To live your life without having known
love is a shame. To live one's life and not make allowances
for love is more shameful." The black and white of it was she
loved Steven and he loved her. In a city known for gambling,

Nachelle decided to throw the dice in their favor. A decision that effectively sealed the vault to the past.

Nachelle ran back to her hotel room and picked up the key Steven had deposited on the bed. With her heart in her throat, she rode the elevator to the top floor and put the key in the door.

Steven turned from the window to look at the woman who had power over him. His throat worked convulsively. Fear of rejection consumed him. He dared not second-guess the reason for her coming.

Without taking her eyes off Steven, Nachelle approached him. When she was within a heartbeat, she placed her hands on his chest and said, "Apology accepted." She raised herself on tiptoe and kissed him softly on the lips.

Unlocking the gates of self-control, Steven wrapped her tightly in his arms and pressed her close to him. He laid his head against her hair and closed his eyes, whispering a silent, thankful prayer. The emotions that had been building since he'd boarded the westbound plane finally settled down.

He drew back slightly, seeking her eyes. "I love you, Nachelle. I promise I'll never hurt you again."

Nachelle smiled and Steven thought the sun could never shine so brightly. "I believe you."

Her arms circled his neck and she whispered in his ear. "Make love to me, Steven."

Desires, that had too long been held back, flared and engulfed them. In a dreamlike state, Nachelle felt Steven lift and carry her to the bed. Not an inch separated them and even as they shed the clothing barriers that prevented them from being one, they let nothing keep them apart.

Steven worshipped her with kisses that trailed from her full heaving breasts to the tip of her toes. His hot tongue and breath branded her a DuCloux woman. Beneath his fiery touch, Nachelle squirmed and moaned, begging for more although she was on the periphery of climax. Steven regained her lips in a kiss that merged their souls forever and in one fluid move, he joined them. Their cry of joy echoed off the walls. Holding tight to each other, never wanting to let go, loving words filled their senses, carrying them to new, dizzying heights. A violent shudder racked their bodies bringing them to culmination and time ticked on, allowing them to gather their breaths.

Steven raised his head from the softness of her neck. He kissed her lightly, and asked, "Will you marry me here? Now?"

Nachelle's eyes answered his question before her mouth formed the one word he held his breath to hear. "Yes," she whispered as Steven took possession of her lips.

A series of small, suffocating kisses, nips, and caresses erupted, drawing them into a new circle of passion. The dance of love started again. And, it was hours later before they rejoined civilization.

Seventeen

Steven carried his bride across the threshold of the honeymoon suite and straight to the enormous circular bed.

Nachelle smiled up into his eyes and sweetly asked, "Don't you think we should call and let our family and friends know?"

Steven let her slide down his length until she stood facing him. He put his hands on her shoulders and turned her around. "Sure," he agreed, as he continued to unzip the simple white sheath, adorned with silver sequins and small white pearls, that had acted as a wedding dress. With the dress out of the way, he pulled her against him and planted kisses along the curve of her neck and shoulders. With a moan, he turned her around to face him and captured her lips in a passionate kiss.

When the kiss ended and Steven moved to plant bite-size kisses along her jawbone, temple, and neck, Nachelle asked, "When?"

"When what?" Steven murmured, intent on nothing but devouring his new wife.

"When should we call our friends and families? They *might* be interested in the fact that we're married."

"Soon." Steven didn't hear a word Nachelle spoke. He was busy unfastening fancy, lacy undergarments and stroking smooth, satiny skin. When his hand landed between her legs, she too forgot what she'd been asking. Arching her back, she moved against his hand, letting their bodies take over when their minds stopped. She moaned delightfully when a finger, then two, entered the moist warmth of her feminine core. All thoughts flew from her mind. Sensation was the only thing she now recognized.

Laying her gently on her back, Steven used his tongue and hands to unclasp her stockings from her garter belt. Her stockings and shoes lay on top of her underclothes and dress; all discarded items, no longer useful.

Standing over her, Steven looked down at the lovely picture stretched out on the bed. "I love you, Nachelle."

Nachelle sat up and reached for his tie. She grabbed it at the knot and pulled him down on top of her. "Prove it." She whispered boldly in his ear.

In seconds, Steven had shucked his jacket, Nachelle had discarded his tie and unbuttoned his shirt. A deep driving need to be one escalated their actions. With pants pooled around his ankles, Nachelle pulled Steven's briefs down and guided his male organ to the place where his fingers had just vacated. They moved frantically, up and down, in and out. With each stroke the pleasure intensified, until finally Steven grabbed her backside and drove deep. They cried out in unison as the waves of pleasure hit one after another as they peaked.

When she recovered her breath, Nachelle kissed her husband. "I'm convinced." She purred like a cat.

Unwilling to part for more than a second, they did so only to position themselves more securely on the bed. With a final kiss and arms wrapped tight around each other, they drifted off into a light sleep.

The ringing of the telephone interrupted their nap. Steven growled, "I'm taking it off the hook."

Nachelle smiled, and almost agreed, when she realized they had never got around to calling their loved ones back home with the good news. She stopped Steven's hand in the act of hanging up and snared the phone. "It could be important."

"Not more important than what I have planned." Steven looked at her wickedly, yet indulgently. "Thirty seconds or less." He tapped his watch meaningfully.

"Yes, sir." She playfully saluted. Behind her she heard the rustle of clothes and knew Steven meant what he said.

"Hello."

"Hi, Nachelle. It's Sheila."

"Sheila, hi." At the mention of her ex-roommate's name, Steven stilled his movements. Nachelle sat up, swinging her legs over the side of the bed. "How are you? What's going on?" The happy, idyllic bubble they had trapped themselves in burst. Sheila could only be calling about Computermation business.

Nachelle shifted so she half-faced Steven who lay on his back staring at her. It was obvious by the dark expression on his face that he recognized Sheila's name and realized what she had to be calling about.

"I'm doing okay, considering. Hey, did you change hotel rooms? The other day when we talked I could have sworn you were in a room number with a two in it. But, oh well, I was calling to tell you the latest and greatest."

Nachelle remembered that as she checked out of her previous hotel room to move in with Steven, the staff had cross-referenced her name to both rooms. She was suddenly glad they had thought to be so considerate; otherwise, she could have missed this call.

"What? What's going on?"

Steven rolled over to face Nachelle and took her free hand

in his own. He held it gently, reassuringly. In the midst of discovering joy, they had forgotten this one loose end.

"First of all, I want to say thanks. Thanks for being my friend, thanks for sending me information, thanks for listening to me. You're a good friend, Nachelle." Without pause, Sheila continued talking in her usual mile-a-minute speech, "I decided to risk everything and come clean. You were right. I have never felt better in my whole life."

"Sheila, you did it!" Nachelle asked, incredulously.

Sheila laughed on the other end. "Yes, and I feel GREAT!"

"I'm very proud of you. I know this couldn't have been easy."

"You're right about that. I lost a lot of sleep behind this mess. Anyway, I called the U. S. Attorney General's office and we met last night, and now they have all the documents. As a matter of fact, I'm calling from Washington D. C. They're getting ready to have a press conference."

Nachelle whooped in Sheila's and Steven's ear. "A press conference?"

"Yeah, go turn on the TV."

Nachelle whispered to Steven. "Go turn the TV on."

Steven's curiosity was peaked. The one-sided conversation left him dizzy with questions, but he did as his wife requested.

"Oh, Nachelle, you should have told me you have company. I'm sorry to interrupt."

"Don't worry about it. You might as well know, it's Steven DuCloux."

"The CEO of DuCloux Enterprises?"

Nachelle's excitement and pride loosened her tongue. "Yes, we got married earlier today. You're talking to *Mrs*. Steven DuCloux."

It was Sheila's turn to squeal. "That's great! I'm so happy for you and please pass my best wishes on to the groom."

Nachelle laughed. Happiness overflowed from her. "I will."

"Now I'm doubly glad I turned Computermation in."

"So am I."

"Well, listen, I see my attorney signaling frantically for me. And boy, Nachelle, you should see him. He *is* cute. Anyway, gotta go. They must be ready to start the press conference so turn to CNN. And Nachelle . . ."

"Yes."

"I don't want to hear any remarks later about how much weight I've gained."

Both ladies laughed and disconnected the call.

Nachelle ran to join Steven on the couch where he had already tuned into the airing of a special news bulletin on CNN.

Ten minutes later, with jaws unhinged, Steven sat with a blank look on his face. "I can't believe it." He kept repeating that phrase during the entire thirty-minute newscast. Nachelle tried to temper her excitement, but she couldn't. She and Sheila had been through a lot during the past few weeks.

Steven turned his head to stare at her. Dazed, he spoke to his wife, needlessly recounting the news broadcast. "The United States Attorney General filed formal charges against Computermation for several counts of fraud relating to government contracts." Steven swallowed a thick lump in his throat. "Supposedly, an accountant at Computermation handed over reports showing evidence of kickbacks, fraud, and overcharging. I don't suppose you know anything about that?"

Nachelle smiled, "As a matter of fact, I just spoke with that accountant and she told me to tell you hi and congrats."

Steven clicked off the TV and turned to face his wife. "Tell me everything."

"You know most of it now, but I'll give you the full effect. Many months ago Sheila started calling, complaining about the new executives. She said they were trying to get her to falsify government reporting records so they could get more money out of the government. Apparently, they have enough government contracts so that if Sheila had falsified the records they would have made millions in unearned money. Sheila refused to do it, but they kept riding and threatening her. That was when she called me and asked for a different reporting format which I faxed to her. She thought if she could use another format and some fudged numbers that she would hand that copy to them and keep the authentic copy with the real numbers in her personal file at home. That fooled the executives for a while, but then, somehow, they caught on and the situation started escalating until they finally forced Sheila into a leave of absence so they could get someone else in the Accounting Department to do their dirty work and so she could, as they told her, get her head together and think about her future. When she returned to work from her leave of absence, they fired her, but by that time, she had all the documentation she needed to go to the U. S. Attorney General's Office."

Steven stood and began pacing the sitting area. "I can't believe it."

"Believe it and apparently that wasn't all they were into which leads me to DE. When Sheila and I spoke a few days ago, we figured out the new executives were living too high off the hog, so, to support their rich lifestyles, they decided to put the squeeze on some smaller companies with accounts due. It wasn't just DE who got the notice to pay up or be forced into bankruptcy, there were several other companies. Computermation's intent was to buy these companies relatively cheap and then rape them of their profits."

"My God! I knew there was something deeper behind their request. I can't believe DE was in jeopardy because some boys on high were greedy." Steven almost skipped in excitement.

"I'll bet if we call the Atlanta office, we'll find the ten-day notice has been withdrawn."

The words weren't out of Nachelle's mouth before Steven had his hand on the phone.

Three minutes later, Steven confirmed the truth of Nachelle's words. According to Nathaniel, he had just gotten a call from the acting President of Computermation, apologizing for the "mix-up in paperwork." The President had gone on to say Computermation valued DE's business and would like to remain partners. The agreed upon terms of the contract would remain in place and if DE continued to be their customer, they would knock ten percent off the next negotiated contract.

Not giving Nathaniel a chance to ask any questions, Steven hung up quickly. His eyes were bright when he turned to Nachelle. "Apparently, Computermation is going to be busy for a long time trying to defend their actions. They just offered us the sweetest deal." An overwhelming feeling of gratitude reflected in Steven's dark, handsome face. He curved a hand to the side of Nachelle's cheek and said, "I owe you a big thank you. If it hadn't been for you faxing that report to Sheila, DE wouldn't have a future." His eyes clouded over, "You saved DuCloux Enterprises and I did everything but stab a knife through your heart. How can I ever make this up to you?"

Nachelle moved his hand so she could place a kiss in his palm. "Knowing you chose to come find me instead of staying to fight for DE makes it alright. It's good to know I'm, no, *our* love, is more important than anything else on this earth."

"Oh baby, you bet it is. And, I'll cherish it forever and never take it for granted."

A slow, easy smile graced her face. Leading him to the couch, she sat him down, then straddled his lap. Seductively, she put his hand on her bare breast. "You mended my heart and made me the happiest woman in the world."

Steven needed no coaxing from that point. He knew how to make them both happy. "I love you, Mrs. DuCloux."

"I love you, Mr. DuCloux."

Their matching smiles dissolved as their lips began an enticing dance of desire.

Later. Much, much later, Nachelle and Steven agreed that after-hours love affairs always lead to a love-lasting contract.

Dear Reader—

I started reading romance novels at age twelve. In those days romance novels were lopsided in favor of merry old England, and while I enjoyed the stories, I thirsted for romance novels with "color."

Luckily, the passing of time brings changes. And, I don't know about you, but I'm thrilled to death that romances have finally crossed the ocean and cultural lines. We, African-Americans, now have characters, settings, history and terminology we can relate to!

And, Steven and Nachelle DuCloux told me to tell you they're glad too; otherwise, their story may have ended up in an empty manila file box under my bed.

It took four years to create Nachelle and Steven's world (they just wouldn't act right!), but I'm hoping I won't have to wait that long to read your feedback regarding their story. Heather and Gerald's story is still under construction so please stay tuned for the 411 on their juicy love story. (I promise it won't take four years.)

Please write to me at the post office box listed below and thank you for supporting Arabesque!

Sincerely,

Anna Larence
Post Office Box 17875
Dallas, TX 75217-0875

About the Author

Anna Larence, currently living in Dallas, develops promotions for a major telecommunications company, serves on the board for several non-profit organizations, is a member of St. Luke "Community" United Methodist Church, is single and spends "free" time with a multitude of family and friends.